Last Days in Eden

By the same author:

Born and Bred, Cornwall Books, 1988 (photographs)
Nine Lives, Halsgrove, 1998 (audio book, stories)
The Poetry Remedy, Patten Press, 1999 (poetry workshops handbook for patients)
Paper Whites, London Magazine Editions, 2001 (poems and photographs)
The Burying Beetle, Luath Press, 2005 (a novel)
Sea Front, Truran, 2005 (photographs)
Because We Have Reached That Place, Oversteps Books, 2006 (poems)
The Bower Bird, Luath Press, 2007 (a novel)
Inchworm, Luath Press, 2008 (a novel)
A Snail's Broken Shell, Luath Press, 2010 (a novel)
The Light at St Ives, Luath Press, 2010 (photographs)
Koh Tabu, Oxford University Press, 2010 (a novel)
Lost Girls, Little, Brown US, 2012 (a novel)
Telling the Bees, Oversteps, 2012 (poems)
Runners, Luath Press, 2013 (a novel)
On a Night of Snow, Ebook, 2013 (a novella)

Last Days in Eden

ANN KELLEY

Luath Press Limited

EDINBURGH

www.luath.co.uk

First published 2014

ISBN: 978-1-910021-27-9

The publisher acknowledges the support of

towards the publication of this book.

The author's right to be identified as author of this book
under the Copyright, Designs and Patents Act 1988 has been asserted.

The paper used in this book is recyclable.
It is made from low chlorine pulps
produced in a low energy, low emission manner
from renewable forests.

Printed and bound by
CPI Anthony Rowe Ltd., Wiltshire

Typeset in 10 point Sabon

For Jennie Renton.
What would I have done without you?

CHAPTER ONE

ON THE DAY the girl first came to Shell Shack, fog lay unshifting on the meadow, smothering the garden and the broad estuary. The constant screech of invisible parakeets split the heavy sky.

Nano would have been up at daybreak, letting me stay in bed until she had roused the fire, fed the chickens and pigeons, seen to the bees and made the bread. But that day the bees kept to their straw skep and the chickens were silent, as if they too were still mourning her. It was mid-morning when I clambered out of bed, my limbs heavy and unwilling, and tried to catch up with the day.

No travs had come to Eden Spit for weeks, if not months. Certainly not since Nano died. I hadn't sold a thing – not one measly apple. I was getting desperate. That morning, as every morning since I'd been alone, I chopped some firewood and added it to the small pile outside the door of Shell Shack. I would have to find more fuel soon. The kitchen range had a never-ending hunger, like a cuckoo, and I was its mother now.

I raked out the soiled straw and earth from the chicken house, replenished it, and gave the birds their feed of cooked potato skins and left-over rice and rye. The iodine smell of bladderwrack hung in the air, reminding me that it was time to gather seaweed to manure the vegetable garden.

Indoors, eating the end of a stale rice-cake for lunch, I watched a pretty harvest mouse scamper out from under the kitchen dresser, sit up and wash its face delicately. Cat was nowhere to be seen. The minute I moved, the mouse raced back to the safety of darkness. Nano wouldn't have rested until the mouse was gone. Preferably dead and gone. But why shouldn't it live there, part of the old place? It had every right to take advantage of the crumbs that dropped. Not that many crumbs dropped nowadays. I surveyed my fast diminishing stores. They wouldn't last much longer. How on earth had Nano managed to provide for us, to always put something on the table that was filling and satisfying? My mouth watered as I remembered her vegetable stews and soups, the cakes she conjured from rye flour, oranges, honey and eggs. She had tried to teach me how to cook, but I hadn't taken much notice. I was always more interested in making clothes for myself out of the beautiful garments I had inherited from my mother. And Nano had been happy to indulge me. Only six months ago there had been three of us – Nano, Grandpa Noah and me. Now there was only me.

It was early afternoon when the gate bell sounded. Manga yelped and pressed his nose against the door, desperate to get out. I pushed my unruly hair behind my ears, smoothed the red net petticoat I wore over my denims and shrugged an apron over the lot. Could it be a trav at last, wanting to buy eggs and apples, or perhaps they'd take a digigraph of Shell Shack with me in front of it?

I peered out of the salt-smeared window, trying not be seen. A child-like figure was checking through the meagre collection of jars on the produce table. A trav, definitely, but not dressed in the usual drab, shapeless overalls. She was smartly turned out in yellow jodhpurs and a black velvet jacket, with a scarlet scarf knotted around her neck. They were the kind of colours I loved. Looped over the gatepost were the reins of a small black mare, which snickered and nodded her head in a pretty manner.

'Hi,' she said, as I emerged, Manga tucked under my arm. She was not a child; I could see that now. She looked scrubbed clean, cleaner than I'd ever been in my life. Her fingernails were perfect – I instinctively hid mine. Her black hair was smooth and neat, tied back under a riding hat. Her lips were stained bright red. She looked at me with eyes wide as a kitten's, barely hiding her amusement at my appearance, so different from her own.

She picked a bruised apple from the box and fed it to her pony.

'No pickled shallots? It's the season, surely?'

'None today.'

I felt awkward in the presence of this diminutive beauty. I towered over her, a clodhopper in ugly, mud-splattered boots.

'What a shame!' she wailed as if it was a major disaster. 'My father loves pickles. Will you have some soon?'

'Er, perhaps. Come next week.'

Why did I say that? I would have to bottle them especially for her!

The pony lifted its forefeet impatiently. She gave it a smart sting with her crop.

'What an unusual home you have.'

'My grandfather built it,' I said, holding tight to Manga, who whined, excited by the horse.

'He did?' She raised her eyebrows disdainfully.

How dare she! Grandpa Noah had built Shell Shack with his own hands from driftwood, the remains of old vehicles, mud and straw. When I was little I had helped him gather pretty pebbles, coloured glass and shells from the beach to decorate the outside walls. That was before he lost his wits and started shaking his fist at pelicans and shouting, '*We shall overcome!*' I suddenly remembered the day I had seen him sitting on the beach, sobbing over a dolphin skull, and my eyes prickled treacherously. He had died after years of ill health and Nano had followed him seven long weeks ago, from a broken heart I think. She had died on my sixteenth birthday.

'So...' the girl said, returning me to the present. She took the reins, mounted elegantly, sat back, pulled the reins tight and struck the pony's withers again with the crop. 'And the funny animals?' She pointed across the garden to the sculptures.

'He made those too.'

'Hmm, fascinating. I suppose he built the dovecot as well? I would like to have that.'

Have the dovecot? How could she *have* the dovecot? It belonged to Shell Shack.

Before I could even respond, the girl kicked the pony with her shiny black boots and rode off a few paces. Then she stopped and looked back at me. 'I do like your petticoat,' she said. And I think she laughed as she cantered away, sending up a spray of sand behind her.

I watched the mist swallow her, almost sad that she had gone despite her high-handed manner, because I was alone again. I let Manga loose and the little terrier staggered off out of the gate on his three short legs to sniff at the steaming dung the pony had deposited. I followed him and started shovelling it up for the compost heap. Nano had instilled in me the importance of wasting nothing, and horse manure was a great source of vital minerals for the veggie garden and the orchard. Whenever the Uzi soldiers rode by on their huge horses I would wait until they had passed and then go out onto the path with the shovel to do the same thing.

I called Manga back inside, trying to work out what the trav girl had really been after. Pickles? Sculptures? Grandpa Noah's pigeon palace? Certainly not my red petticoat! I washed my hands, despairing of my ragged nails. What was the point? There was nothing pretty or delicate about me. There was just work to be done. There always was, and there always would be. And on top of everything, I'd have to make pickles now, thanks to my foolish offer. I'd have to peel shallots, look out the spices, find the right containers. Why hadn't she just taken the apples like any normal trav?

I took out my anger on the chimney, knocking down the soot and removing the ash from the grate of the iron range, as I'd seen Nano do day after day after day. I carried the ash-pan outside to the compost heap. On my way back, I picked up a bundle of kindling and firewood, heaped a few small pieces of sea-coal and dried furze on top, and relit it. There was hardly any sea-coal left, I noticed. I hadn't made time to gather any. Oh, how my back ached!

Nano had made rye bread twice a week, but she did everything from memory. There were so many things she'd not got round to teaching me. And I had never imagined a world without her.

My supplies of basics, like salt and rice, were running very low, but so were the dees in the earthenware pot on the mantelshelf. Nano had saved them carefully, spending them only when bartering was impossible. I hadn't earned a single dee.

The pullets had laid three small eggs the day before. But it hadn't even occurred to me to sell them. I had cooked them for my supper, mixing in parsley and wild garlic with the omelette.

That evening, on my way towards the tool shed, I noticed that the strong wind the previous night had torn a huge rent in the nets that protected the soft fruit plants. Where on earth would I find the time to mend them? And *how*? My spirits plummeted. Nano's voice was loud in my head – *Don't leave a hole to get any bigger... plan ahead to let things grow... prepare the ground properly.* I took a hoe to the weeds in the vegetable patch and started to dig a second trench for new planting, my hands already sore with blisters from an earlier attempt. Nano had made it look easy, but I sweated with the effort. The ground was so hard! I stabbed at it furiously. How could she have left me so suddenly, so unprepared for all this?

By the time I'd created what passed for a new trench, the fog was lifting, so I went to sit on the gate to watch the sunset. On clear nights I had often perched there between my grandparents, all three of us gazing over the water meadows as the last rays bloodied Eden Bay.

This evening there was a green haze to the sky and a wind sprang up which riffled the water into waves. I ambled down to the strand, Manga grumbling along beside me. Usually the sunset and a walk calmed me, but my thoughts remained troubled. The surrounding landscape seemed melancholy, suffused with sadness. This was where I belonged, surrounded by the singing of tall grass, part of the world of shingle and sand, the smell of black mud and cockle-shells in my nostrils, the big sky racing from horizon to horizon. But I felt dislocated, like a spider plucked from a warm corner and put out into the night. I hugged myself and turned slowly in a full circle. It was all so familiar, so loved, but...

In the past there had been days when I'd complained – about the monotony of our diet, the draughts and dust, my chores – but no more than any other child on Eden Spit. Now, for the first time as I looked out across the darkening water that evening, I wanted something different, a life in which I could have pretty clothes and clean, smooth hands. Like the trav girl. She had made me envious. Strange as it might seem, I had not known envy before. Surely there must be other ways of living, I thought, not hand-to-mouth, alone, in a draughty old shack looking out at the same scene, day after day. Was this to be my future?

That night the wind howled down the chimney, moaned in the timbers and rippled the metal roof, slamming it down again and again, even though it was weighed down with large stones. I could hear the Shell sign creaking ominously. Grandpa Noah had been so proud of it that he'd bolted it to the chimney stack. It was from the olden days before the Oil Wars, when people used petrol for fuel. 'Relic of a bygone age,' he'd say. 'Your mother thought it was ugly, but it's part of history. And we all need history.' He could never get enough of stories from the past. '*Remember when...*' he was always saying, and Nano would shush him. Until he began to forget everything. But he never forgot to wear his war medals, even when he was confined to bed in his final illness he had them pinned onto his dressing gown.

Peering out into the darkness, I could see what looked like Portuguese Men o' War floating wraith-like across the marshes: white polythene bags blown all the way from somewhere. I hoped some would catch on brambles so that I could gather them in the morning. I wasn't going to risk going out in a wind like this, anything could be flying about and the sand would stop me from seeing properly. Those bags were useful for all sorts of things – as containers for food in the kitchen, to plug holes in the walls and to waterproof the leaking roof.

I shuddered at the thought of the never-ending list of repairs and turned back to the range. Smoke puffed into the small room. The image of the trav kept coming into my mind: the lovely clothes, the shiny boots, the manicured hands. I stoked the fire, more in temper than in hope. *It wasn't fair! It wasn't fair!*

I lit the candle and turned to the consolation of *Pride and Prejudice*, which had belonged to my mother, who had worked for the Great Flood Library. It had been her treasure. Thumbed and torn, it had lost some pages, but as usual the magic of the words began to relax me as soon as I opened it, Within minutes I was immersed in the warmth of the Bennett family, no longer cold and lonely and anxious, free from the bitterness and anger that had been with me all day.

This had been our only book. Grandpa Noah had kept it hidden against the occasions when the shack was spot-searched by Uzi soldiers. I was never allowed to read it outside in case I was seen.

'Why not?' I asked.

'Forbidden, books are. Dangerous things, books,' Nano tutted.

'Let the girl be,' said Grandpa.

He had read and reread the story to me. When I was small, I had begged him, 'Talk to the book, talk to it, Grandpa.' That was how I'd learned to read. I knew half of it by heart. Although there were things I didn't understand, things that made no sense to me, I could escape into that world, take part in that family's strange existence. But following the visit from the beautiful girl that morning, the book's power to distract had weakened. Now I imagined *her* mixing easily with the Bennett sisters in the story, making mischief with the younger ones. Her life was stylish and privileged like theirs – and it was real, not made up by someone called Jane Austen hundreds of years ago.

One day I wanted to write a story made up out of my own head. I had started so many times, but never got beyond the beginning. What could I expect? I asked myself, surging with resentment. What story had I to tell, a sixteen-year-old orphan who had travelled nowhere, and who had hardly any schooling, and only homemade ink and rough paper to write on? Nano had not approved, shaking her head at the sight of me writing, but Grandpa would encourage me.

How I wished Nano was here now, shaking her head.

The fire finally gave up the struggle. I had not brought in enough wood or coal to keep the range alight. I wrapped my book carefully and hid it away beside my tattered notebook, then went to bed to keep warm. With no one there to hear me apart from Manga, I cried myself to sleep.

CHAPTER TWO

ALL THAT NIGHT I tossed and turned and the next day I rose late, after only a few hours' sleep. I was peeling an orange for breakfast when I heard the screech of parakeets. They sounded unusually close. And it hit me – I hadn't mended the soft-fruit nets yesterday. I rushed out, still in my nightdress, waving my hands at the flock of red and green birds, Manga yapping helpfully. However vigorously I shooed them away, they ignored me, too hungry to be frightened off. In the end, all I could do was watch as they shredded the ripe currants and gooseberries, squabbling for the best perches.

Nano's voice shimmered in my mind, chiding me into action: '*Do something, child! Make something of the day!*'

I turned on my heel. What I needed was a scarecrow – a *scarekeet*, that was it. I searched the cottage for something to dress the crossed poles that were to become its arms and legs. I hadn't had the heart to destroy any of Nano's clothes, not yet. Not that I could wear any of them, they were all the wrong size and shape for me, except for her apron. But they still smelled of her.

My mother's clothes were precious to me, but in a different way. I had never really known her – Faith Mandela – she had died a few days after I was born, Nano told me, of an infection that couldn't be cured. All I had of her was a digigraph, a portrait painted by an artist, and her clothes – which were gorgeous – mostly given to her by the artist, in payment, I suppose, for modelling. I often used little bits of her lace, velvet, nylon, polycotton and lycra to adorn my work things, and sometimes I wore her dresses. '*Make-do and mend*,' as Nano was fond of saying.

Luckily my mother had been the same build as me. As I picked through the pile of garments I was distracted by a couple of flower-patterned remnants; I put them aside to patch my cloak and kept back a length of purple lace to add to Nano's apron. This was one of my favourite pastimes, altering and adding to my old clothes. Kit and Annie and the other kids at school had thought I looked outlandish. Well, I didn't care. What did they know anyway?

In the digigraph, my mother is standing next to my father. She's wearing a white dress that billows over her slightly swollen belly – that was me, floating inside her. But in the portrait on the wall opposite the one of the Rice King, she's alone, younger, wearing the red net petticoat under a white linen full-skirted dress. She always dressed beautifully, Nano said. I reached into the bottom of the cedarwood trunk where I'd stuffed Nano's clothes next to my mother's. There was nothing there to waste on a scarekeet. Grandpa Noah's clothes would have been ideal – he had looked like one at the best of times! But most of them had been recycled into the rag rugs he and Nano had made to sell.

I felt around under my grandparents' bed, hoping for something discarded, and my fingers touched something cold and heavy. With difficulty I hauled it out and wiped the dust from its rusty lid. It was a metal chest. Now I remembered! What a rumpus there had been, years before, when Nano found me trying to open it.

'Why must you decide to play with the one thing I want you to leave well alone? These are your grandfather's things in there. Private things. Things to do with fighting and horrors. Not for your eyes.'

'No need to raise the roof,' Grandpa had said. 'But Nano's right, Flora. When the time's right I'll show you. For the moment, I'd like the past left where it belongs. In the past.' The time had never been right and, to be honest, I'd forgotten the chest's very existence.

I tried to open it but it was locked. Why would that be? We never locked doors or cupboards. We had nothing to steal and no pirates, thanks to the battlements and ramparts of the Tescopec Mountains to the north-west, and the vast reef of drowned towers and skyscrapers that had once been the city of Sainsburyness to the east and south. A large fort and barracks on the hill at the end of the narrow peninsula guarded Eden Spit.

Nano and Grandpa Noah must have had a very particular reason for keeping this chest locked. I searched in every pot and jug, drawer and cupboard, but there was no key to be found.

I was racking my brains, trying to think of a hiding place I might have missed, when the gate bell sounded. My heart stood still. The girl from yesterday? I hurried to the window, trying to decide whether I wanted it to be her or not. But no, it was Kit, shielding his eyes from the sun, surveying the damage the parakeets had done. I hadn't seen him in days.

'Hi,' I went out, braced for the lecture I knew I'd get for not having mended the netting.

'There are parakeets...'

'I know...'

'...eating you out of house and home.'

'Kit, I told you, I know. I was just going to make a scarecrow.'

He dropped his canvas bag, told his collie, Jess, to stay, and followed me into the house. 'Bit late,' he said, but not unkindly. 'That's this year's crop gone.'

'It wasn't my fault!' There was a whine in my voice that I hated.

'You just have to attend to things as soon as they go wrong.'

I rolled my eyes at him and he gave a half smile. He knew me well enough not to push too much further.

'So, apart from pointing out my shortcomings as a smallholder, to what do I owe the pleasure of your company?'

Kit smiled at my *Pride and Prejudice* style language. He was used to it, but it always amused him.

'Flora, I want you to come with me.'

'Come where?'

'Eel-catching. Better than dressing up a couple of old sticks, anyway.'

He knew how much I loathed eel-catching expeditions! But anything was better than being stuck here with nobody to talk to, with the place collapsing round my ears.

'And I'm not sure you're quite dressed for it...' He indicated my fleecy nightgown.

'OK.' I went behind the curtain that cut off the ladder to my sleeping platform from the rest of the room and changed into my outdoor clothes. 'But don't ask me to bait the basket again. I was nearly sick last time,' I called.

'Not a problem. I've got a nice rotting rat for them.'

'Thought you smelled worse than usual.'

He rattled the curtains and I wailed in pretend horror.

'How's your dad?' I asked as Kit and I trudged along towards the estuary. 'Leave off, Manga!' The terrier was practically hanging onto Kit's bag. I threw a stick and both dogs ran pell-mell after it, barking.

'Same as always, grumpy old sod,' Kit said, thrashing at reeds. Kit's father was a Water War veteran like Grandpa Noah. Born and bred on Eden Spit. But he was a very different kind of man. I had known Kit all my life. He'd left school when he was ten, after polio ruined his leg. Then his mum died, and he had to look after his shell-shocked dad. '*That lad's had to grow up ahead of his time*,' Nano would say. She had been very fond of Kit.

I watched him drag a hand through his dark mop of hair. His shoulders were broader these days.

Then he sniffed deeply and spat.

'Charming!' I moved upwind of him to lessen the smell of dead rat.

Kit grinned, ignoring my grimace. 'I've seen you spit like the best of us,' he said. 'Clears the tubes.'

I punched his arm. It was hard to be cross with Kit.

When we reached the small wooden pier where he kept his boat, he untied it and we climbed aboard. 'I've got traps up by the Ede, should be good catchings there.' The dogs sat on the shore, watching us. The boat was too small for them as well.

'Stay and be good!' I called. They knew the routine.

Kit rowed while I scanned the shoreline.

'Still hanging around, is he?'

'Who?' I pretended not to know what he was talking about.

'Scav kid.'

'Oh, him. Haven't seen him lately,' I fibbed. Actually, I had seen the boy a couple of days before. I reckoned he sometimes slept in the big barn, but after I'd caught him stealing chicken feed, he made sure he stayed out of sight. I knew he helped himself to oranges from the orchard but I didn't mind. If he was living rough, the odd pilfered orange wasn't such a terrible crime. I thought briefly about the missing key, then decided against mentioning it. Kit would only draw the wrong conclusion.

'He's harmless,' I assured him. For me, the youngster's shadowy presence was almost comforting. He could only have been about seven years old, a timid bag of bones with a mass of unwashed dreadlocks, fast as a hare on his bare feet. Manga never barked or growled when he was about and I trusted the dog's instincts. I didn't begrudge the boy a little food any more than the mouse who waited for my crumbs.

'Not encouraging him, are you?'

'Course not.'

'Could be a toxic.'

'Don't be daft. He's not covered in boils,' I pointed out.

'Doesn't mean he's not carrying something bad in him. You have to be careful, Flora.'

I said nothing. Kit might be two years older than me but that didn't mean he could tell me what to do, how to think.

'I've seen him quite a lot recently in the dunes,' he continued, frowning, as we came alongside one of the buoys. 'Not far from Shell Shack. Don't take risks, Flora. Have nothing to do with him.'

We hauled the eel traps out of the water. They were empty.

'All that effort for nothing,' I complained.

Kit quietly baited the traps again with the stinking rat corpse and lowered them into the water without uttering a word, while I held my nose and tried not to retch.

'You can row,' he said, handing me the oars and sliding forward to let me take his place. 'I've done all the work this morning.' The rain started and it was a long haul against the wind. By the time we reached the pier I was damp and exhausted. Our patient dogs appeared from the long grass when we whistled, woofing happily. 'We'll do better next time,' said Kit, waving goodbye and taking

Jess off home to his yurt on the far side of the Spit.

'What next time?' I retorted under my breath and Manga groaned in agreement.

That evening things went from bad to worse. I peeled shallots and boiled up vinegar with spices until my eyes streamed. I scalded glass jars in the oven, singeing my hair in the process. I had only just sat down with a bowl of soup when from somewhere outside there was a muffled bang and the sound of shattering glass. I rushed out, looking into each shed in turn before I finally discovered that Nano's bottled elderflower wine had exploded. I surveyed the chaos, my eyes weary from the shallots and lack of sleep. The walls dripped with the sticky mess, the floor glittered with shattered glass from the precious colas that Grandpa, Nano and I had collected from the shore over the years. I was too weary to sort it out tonight. I shut the door behind me and scuttled back to Shell Shack, the panic rising in my chest. This was exactly the kind of disaster Nano had warned me about. What had she done to avoid it happening? She'd probably told me and I hadn't listened.

Beaten and wretched, I retreated to bed.

Manga's frantic barks in the early hours woke me, but it was too late. In the aftermath of the exploding wine bottles, I had failed to lock up the chicken house securely. By the time I reached it there was nothing I could have done. Taking only two of the hens, the fox had left the others torn apart, their bloody feathers stuck to the straw. The carnage would look even worse in daylight.

I put my head in my hands and wept. No more eggs! What was I going to do? The pigeons fluttered around, disturbed from their roosts in the dovecot. Why couldn't the fox have killed them? Perhaps I *should* sell their palatial home to the trav girl? And she could take the useless pigeons with it. She wasn't the first to have commented on Grandpa's folly. It was more like a silvered wooden palace than a shelter for pigeons, completely out of place here at Shell Shack, where everything else was shabby and worn. I wondered how many dees she might pay. But no, I could never do that. I hadn't had the heart to wring the pigeons' necks and cook them, even though their stupid cooing drove me potty. They had been Grandpa's pride and joy. The two survivors had hung around, dusty and bedraggled, looking sorry for themselves and laying no eggs. But they were his pigeons.

When I was little, Grandpa Noah often used to climb the ladder up to the pigeon palace with Doc and Mr Mackenzie and they'd be in there for hours. No matter how much I begged to join them, Nano always refused.

'*Why* can't I go?' I'd pull at her apron and look beseechingly into her sky-washed eyes.

'You don't want nothing to do with that. Stupid talk!' was all she'd say. Grandpa always smelt of rice wine when at last he stumbled cheerily into the kitchen after one of these visits. He was always keen to talk, but Nano would shush him off to his bed, determined that he'd sleep it off.

There was nothing for it. I cleaned up the chicken shed the next morning. Stripping the remaining feathers from the slaughtered hens was a horrible task. I had watched Nano gut them over the years, tearing the innards out with bloody fingers, but I loathed the smell and would find an excuse to be anywhere else if I could. If only Kit were here to help – he wasn't the least bit squeamish and often gave me game birds already drawn and plucked.

Eventually, the job was done. I scrubbed my hands for ages to rid myself of the whiff of guts. At least I had the makings of several days' food. I put the remains of the birds into a stewpot with onions, carrots and herbs and put it on the range to cook. I watched, pleased with myself as the mixture heated, and began to simmer gently.

But the feeling of wellbeing was short-lived.

When I went back outside I discovered something even more awful. There was an overwhelming silence. The mutan bees had abandoned the hive. And as I stood there, helplessly gazing at the empty boxes, it came into my head that I hadn't told them when Nano died, so it was my fault – you are always meant to tell the bees when there's a death in the family. 'They'll take off and go if they're not told,' Nano had warned as she'd waddled out there the day Grandpa died.

And now they'd done exactly that. Without bees, the fruit would not get pollinated. I had listened and learned enough to know that. There would be no sweetener, no beeswax for long-lasting candles, no fruit next year.

I stared and stared at the empty hive. It seemed as if everywhere I looked there was mayhem. My entire livelihood was being ruined. That winter had been hotter than ever, scorching the salad crops, then winds and rainstorms had battered the soft fruit. What hadn't been flattened or spoiled was being eaten by slugs and snails, or finished off by the parakeets, thanks to my own laziness. Even the orange trees had been attacked by fungus and root rot.

I couldn't carry on like this.

I ran back into the shack. Maybe there were some dees in the mysterious chest under the bed? I had another search for the key, in all the same places I'd looked before, with the same result. Perhaps I could force the lid open with a crowbar? Did I even have a crowbar? I'd have to ask Kit to help. Perhaps he'd know how to entice the bees back too.

After a while with the familiar calls of terns and oyster-catchers in my ears, I took a walk in search of herbs. I watched a flock of lugubrious pelicans heading off towards their feeding grounds. As I breathed in the salty aroma of seaweed, I wondered, what did I actually want? For things to go on as they always had? But what else was possible? There no point thinking about leaving Eden Spit. No one ever did, not even to other parts of Eden, let alone the rest of Nortland. Except the travs and privs, of course.

I hadn't even met my other set of grandparents. My father's family had lived in Spitsea, I'd been told. Nano had never explained why I'd never met any of them, except to say Spitsea was out of bounds. And once, when I was about ten, I'd overheard Grandpa Noah telling her that they were among 'the disappeared'. Later, I'd asked Nano, 'What are "the disappeared"?' She'd put her hand over my mouth and said, 'Never say that again, Flora!' The fear in her eyes came back to me now. What was that about?

'*Stay, Flora. Don't leave Shell Shack,*' she'd implored as she lay dying. 'You're safe here.'

I sat down on the damp grass, a tight feeling in my chest. What was it she'd left unspoken?

I tried to pull myself together. I had to be more practical.

I mustn't let everything go. That would be failing Nano and Grandpa. I had to make the place work now I was on my own. And I did love Shell Shack, and the barren beauty of Eden Spit.

I recalled how, when I was little, the creaking of the timbers on a stormy winter's night used to make me feel like I was on a galleon riding the waves in one of Grandpa's beautiful ships in a cola. The screech of parakeets, the scent of apples and orange blossom wafting through my window, the tall grasses whispering in the meadow, the rabbit warrens in the dunes, the constant boom of the sea – no, I couldn't imagine living anywhere else. But then I'd never imagined what it would be like without Nano and Grandpa Noah, the weight of responsibility for everything on my shoulders. This was my reality. I was on my own.

I had no father to turn to. He had sailed away before I was born. Nano once told me that he had gone to find us a better place to live. But he never came back. He never knew me, perhaps never even knew my mother had died. Maybe he liked it so much wherever it was that he went that he couldn't be bothered to come back for us. Or maybe there was no other place to live, no better way. Maybe he drowned somewhere out on the ocean in his little yacht. It must have been very dangerous, all on his own, with all the reefs and rocks and storms. Nano said he had dreams the size of the ocean – and that he was as easy to control.

One night when he was tucking me up in bed, I asked Grandpa Noah if my father would ever return, and he had whispered to me that he would. He had never repeated the promise, but one day when he was totally doolally, he stood on the beach shouting into the sky, 'Where are you, Redvers Mandela, we need you! We need you to kill these fecking fascist bastards!'

Nano and I had dragged him back to the shack and tried to quieten him. I'd never seen him so agitated.

No father, and no mother, and now no grandparents.

I'd have to face the searches all by myself in future. You could never tell when the Uzis would descend on us. 'Fascist bullies,' Grandpa used to say after they'd gone, and he would turn the digigraph of the Rice King to the wall again.

'You stupid old man, you'll get us all shot!' Nano would scold him and turn it back, then tut at me as I unearthed my book from the straw in the pigeon palace where Grandpa had hidden it.

All the stories that made me who I was were tied up in this place. Who would I be if I left Shell Shack? There was no choice anyway, was there? I had to make the best of things.

On the way back home I found six polythene bags that had been snagged on the thorns after the storm, all remarkably undamaged. I would fill them with grain and hang them high on ceiling hooks. That way the ants couldn't get at them. Nano would have been proud of me.

Kit arrived as I was adding mushroom stalks to the chicken stew.

'My bees have left and a fox got the hens,' I blurted out, trying not to cry.

Kit hugged me. Close to, he stank of his beloved ferret, but I was glad he was there.

Delighted to see each other again, the dogs started running about the small space and knocked over a chair.

'For Rice sake!' I shouted at them.

'Behave,' Kit said and let them out into the yard. 'What's cooking?'

'Chicken stew. Lots of it. Courtesy of Mr Fox. Better take some home for your dad.'

He grinned. 'Don't go giving it to the scav kid.'

'I'll do what I like with my food, thank you very much.' I lifted the lid and we both breathed in the delicious scent, our heads wreathed in steam.

CHAPTER THREE

THE RASPING SOUND of sawing wood woke me the next morning. Kit had made a list of things that needed doing and, as promised, he had come back to take down a dead orange tree in the orchard. He stopped as I handed him a tin mug of orange leaf tea.

'Thanks,' I said, 'I really needed more firewood.'

'Time it came down anyway.' He sipped the hot tea, and the pair of us leaned our backs against one of the other trees, looking out towards the water.

'Bit much for you, all this?' Kit asked.

I shrugged. Wasn't it obvious? He took one of my blistered hands in his. I had run out of ointment for them, just as I had run out of all sorts of things that Nano had made. I didn't know what the ingredients were. Some sort of mashed herbs and seaweed. I pulled it away, embarrassed.

'Nano managed.'

'You're not Nano.' He nodded at my bare legs. I had pulled on a pair of shorts when I woke – cut-off denims with lace edges – the lace from one of my mother's petticoats. 'I would never have caught her in that get-up,' Kit grinned.

I play-punched his shoulder and he pretended to punch me back. I wrestled him to the ground, the dogs barking in excitement at us. We ended up in a tangle of limbs, him tickling me until I screamed for mercy. It was good to laugh.

I watched as he sawed the branches into smaller lengths, then chopped them up. I helped him stack the logs into a pile that would last for ages, keeping the range lit.

Kit greased the axe and frowned at the state of my other garden tools. 'Flora, you really need to... you know... look after these, make them last,' he said with a rueful smile, obviously afraid that I'd bite his head off.

'I'll get a bucket of water, shall I?'

When I returned he was already busy cleaning the spades and hoes with a rag, greasing the metal parts and oiling the wood until they gleamed. 'Found a cloth – and this.' He held up a canister. 'Soya oil. There's plenty left in here,' he said, shaking it. Found it in the shed. Look after your tools and they'll look after you.'

It was something Grandpa Noah might have said.

'I know. Do you want something to eat? There's lots of chicken stew left.'

'I'd better get back to see to the old man. Frets if I'm gone too long.' Kit slotted the tools back into their stands in the shed, and swept the sawdust into a pan. 'A sprinkle of that should help get the range started,' he suggested.

'Thanks, Kit, I don't know what I'd do without you.' I felt my eyes fill with tears. 'The place hasn't looked so organised since...'

'Let's get some sea-coal, shall we? Day after tomorrow?'

'Yes, and we'll have that stew then, if there's any left.'

He gave me a quick hug and limped off, Jess at his heels.

And then the girl rode up.

Kit stopped dead at the sight of her.

This time she was wearing a riding skirt of red velveteen with a black jacket and a black felt hat decorated with red feathers. Dark curls fell loose on her shoulders like rippling water, and her black eyes sparkled. She was, quite simply, dazzling. She ignored Kit, rode straight past him; he might as well have been invisible.

'No red petticoat today?' she mocked, making me feel even more ridiculous in my lace-trimmed shorts. 'And where's your mutan terrier?' she added.

'He's not mutan,' I mumbled. Where was he, anyway? Manga was nowhere to be seen.

'I'll take them all.' She nodded towards the pickles then made a gesture of hopelessness. 'Oh dear, how in World will I carry them?

You'll have to deliver.'

'Deliver?' Nobody had ever asked me to deliver. Nobody ever bought enough of anything.

She nodded, as if it was a perfectly reasonable thing to ask.

'Where are you staying?' I heard myself asking.

'The Hall. The private wing of the Travilla up beyond the rice fields. You know where that is? Yes, you'd better deliver. Tomorrow.'

I clenched my jaw. 'Is there anything else you'd like?'

'What else do you have?'

'Potatoes, beeswax, preserves, apples, beans, eggs – oh no, no eggs, I forgot. Fox got the hens.'

'Beeswax, pickles, beans.' She counted them off on her delicate fingers. 'Tomorrow, remember.' Her tone suggested she was doing me a favour. Without waiting for any confirmation she flicked her little whip at the mare's flank and off she went.

I stared after her, furious. Why should I deliver to The Hall? I wasn't a skiv or a mart-keeper. But the thought of my empty cupboards and shelves forced me to button my lip.

'Who in the name of Rice was that?' Kit asked, clearly impressed.

I'd almost forgotten he was there.

'Looks like trouble, she does.'

'She knows what she wants, all right.'

'Has she been before?'

'A couple of days ago.'

'You didn't mention it.'

He was right, and I wasn't sure why not.

'She said her father wanted pickles. I'd run out, so I made some fresh ones. I didn't offer to deliver though.'

'I'll deliver to her.' Kit's lopsided grin was starting to annoy me.

'No you won't.'

'Please yourself…' Kit shrugged and started to walk away. 'But if you want company…? It's quite a long way to The Hall.'

Manga suddenly appeared in his path with a young doe in his jaws. That dog's passion for rabbits was bordering on an obsession. Kit bent to rub his ears, then turned back to me.

'I meant to say, better watch out, Flora. The scav kid's getting bold. He didn't even run away when he saw me earlier. Been thieving, more than likely.'

'There's not much left to take,' I pointed out.

'He could be toxic,' Kit warned as a parting shot. 'I've told you before.'

'And I've told you, I can handle the likes of that little tyke.'

Next morning I opened the wooden chest that had been Nano's pride and joy. I was quite excited by the prospect of visiting The Hall. All my mother's clothes lay neatly folded, smelling of lavender and aromatic cedar wood. I meant to show Miss Hoity-Toity that I, too, could be a lady. After much consideration I settled on an apple-green divided skirt, a denim shirt, a wide tan leather belt and sleeveless leather jerkin. And my work boots – my mother's feet had been much smaller than mine, so I had no choice. However, I decided to wear the yellow stockings. They might distract from the boots.

Manga found me as I was preparing to leave. He was sleepy and plump after his feast of rabbit the previous day but he sniffed at my clothes. He knew something was up. I put a good bundle of beans into a basket along with a stoneware jar of beeswax (the last I would have until I managed to re-establish the hive), added three jars of pickled shallots and set off across the fields. The day was muggy with a hazy sun, and the distant Tescopec Mountains to the north-west were obscured by a brown fug. It wasn't pleasant walking weather. The basket was heavy on my arm so I decided to turn back and head for the wooden pier. I would row around the bay in my dinghy instead of walking. It would be cooler on the water.

Between the beach and dunes I caught sight of the scav. At first I thought it was one of Annie Wang's little brothers. But no, it was definitely the boy who worried Kit so much, the one I'd caught at Shell Shack a couple of times stealing chicken feed. Over his matted brown dreadlocks he wore a peaked cap which had probably once been grass-green, but was now faded and salt-stained. He was sitting among the marram grass stripping black and white snails from the tips of stems. He put them whole into his mouth, chewing rapidly before spitting out fragments of shell. So intent was he on his snack that he started at my arrival and cringed away.

'Hello,' I said, glad to put down my basket. Manga bounced up the dune from where he'd been sniffing out rabbits and wagged his stumpy tail. The boy was wary of me but not prepared to leave the harvest of snails. Flies hovered over and around him, like an aura, a halo. His skin was grey, ingrained with grime. No wonder Manga was so keen on him. He stank even worse than Kit's ferret.

'Don't worry, I won't hurt you, and my dog's friendly, look!' I smiled and ruffled Manga's fur, and the terrier barked excitedly and ran in circles. I threw a stick and he fetched it. Then I handed the stick to the boy. 'You throw it, go on.'

He hurled the stick hard and Manga ran off to find it. When he returned and placed it at the boy's feet, the grubby child smiled broadly, showing gaps in his broken teeth, and threw it again. He giggled and offered me a snail, his jagged fingernails black with dirt.

'No, thanks. What's your name?'

He seemed not to understand. Snail slime dribbled from the corners of his mouth.

'I'm Flora Mandela.' I spoke slowly and held a hand to my chest. 'Flora Mandela.'

'Barcode!' he shouted out. 'Barcode, Barcode,' and he leapt up and down. I noticed a knife tucked in his belt.

'Where are you from, Barcode?' A stranger was a rare event on the Spit; a strange child was unheard of.

'Barcode, Barcode, Barcode.'

I nodded, smiling. That was as much as I was going to get.

Was he a rice-slave child escaped from the paddy fields near The Hall? Had he travved from the toxic mountains of Tescopec? How had he survived? Scav skills, I supposed. He was on his own too. Like me. I offered him a few beans from the basket. Delighted, he grabbed them, gathered his rags around him like tattered feathers and ran off like a tiny shore bird, moving lightly over the dunes on stick legs, his flat feet making hardly any impression on the sand.

A bittern boomed in the reeds and curlews piped their sobbing call as I made my way slowly down towards the water. The bay was as still as a silver plate and tiny wavelets licked the sloping shingle, dragging pebbles back and forth with a sucking, clicking sound. I shoved my boat out from the little wooden pier and rowed hard, enjoying the feel of my muscles working, glad I'd decided to come via the bay.

As the morning turned into afternoon, an easterly wind blew up. Manga stood at the prow, like a miniature figurehead, enjoying the wind ruffling his head and back. The day was becoming chilly. The sky ahead was an ominous mauve-grey. Lucky I had worn my jerkin.

I heard the bark of a dog on the shore and Manga answered, his tail quivering with excitement. Kit waved, Jess by his side. He called, but I couldn't hear what he said. I shrugged and waved back and pointed in the direction of The Hall. He would be wise to stay well clear. He probably had a duck or two in the canvas bag slung over his shoulder. His poaching was something I disapproved of. Not because I disapproved of poaching, but I worried that Kit would get caught and incarcerated in Maxsec. Nano had told me it was full of murderers and rapists, debtors and pirates. He might not even get that far – there were many tales of poachers being shot by the Uzi guards. Was Miss Hoity-Toity's pickle-loving father a hunting man? I wondered briefly.

The mechanical pull and thrust of my arms and body allowed me time to think. The girl's second visit hadn't affected me as much as the first had. Admittedly I'd agreed to this delivery against my better judgement, but now it suited me to go. I was mistress of Shell Shack, I told myself. She was just another trav, passing through. She must be rich if she was staying at The Hall, but she would be gone soon.

The previous day's anxiety gradually evaporated as I rowed onwards. There was no reason why I shouldn't be able to run Shell Shack properly, why I couldn't get help when I needed it. Kit had made short work of the orange tree. I only needed to ask for help, rather than pretending I could do everything myself. I was suddenly confident, mentally listing the high quality produce I'd take to Bartermart. I could make a decent living, I could refill the jar of dees. Today was just the start of good times, I decided.

Our neighbours used to trade with Nano for cheese and goat's milk, but the she-goat had died a year ago. At the time I wasn't sorry. The goat had taken a dislike to me after Nano became too weak to milk her, and she would charge me at every opportunity. We sold her kid when Grandpa Noah was at his worst and we needed dees to buy medicines Nano couldn't make. Although I'd been scared of the nanny goat, I sobbed hard over that kid. I'd thought of him as mine. Even gave him a name – Wicky (after Mr Wickham in our book).

But Nano had no time for my tears. 'You see something soft and cuddly where I see dairy and meat and the makings of a good stockpot,' she'd told me. Grandpa was as sentimental as me, though, over his pigeons or any hurt bird he came across, mending broken wings, feeding the wild birds with crumbs and precious grain.

I would buy a new goat – that would save me buying milk and cheese, and I could sell what I couldn't use. Transport was still going to be a problem. Other than my little boat or my own two feet I would have to rely on friends to get my produce to the Bartermart. I had no mule. If I had a pony as pretty as Miss Hoity-Toity's, I would teach it to pull a large skimboard. I could float stuff a long way using the water meadow or the shallows of the bay.

Kit would be amused at all my plans and ideas. He would point out that I had to prove that I could cope with the day-to-day chores needed to keep Shell Shack going for a start. I hadn't done terribly well so far. Then I had to earn the dees. But I was sure he'd be impressed too.

My arms were tiring. The wind was dancing, making even the shallows slap at the bow and Manga had taken refuge under my seat. It couldn't be much further now. I should have read the weather as Grandpa Noah had taught me. For a moment I wished I had asked Kit to come, but then I remembered that this gave me a chance to prove to him that I wasn't completely useless, that I had a proper business head on my shoulders.

The idea of having a business head made me smile, perked me

up. Perhaps I should go into business with Kit. *Business partners.* The idea appealed to me. Yes, I would ask him if he would consider working on Shell Shack, not just the occasional generous bit of chopping and carrying, but a real partnership. Although he had his father to look after, he might welcome the chance to work for me – *with* me. We could share the profits.

I was relieved when eventually I recognised a kink in the shoreline where I'd sometimes sat fishing with Grandpa Noah over the years. It was well hidden from The Hall, but not far away. I felt almost excited as I rowed towards a likely looking landing point. Despite the weather, I'd managed the trip well so far and I'd sorted out my muddled head, too. And if Kit didn't want to work for me maybe I could hide the young scav from the authorities and he would turn out to be an ace worker. There was something about him that I liked. He didn't judge me, or make me feel foolish. Even a small boy would be better than none. I would cope. Shell Shack would thrive.

Instead of feeling overwhelmed and useless, as I steered my dinghy towards the shore, I began to picture the kind of future I could look forward to.

CHAPTER FOUR

AS I ROWED through the reeds, I kept well in, nearly scraping the keel on the stony bottom. I didn't want to get lost on the outgoing tide. I had heard stories of others whose boats had floundered in fog, to be wrecked on the reef. Travs and scavs who didn't know the danger of gathering cockles on the mudflats had been caught out by sudden fog and the fast flooding tide. Many people had been lost in Eden Bay.

At the small cove just down the hill from The Hall I jumped out of the boat and pulled it up well beyond the high tide mark, leaving a sack under the thwart for Manga to lie on. 'Stay and guard the boat,' I instructed him. He wagged his excuse for a tail, his whole body swaying. Taking up the basket, I walked, then scrambled the few hundred yards up the lush valley towards the razor-wire fence surrounding the large house. I was wetter than I'd realised. My skirt clung heavily to my thighs, the shirt was plastered cold to my arms. So much for the elegant impression I had planned to make. Nothing I could do now, though. And anyway, I was only there to deliver the goods and collect my payment. This wasn't a social call.

The last occupant of The Hall had been an independent rice farmer who lived there with only a female skiv for company. After he died the place stood empty for ages, the haunt of owls and bats. The surrounding rice fields had been taken over by a syndicate of rice and water bankers, Beijing and Nortland Growers (B&NG) – *Buccaneers and Nasty Grab-alls,* Grandpa and his friends had called them.

Just a few months ago Eden County Council had announced that The Hall was being renovated as a Travilla. No one I knew had ever clapped eyes on a Council member, but we had to live by their edicts.

At the gates to The Hall an Uzi guard glanced at my basket, examined my identity card and nodded me through to the private wing, past a cage of slavering guard dogs which jumped up to the wire and snarled at me. I'd never been this close to the place before. Grandpa had always avoided it. I walked past dripping daturas, the bell flowers sweetly pungent, and squeezing by a giant gunnera's prickly stems, turned a corner into the driveway. Wreaths of wisteria festooned one wall. I was so taken aback by the size of the place that I almost walked into a grove of bamboo that was bent low under the weight of rain.

There was an obvious path round to the back of the private wing, but why should I go to the barterers' entrance? I carried my basket past a ruined dovecot and strode up the granite steps. With its large iron studs, the huge oak door was how I imagined a Maxsec entrance would look.

As I rang the bell I shivered, not just with cold.

Now that I was standing here, I wasn't as sure of myself. My clothes were drenched, my feet soaking, my arms ached from the heavy basket. I laid it down and, hands on hips, stretched back from my waist to ease my spine.

'Hey, what have we here?'

I dropped my hands to my sides.

'Is it a drowned rat?' the young man asked.

'I've come with the pickles,' I muttered, embarrassed.

'Where's your horse?'

'I came by boat.'

'By yourself?'

It was the girl's brother; it had to be. He looked so like her. His skin glowed with a bronze sheen, his hair shimmered like the feathers of a black swan.

Before I could reply, the girl appeared at his shoulder. 'Let her in, for Rice sake, she'll get pneumonia standing there.'

Before I could protest, I was whisked along corridors and down a stairway into a vast kitchen where there was a fire blazing. The girl wrapped me in a blanket and steered me towards the warmth, shooing away two lurchers who reluctantly moved towards the door and stood side by side, wagging their shaggy tails. Huge sides of salted hams, long strings of red onions and copper pans in all sizes hung from hooks on the beams. I had never been in a room that big.

My teeth chattered.

'You're cold. We must get you out of those wet clothes. Come with me.' The girl ignored my protestations, leading me up the back stairs to the next floor, along an oak panelled passageway and into an even larger room lined with a pink flower-patterned wallpaper. A fire burned brightly in the hearth, reminding me of some of the descriptions I'd read in *Pride and Prejudice*. In Shell Shack the fire was in the cooking range – we never had enough wood for a fire like this. There were two wide beds with white muslin curtains draped between carved corner posts, and on the ceiling above each bed hung a knotted mosquito net. Polar bear skin rugs littered the wooden floor, and red velvet sofas stood by the fire. I couldn't believe my eyes.

The girl handed me a cotton towel. 'Here – dry your hair.'

I stood, stranded, while she opened a wardrobe and flung several dresses onto the bed. 'Change your clothes.'

'I can't wear your clothes. I have to row back home.'

'You'll do as I say,' she insisted – I thought she was going to stamp her foot. 'We won't be held responsible if you catch your death.'

I had never undressed in front of anyone in my life. It was humiliating. As if she was dealing with a small child, the girl pointed towards a folding screen made of inlaid wood.

'Hang your wet things over the top. And hurry up –before you catch a chill!'

I crept behind the screen, peeled off my soaking clothes and flipped them across the top. So much for my earlier bravado. This was somebody used to getting her way.

'Skiv! Come here at once,' she shouted.

For a moment I wondered if she was talking to me. But someone opened the door and came softly into the room.

'Get these dried.' My wet clothes were pulled away. 'And clean the boots.'

The longest of the dresses was made of very fine soft grey blue wool, but it was still far too short for a girl my height. I pulled thick black stockings over my knees. I couldn't possibly get my feet into the tiny shoes the girl had brought me. I walked out from behind the screen to be greeted by a peal of laughter. I didn't need a mirror to know how silly I looked.

'Here, wear this.'

She handed me a heavy silk and wool kimono, embroidered in red and yellow and green, so gorgeous it could have been one of my mother's garments. I wrapped myself in it, admiring its elaborate pattern. I noticed the girl had changed into a scarlet silk cheongsam with daring side slits. It looked so sophisticated.

'Now, come with me...'

I followed the imperious creature along corridors hung with paintings in ornate gilt frames, somehow reminded of the tales about the Snow Queen that Grandpa had told me when I was little. The Snow Queen had been ravishingly beautiful, but...

Eventually the girl stopped at a door, rapped on it with her fist and burst in without waiting for a response.

'Papa, this is...' she faltered, giggling. 'I don't even know your name.'

'It's Flora,' I whispered.

Her father was a slender man with dark hair greying at the temples, almond-shaped eyes and a waxed moustache that was twisted up at the ends in stiff little horns. He looked up at us from an elegant writing desk. 'Flora who?'

'Flora of the red petticoat, Papa. Remember? I told you about her. From Eden Spit. She's brought your pickles and beans.'

'Ah, *that* Flora.'

The brother and sister had foreign accents, like all the travs, but their father's was stronger. He rose from his chair and kissed his daughter on both cheeks, then held out his hand to me. It was cool and smooth. I was horribly aware of the roughness of my own hands.

'She was soaked right through, Papa, you wouldn't believe it.

But look at her now. Doesn't she suit Mama's kimono?'

It was her mother's? I concentrated my gaze on the black spaniel that had appeared by my side and bent to stroke him, trying not to stare at the shelves of books that surrounded me.

'If you say so, *ma petite*.' The man smiled at me, and I caught a glimpse of gold teeth. 'Your mother's clothes will fit her better than yours. But please find her some shoes.'

I curled my toes when he glanced down at my stockinged feet.

The girl – I still didn't know her name – giggled again, took my hand and dragged me downstairs to the kitchen, where my own clothes hung, steaming, on the wooden clothes drier above the huge iron oven. On the other side of the kitchen a skiv stood with her back to us, transferring hot scones from an oven tray to a cooling rack. The smell was delicious and the sudden growl of my stomach reminded me of how long it had been since breakfast.

'Annie, give Flora a scone.'

The skiv turned and our eyes met. I felt a rush of relief.

'Hello, Annie, how's the new baby brother?' I was delighted to find a friendly face. Annie and I had been in the same class. I hadn't seen much of her in the couple of years since we left school, though we heard news of her family. But not the news she was about to give me.

'Died. Four weeks ago,' she replied in a low voice.

The trav moved to the window, ignoring our conversation.

'Oh, I'm so sorry. I hadn't heard. How's your mother?'

'Not so good.' Annie put some honey on a scone and silently indicated that it was for me. But at my very first bite, I began to choke.

Impatiently nodding to Annie to get on with her work, the girl took a glass and poured some liquid into it from a bottle on the sideboard. 'Drink this, it's rice raki,' she instructed, pressing the glass to my lips.

The strong liquid burnt my throat and made me cough even more. My eyes streamed as I tried to regain my breath.

The girl watched me. She was, I realised, absolutely unconcerned.

My humiliation was complete when, just as I thought things

couldn't get worse, her brother strode into the kitchen.

Overwhelmed with self-consciousness and still coughing, I clutched the kimono round my body.

He waited until I had recovered before offering his hand in the manner of his father.

'We haven't been properly introduced. Yo-yo Lao,' he said, bowing slightly.

'Flora Mandela,' I said, my voice squeaky.

'And of course you already know my sister, Li-li. You will stay for supper?' he asked.

'I'm sorry, I can't. My dog's waiting in the boat, there's the chickens to…' I trailed off, remembering that there were no longer any chickens.

'You *will* stay and eat with us,' declared Li-li, allowing no room for argument.

I had no doubt of my ability to row back home in the dark. A hunter's moon would light my way. But, 'You will stay and eat with us,' repeated Yo-yo, his gaze holding mine. And the truth was, at that precise moment I wanted nothing more than to stay.

Before supper I was offered the chance to select a different outfit, this time from clothes that had belonged to Li-li's mother, who had evidently been a tall woman. Encouraged by Li-li, I tried on various combinations while she explained that her mother had come from Murdoch, in the far north, while her father was from Indo-Aje. I tried to look knowledgeable. In fact I knew nothing of what lay beyond the boundaries of Eden.

'Is that your mother?' A large framed digigraph of a strikingly pretty Indo-Aje woman hung on the pink silk-lined wall of her mother's opulent room.

'Yes, that's her. She's lovely, isn't she? She died when I was three.'

'I'm sorry. My mother died too.' At least we had that in common.

My reflection in the huge mirror in Li li's room showed that the brown woollen dress embroidered with bright pink silk flowers I finally selected could have been made for me. It was a perfect fit and I'd never seen myself looking so graceful, so adult. I loved it.

Li-li found a pair of almost unworn suede shoes that fitted perfectly. My hair, brushed by an enthusiastic Li-li into submission, looked sleek and golden rather than the usual unruly orange fuzz.

'I do wish I had your height,' sighed Li-li. 'I'm so small I could be in a circus!'

'A circus?' I'd heard of those from one of Nano's friends. 'Are there circuses still?'

'Of course there are! Have you never been to a Mutan-Cirque?' Li-li looked appalled at this inconceivable void in my experience. 'I have been to circuses all over World,' she boasted. 'I love them! I might run away to be a trapeze artist one day.' With that, she hitched up her skirt and performed a neat cart-wheel.

She looked as if she expected me to applaud her gymnastic skills, but I found myself struggling against an insane desire to laugh. I didn't know what to think. Somehow I managed to stutter something complimentary. That seemed to do the trick and she beamed at me, as if my appreciation was to be expected.

I began to hang the other clothes back in the wardrobe.

'Oh leave that to the skiv,' Li-li interrupted, seizing them from me and dropping them in a heap on the floor. 'Come...'

Supper was a succulent bean and meat stew, flavoured with herbs and spices that I had never tasted before, served with a large silver bowl full of fragrant top-grade rice. As I ate, I watched the way the family enjoyed each other's company. There was no silent eating here. They all talked at the same time, laughing, licking their greasy fingers, shouting, interrupting each other, in an Indo language I couldn't make head or tail of. I tried to follow, but my expression must have given me away.

'I apologise for my unruly children,' said Li-li's father. 'In Nortland we must speak only Nort,' he admonished them, though he smiled proudly.

Rich drapes of purple velvet hung over the mullioned windows and tall candles cast a flickering glow over the scene. It was like a cameo from my Jane Austen book, except that I was one of the characters.

The Laos must have moved in as soon as the The Hall was renovated. There were wooden crates still unopened in the corners of the dining room. I couldn't help comparing this place with home. I watched and ate and drank, enjoying the kind of meal of which I might have dreamed in the past, had I known such a thing was possible.

As the evening went on I felt my cheeks grew fiery – it was probably the fault of the rice wine. Nano's elderflower cordial had never had this effect. But it was also because I was so happy to be there. I could almost pretend my life on the Spit didn't exist. Every so often, the Laos would turn their attention to me, asking my opinion on a topic, or demanding that I adjudicate in one of their light-hearted quarrels. I stuttered and blushed, but their encouraging looks reassured me, and gradually I relaxed. Li-li's laughter sounded warmer than it had earlier, but it was when Yo-yo's eyes met mine that I felt my heart soar.

Reality re-entered once we had finished eating, when Annie came to clear the plates away. She avoided my glance. The others ignored her completely, and I could tell they were uncomfortable when I offered a muttered 'Thank you.'

'Come…' Li-li took my hand and led me into what she called 'the sitting room'. 'We'll leave the men to their water pipes,' she said, as if she was talking about children and their toys. The sitting room had red silk wall coverings, and huge sofas of white leather strewn with velvet cushions. On the floor were large silk rugs in deep purples and pinks. All around were glass cabinets full of books. They were everywhere.

'Disgusting habit! Why do they do it?'

Waterpipes were almost unknown on the Spit, except amongst off duty Uzi guards, lolling on the dunes.

'I don't know…' I said. I'd never really thought about it.

Li-li threw her slender arms in the air, exasperated. All her movements were graceful. I was a gawky stork next to her. When I went to look out of the window I almost fell over my feet. What was wrong with me? Until this evening they had always been perfectly able to do what they were supposed to do.

Rain streaked the glass, but I noticed a lightness to the west.

Li-li suddenly appeared close to me, so close I could have counted the eyelashes that curled around her eyes.

'How did you get the scar on your chin?'

'Fell out of a tree when I was six. That's how this happened.' I pointed to my chipped front tooth. 'Broke this too.' I wiggled my bent nose. 'I told my grandma that the tree had thrown me out.'

We giggled together.

'It adds to your interesting looks,' Li-li said as if she meant it. 'You could be very attractive, do you know that? Though I disapprove of your rough hands. We'll have to do something about that. Wait here.' She disappeared for a few moments, then returned with a blue jar. Sitting me down, she took my hands and stroked soothing cream into them.

'Isn't Yo-yo marvellous? I love him so much,' she said in a confiding tone. 'He's my absolute hero.'

'Your hero?'

'Yes. He's so clever. He's studying astronomy, you know.'

'What's that?' I had to ask.

'Oh... Astronomy? He examines the planets through a telescope.'

'How wonderful!' I had never met an astronomer, nor even known that there was a name for such people. Imagine spending your life gazing at the stars! I couldn't wait to tell Kit, who was forever staring up at them. He would love the idea that he was an astronomer.

'Yo-yo is building a telescope to view a comet that will soon be visible. Eden Spit will be a good place to observe it from – that's one of the reasons we're here. Papa is also interested in astronomy, though he knows all about the other sciences too. He's a googler. A collector. He collects, not just things, but ideas as well. He is a patron of the Great Flood Museum.'

I stared at Li-li. Had she any idea how different we were? Or did she simply assume that everybody knew what she knew?

There was nothing familiar about this situation. Nothing that connected it with my life at Shell Shack. I had never felt this sense of excitement before. It was as if I had been waiting all my life for this opportunity, and for these people.

CHAPTER FIVE

IT WAS LATE. And I wanted to stay with the Laos forever. I hadn't contributed much to the conversation, but I had listened and admired. Yo-yo smiled often at me and his father poured me more wine than I should have had. Li-li and I were curled up on a pink sofa, surrounded by black fur cushions.

Through the windows I could see the sun setting into the sea beyond the trees. The rain had stopped.

'I must get going,' I announced, standing. The wine had made my head spin.

'Oh, must you? Won't you stay the night?' Li-li implored.

'No, I must go while the tide is right.' I longed for her to forbid me but she didn't.

'Very well, but you must come again. Soon! You could ride my pony. You could see my doll-houses and all my dolls.'

I smiled to think that Li-li still played with dolls. Perhaps she was younger than I had imagined. The only 'doll' I had ever owned was actually a hollow plastic head, bald and eyeless, which Grandpa Noah had found on the beach. Dolly still sat on the mantelshelf alongside the one surviving ship in a cola that Grandpa had made, and his tin whistle. Li-li would be less than impressed at my solitary excuse for a doll.

'Promise?'

'If I have time, Li-li.' I smiled. 'But now I must change back into my own clothes and get going.'

'No, child, keep those for your journey home, bring them back another day.' Mr Lao went to a drawer and pulled out a handful of dees. He counted them into my hands. 'It has been a pleasure to meet you, my dear. You must come again and amuse my beloved daughter. She is so easily bored with just her father and brother for company.'

His manner was impeccably courteous, his tone so warm and considerate that I was completely bowled over. I nodded.

Annie was summoned. She had bundled up my still damp clothes in a canvas bag which she handed me in silence. She kept her eyes lowered.

'Will you be safe rowing home all alone?' Yo-yo asked, as we walked towards the door.

'I've rowed these waters all my life,' I said briskly, although that wasn't strictly true. I had only been able to row since I was seven, when Kit had taught me. But I probably knew the bay and its shifting sands and currents as well as anybody. The real world was creeping back towards me now and the thought of Manga waiting in the boat made me anxious to take my leave. He had gone supperless, poor thing. 'It's a while yet until the Hurricane Weeks,' I said, hoping I sounded like an expert.

'Well, if you're sure,' said Yo-yo.

I stepped out of the pretty shoes and pulled on my boots, which had not looked this shiny since Grandpa was alive. He had cleaned all our shoes once a week, resoling them, if they needed it, on a metal last.

'I suppose... could I possibly take a bone for my dog?'

Yo-yo nodded and called for Annie. A few minutes later, she came back with a wrapped parcel.

'Tell your mother I'm sorry for your loss,' I said as she handed it over. I didn't want to leave without making more of a connection with my old school friend. Annie hesitated, but said nothing.

'Back to the kitchen, skiv. Haven't you work to do?' Li-li clapped her hands.

Annie ducked down and up again in what might have been a curtsey, then scuttled off.

'See you soon, Flora, do come again, any time.'

Li-li's voice was suddenly cold. It was only minutes since she had begged me to come back and I was taken aback at the abrupt change in her tone. Perhaps her invitation hadn't been genuine.

'I'd like to see this boat of yours,' said Yo-yo, cheerfully ignoring the chill in the air. He pulled a cloak from a row of hooks by the door and wrapped it around his shoulders.

Li-li showed no signs of coming too.

'But Yo-yo, I want you to play chess with me,' she protested. 'You promised.'

'Set up the board. I'll be back before you know it,' Yo-yo said, unmoved.

I couldn't help smiling. 'Goodbye!' I waved to Li-li. 'And thank you.'

She raised her hand briefly and closed the door with a bang.

Yo-yo and I walked side by side in the gathering dusk. Next to him I felt clumsy and inelegant. I couldn't think what to say. But he seemed perfectly at ease, whistling a tune, his hands in the pockets of his cloak, asking me the occasional question. I was very aware of his faint scent of lemon and spices. I'd never known a man to wear scent. We walked on, neither of us saying much, with me pointing out the way from time to time.

Suddenly, he grabbed my arm.

'Look,' he said, 'close to the horizon – Venus!'

'Is that its name? Beautiful,' I nodded, enjoying the pressure and heat of his hand on my arm.

We continued along the path. Deep darkness was falling fast, but the clouds had dispersed, revealing the large yellow moon.

'Do all the stars have names?' I asked. Grandpa Noah had told me the names for some of the groups of stars but I'd never been sure if they were just made-up. Yo-yo pointed out Mars, Saturn, the Great Bear. Grandpa must have learned these names from others, I realised. I did know something about astronomy after all.

'Halley's Comet will be visible very soon,' Yo-yo enthused. 'It only appears every seventy-six years. The last time was 2061.' He started to spout all sorts of facts about planets and comets. Now he had lost me. It didn't matter though. I was more interested in the sound of his voice than his words.

At the beach Manga flung himself at me, delighted that I'd come back at last.

'Good boy, good dog,' I scratched his ears. He growled at the sight of Yo-yo and I petted him quiet, apologising.

'Did you really come in this?' Yo-yo raised his beautifully curved eyebrows.

'What's wrong with it?' I asked defensively.

'It's so... small.'

'Big enough and seaworthy enough for me,' I said, throwing the bag of clothes into the bottom of the boat. 'And for your father's pickles.'

'You are quite something,' Yo-yo said.

'What do you mean?'

His gaze was direct. 'You are completely different from all the girls I usually meet.'

'Am I? In what way?' I couldn't help it – I wanted him to flatter me. Nano would have been appalled.

'You are so natural. A child of nature. Self-sufficient.'

I turned my back on him. How wrong he was. But he need never know how hopeless I was at looking after myself. Things were going to change.

'Do you think so?' My blush would not be visible in the moonlight. I untied the ropes.

'Go on, I can't wait to see you rowing.' He helped me push the boat down the shingle and into the water. I climbed in and hooked the oars into the rowlocks. I had intended changing out of the lovely dress before I got in the boat, not wanting to spoil it with salt water and sweat, but with Yo-yo there I couldn't. I hitched the skirt up over my knees to keep the hem from getting wet.

'Come, Manga,' I commanded, and the little terrier splashed into the shallow water and scrambled in, then stood on the stern thwart, barking at Yo-yo.

'I think he might be jealous,' Yo-yo shouted.

He stood on the shore, watching.

I could see his silhouette long after I had pulled away.

Then it was gone.

The journey home went faster than I'd expected, not only because the tide was with me: moonlight created a pathway through the water. I couldn't remember having felt this exhilarated and happy before. No one had ever spoken to me as Yo-yo had. No one had ever looked at me that way. And I had never felt this electric feeling on my skin and in the pit of my belly before. What had he said?

You are quite something...

Me, Flora scar-face Mandela!

And I had been invited back to The Hall. Just wait until I told Kit!

I went through every detail in my mind – the hams hanging in the kitchen, the luxurious furniture, the marble fireplaces, the sheer amount of delicious food, the silver plates, the warmth, and most of all, the books. Li-li's behaviour had been difficult to gauge, and I shivered slightly as I recalled the way she had treated Annie. But these people were different, I told myself. They didn't behave as we did on the Spit.

I stowed the boat and set off over the dunes. My spirits remained high until I pushed open the door to Shell Shack. I was on my own.

I busied myself lighting candles, put the precious dees into the jar on the mantelpiece, changed out of my finery, fed Manga with a scrap of meat and a little of the fat from the bone, then put the bone into a covered pan with herbs and shallots to make stock. The range had gone out, so it would have to wait until the morning to cook.

I wiped my hands on my apron and looked around my one-room home. Everything was worn and patched. It was all so faded, so shabby.

I fell into bed, exhausted. But my head was still fuzzy and my thoughts grabbed at me, fending off sleep.

Next morning, Kit came by with Jess. He dumped a sack of sea-coal by the woodpile.

'Oh, thanks,' I said. We were supposed to have gathered it together but it was a tedious, back-breaking task, so I couldn't help feeling relieved.

'So who is she?' he asked.

'Good morning to you too, Kit. Who is who?' I teased.

'Horse-girl.'

'Her name's Li-li Lao, and I had supper with her and her father and brother last night at The Hall, so there!' I couldn't contain my glee.

'I don't believe you.'

'I don't care what you believe,' I replied smugly, wheeling a barrow of compost to the vegetable plot. Nothing was going to sully the experience I'd had. Kit and I forked the sweet-smelling stuff into the earth together. I felt the old fondness for him welling up. He was my oldest and dearest friend and he was doing his best for me.

Perhaps now was the moment to put my proposal to him.

'Could you see yourself working here, Kit? At Shell Shack?'

'Become your slave, you mean?' He leaned on his fork and gave me a cheeky grin.

'No, my business partner. Share profits. I've been thinking about it for a while. I want to make something of this place. Get chickens, ducks, geese, a kid, maybe a mule. More bees. I can't manage on my own.'

Kit said nothing. He leant on his fork, looking at the ground. Annoyed by his silence, I began to babble, partly through anxiety and partly through anger.

'I met that scav boy yesterday,' I told him. 'He's harmless. He's called Barcode. *He* might want to work for me,' I suggested.

Kit sniffed hard and spat on the ground. 'Don't be stupid, Flora.'

'Want some rice cake and an onion?' I knew him well enough not to push him any further. But I couldn't work out what his reaction was to my proposal.

Jess yapped at the word 'cake' and we both laughed.

The forking complete, we sat under the apple tree Grandpa had planted in memory of my mother, the sun in our faces, our dogs, side by side, patiently waiting for scraps. Kit was still subdued. Surely he wasn't offended by my idea?

'Everything all right? How's your dad?'

He chucked a clump of earth at a carrion crow that had come

too close. It looked scornfully at him and flapped off a little way.

He shook his head. 'Worse than usual. He does nothing to help himself and he makes my life miserable too.'

'I'm sorry...'

Nano had often observed that things between Kit and his father weren't helped by their living conditions. Their yurt wasn't far away on the other side of the Spit, but it had none of the homely touches that Nano had given Shell Shack. Untanned wolf skins were spread over the earth floor and dusty blankets hung on the canvas walls. It was always smelly so I hardly ever visited. Kit's ferret ran free around the place.

Eventually Kit scratched his crotch and pulled his grubby cap down over his forehead. I tried not to think of Yo-yo, his delicate scent and his immaculate manners.

'I'll think about it – what you said earlier.'

'What?'

'The job, partnership, whatever.'

'Shared profits and responsibilities,' I reminded him.

'Yeah, business partners.' He looked hopefully at me. 'Do you ever... Don't suppose you'd want a partnership... of a different kind?'

'What do you mean?' I was embarrassed by the dismissive tone of my own voice. He had caught me off guard.

His eyes narrowed and he turned away. 'Nothing, nothing. What else could you possibly want from somebody like me?'

I started fussing, trying to cover up for the way I'd reacted. 'Come eat with me, Kit. Lunch tomorrow? We can talk about it some more? It could work well for both of us. Many hands and all that...'

'Yeah...' He stood up as if to leave, but hesitated.

'You could do with the extra food, couldn't you?' I pressed on. 'You and your dad? What are you eating these days? No fresh veggies, I bet. Not much fruit.'

'We get by.' He jerked his head in the direction of the wrecked fruit cages. 'And you've not got a great deal to offer around here, now have you?'

His tone was friendly and I smiled back.

'Tomorrow,' he said.

He chucked a tiny piece of rice cake to his collie. She caught it and swallowed it whole, then sat, ears cocked as if expecting more. Manga looked at me accusingly, so I threw him my last piece.

Kit looked as if he was waiting for something. Then he tinkered with some kindling, neatening the pile for me. There was still an atmosphere between us.

'What's she like?'

'Who?'

'What's-her-name, Lillo.'

I laughed. So *that* was why he was hanging around. 'Oh. Li-li Lao. Well, Murdoch mother, dead, Indo-Aje father, very good looking. And she has a brother.' I felt myself blushing and dipped my chin. 'Yo-yo Lao.' I relished being able to speak his name, moving my lips around the sound, savouring its strangeness.

'Li-li Lao. And Yo-yo Lao,' Kit said quietly, and smiled. 'Li-li. Pretty. Yeah, well, I'm off.' He threw the fork into the wheelbarrow and took off, Jess at his heels.

But as he was opening the gate, two Uzi soldiers on horseback appeared, trotting towards us.

Ever since I was a child I had disliked their black helmets and uniforms. One of them would stand at the back of the class at Eden Spit School, bored and sullen. He'd lead us all home in a crocodile at the end of the morning – the de Kooning kids, Stefan and Olaf, Sami and Cher Karim, Annie and Wu Wang, Kit and me. I was scared of the anonymous young man who never spoke to us. You couldn't see his eyes through the dark visor.

The Uzis shouted at Kit and pointed at the gate with their guns. He opened it and walked back into the yard, Jess cowering at his heel, followed by the guards, one tall and thin, the other a head shorter, and sturdier. My heartbeat quickened. Had I left my book out? They had done a search only a couple of weeks ago. I had thought myself safe for a while yet. From the corner of my eye I saw Barcode slide out of the barn and slip away. Scavs were shot on sight in Eden, he must have known.

I hoped my face hadn't given away my fear to the soldiers.

They dismounted and pushed us inside the shack, kicking at our dogs, shutting them out. As usual, the Uzi soldiers said nothing as they poked into cupboards, beds and drawers, guns at the ready. Lazy, they had never even looked under the beds properly. My eyes flickered over the room. Where *was* the book? Kit was shoved against the wall and searched. His face was expressionless. Thank Rice he hadn't any poached rabbit or duck on him. And he'd left his gun behind, presumably buried somewhere (he used a different hiding place each time, he once told me). The two dogs were barking and scratching at the door.

When the thin soldier came over to the range to search me, the sturdier one began to climb the ladder to the loft space where I slept. Then I remembered – that morning I'd thought I'd heard the buzzing of bees and had dashed out to see if my swarm had returned. I'd dropped the book on the top step of the ladder. I felt sick.

Without thinking, I pushed the empty kettle onto the floor. The clatter made the soldiers turn in alarm, lifting their guns.

'Oops! Sorry about that.' I raised my hands to show that it had been an accident. 'What about some mint tea? Or an orange?' I pointed at the bowl of fruit and tried to remain calm. The thin one shook his head but the sturdy one wanted to take me up on the offer and climbed back down the ladder. His friend turned back to me.

I hated being felt over like this, hated it more each time, hands prodding and patting. I always scrubbed myself from head to toe afterwards. Once it was over, they said something to each other in their harsh language and shook their heads. Time to move on. Thank Rice they hadn't found the book. The thought of having it confiscated was almost worse than the whipping I'd have to face for having it in my possession.

Kit was still standing where they left him, against the wall on which the portrait of the Rice King hung.

The soldiers went to leave but then the short one's eyes fell on the brown wool embroidered dress. He lifted it off the bed with the barrel of his Uzi gun.

'Where get?' he demanded, fingering the soft fabric with suspicion.

'It's my mother's,' I lied. I walked over to the cedar wood chest and opened it. 'Look, more of her clothes.' I was sweating.

The soldier seemed satisfied. To my huge relief, he dropped the dress back on the chair. I hoped he couldn't see that I was shaking. He took several oranges, throwing some to his mate and pocketing three for himself. When he opened the door the dogs fell back, whining.

The Uzis headed off to their next search, their horses' hooves almost silent on the sandy earth. A flock of lapwing took flight and passed over us. We watched, in silence, until the horses were out of sight.

I burst into tears of relief.

Kit turned to me. 'What were you thinking of?' he said angrily.

'I was only trying to keep him from finding my book.'

'Not that. I mean the scav kid. I saw him run off. You could be shot for harbouring a scav. All that stuff about him working for you is rubbish, you must know that, Flora. He'll be shot when they find him.'

I wiped my eyes with the backs of my hands. Who did he think he was? 'I'll do what I like on my own land,' I said, determined not to give way.

'Well, if you're so clever, maybe you don't need a business partner.'

I shrugged. 'What has Barcode got to do with anything?'

'I'm not going to risk getting shot for your pet scav.'

'Please yourself,' I retorted, 'but how would you feel if it was you with nowhere to live? Poor little kid, it's not his fault.'

Kit gave me a bitter smile. 'And this?' He lifted the hem of the brown dress as if it was contaminated. 'Where did this come from? Accepting presents from the privs now?'

'Don't be ridiculous...' I spluttered to a halt. Explaining the dress to Kit would be even harder than explaining it to the Uzis.

But Kit had had enough. Calling Jess, he went off.

'Don't forget tomorrow,' I shouted after him.

There was no sign that he had heard me.

'Well, see if I care,' I mumbled to myself. Manga leapt up at me and I took him into my arms. He licked my tears away. I hated anyone to think badly of me, especially Kit.

CHAPTER SIX

FIRST THING THE next morning I dug up some potatoes, scrubbed them, sliced a few shallots, carrots, and apples, and put the lot, with the meat stock from the bone, plus a cupful of yesterday's soup, with added seasoning and herbs, into Nano's biggest pot onto the lit range. This was the first time since she'd died that I'd managed to get a proper stock pot brewing. Things were going to change around here.

I left a covered bowl of cold chicken soup by the barn for Barcode. Whatever Kit's warnings, I didn't mind. The boy looked half starved. And I didn't need the barn for storage yet. As far back as I could remember the only thing it had housed was one of Grandpa Noah's sculptures – a dove woven from willow boughs – the biggest thing he had ever made. He'd never got round to dismantling a side of the barn so that he could get it out and Nano referred to it as 'Noah's folly'. I couldn't imagine what the scav boy made of it.

I kept squinting out of the window, hoping to see Kit walking up the path. He would come round to the idea of a partnership here, if only because he needed to grasp any opportunity to earn some dees, given that his income was practically nil. He fed his father and himself mostly on the mutan mussels and the odd eel that he collected from the rocks on the beach beyond his yurt. I was fairly sure that he was bartering poached rabbits for basics like salt and rice. It made sense for him to work with me, to supplement his meagre income.

I opened the door and shook out a cloth. Where was he? I had done more thinking during the night. I would expand the smallholding, be a proper farmer. With time and a bit of help from Kit I could make things work. I had ideas, ambitions. But midday came and went and Kit didn't come. Well let him sulk, I thought. I went to look at the hives but the bees hadn't come back. No sign of Barcode either.

The sun was too hot for me to do any more digging. It wouldn't be too long before the Hurricane Weeks, when the shore and waters were out of bounds. At full moon the tides could rise up to Shell Shack from the waters on either side of the Spit and although I'd never seen that myself, I knew about when it happened before I was born because Grandpa Noah had hammered an old pan handle into the wall to mark the highest point the water reached. Then after the Hurricane Weeks the Big Heats would come. I always dreaded the energy-sapping humidity, the way I had to stay inside in the shade except for an hour or so at dawn and dusk and when it was dark. And with the Big Heats came the droughts. Ever since I was a child I'd had a horror of not having enough drinking water.

Still no Kit.

I don't care what he thinks, I told myself. There were other places I could go for help. I would go where I was appreciated.

You are quite something.

Yo-yo's words kept breaking into my thoughts.

You are quite something.

Yes. I could go to The Hall, to see Li-li of course, play with her dolls if she wanted me to, perhaps get a chance to read some of the books. The Laos would understand my ambition, they might even be prepared to give me some business advice.

But I knew perfectly well that the main reason I wanted to go back was to see Yo-yo. And now that I had made my mind up, I realised that I didn't want Kit to be involved, or even to know that I intended to go there. He would think it stupid of me. Strange. Pig-headed.

By mid-afternoon there was still no sign of him. It was almost as if he had given me his permission to do as I planned, by not turning up.

Impetuous, Nano often called me, said I was just like my father. I went and found the one digigraph I had of my parents and, as I had done thousands of times before, examined it minutely. My blond-haired father stood in front of his sailing boat, arms crossed. Tall, strong, fearless. My mother, next to him in the white dress – the mass of red curly hair, long legs, dark skin. I might *look* like her, but inside I knew I was more like him, and I was glad.

For the first time I saw that my mother looked sad.

I had once asked Nano and Grandpa Noah whether being impetuous was a good or a bad thing. They had looked at each other before Nano answered, 'We're not sure, Flora.'

But now I was sure.

I bathed and washed my hair at the pump and changed from my work clothes into a pretty dress of my mother's – printed blue daisies on white linen. There were violet stockings which went with it. But my clumpy boots were a constant reminder of my actual poverty. I wished I had pretty shoes – and places to wear them. I brushed my hair a hundred times until it shone, refolded the brown dress, placed it carefully in a bag and then decided I should take some flowers. It was only polite to take a gift when one went visiting, as I had learned from Nano. I gathered all I could from the flower garden. It looked so neglected. Marigolds and sunflowers had seeded themselves in the vegetable plot but Grandpa said these plants made 'good companions' as they attracted greenfly away from the crops. However, Japanese knotweed was not good and it was invading everywhere.

I stood up on the gate to give Kit a final chance to appear. No sign? Good!

A strong onshore wind in my face, the scent of the flowers in my nostrils, I called Manga and strode off up the Spit through long grass dotted with pink convolvulus, my boots growing dustier with pollen at every step. As I walked, I played a game I often played: making pictures from the clouds. There a castle, there a boat. I was enjoying myself. If I squinted one way I could see a vast loaf of bread, the other and it was a dragon. And just then, I lost my footing. A rabbit hole! I felt my left ankle twist and collapse and I fell.

While I sat nursing the ankle, moaning with the pain, Manga took the opportunity to disappear down another burrow, but reversed out quickly, his nose caked with sandy earth. He sat waiting for me to get up and set off again, but I couldn't bear to put any weight on my foot.

I called out 'Barcode!' in the hope that he was following, but there was no reply. There was nobody about.

I had no choice. I had to get moving. I pushed myself up and limped a short distance, tears filling my eyes. I had dropped the flowers when I fell but I couldn't face going back.

The pain was so bad I had to sit down again. At least I still had the bag with the brown dress. I hadn't lost that. I tried to take off my boot, but the foot and ankle were already so swollen that I couldn't.

Manga, who was usually so responsive to my mood, suddenly barked and wagged his tail. What was he so cheerful about? I smelled the scav before I heard or saw him. Thank Rice.

'Flora Mandela, Flora Mandela.'

Barcode leaned over me, the bunch of sea pinks I'd dropped clutched in his grubby hands. He tried to help me up. He was too little to be of any use, but he tried.

'Go tell Kit,' I begged him. 'Kit, my friend. The boy with the bad leg.' I pointed to my leg.

But Barcode was too busy glancing behind me to pay attention. His smile had disappeared and he looked scared. Without another sound he shook his head, dropped the posy and vanished into the long grass.

It was as if he had never been there.

I bit back a sob and struggled again to remove my boot.

'What's this? A damsel in distress?'

I looked up to find Yo-yo standing over me. Without another word, he slipped my bag over his shoulder, lifted me into his arms and carried me as if I were a doll.

'Please take me back to my shack,' I said weakly.

'I'm taking you to The Hall. It's closer.'

He strode along, whistling something I didn't recognise. Manga ran along beside us, panting, his tongue hanging out.

I summoned the strength to order, 'Go! Home!' and he obediently took off in the direction of Shell Shack.

'How did he lose his leg?' asked Yo-yo.

'A rat. When he was a pup.'

'Isn't he a Jack Russell – a rat-terrier?'

'Not a very good one.'

We both laughed.

The route Yo-yo chose took us north along a hillside track overlooking flooded rice terraces with rows of men, women and children bent double among the green shoots. Grandpa Noah had brought me this way a couple of times on the way home from the Bartermart and I remembered the tone of his voice as he told me that the rice slaves had to work like that for twelve hours a day, six days a week. Nano made it clear that she didn't like him taking me anywhere near the paddy fields, but she often cited the slaves to remind me how lucky we were. Life on the Spit might be hard, but theirs was far tougher. They lived in horrible communal shacks on the edge of the paddy fields, she told me, with only a bowl of rice each day.

None of the workers looked up as we passed. A little further on we reached stables, four horses peering over half-doors. I recognised Li-li's little mare. A black stallion screeched loudly, showing yellow teeth.

'That's Jupiter. He's gone lame. I'm giving him a rest today.'

Through a haze of pain I could see male skivs scuttling around us carrying buckets and brooms; one was washing a gleaming carriage in the yard. Further up the hill, through the open door of a huge kite-shack, I saw a set of orange sails hanging from the roof beams where two skivs were perched precariously, cleaning the aluminium superstructure.

Orange was the corporate colour of B&NG. Everybody knew that. Did the Laos work for them? I pushed away the thought. I was too dizzy with pain to think about anything that complicated.

I laid my head on Yo-yo's shoulder, and closed my eyes.

CHAPTER SEVEN

I CAME TO on a sofa, Li-li hovering close by, her father slitting my boot with a knife to release my foot. His gold teeth glinted under his moustache. I remember biting my lips to stop myself crying out, then I fainted clean away.

When I came to for the second time, my legs were draped with a paisley wool shawl.

'She's back,' I heard Li-li say. 'Papa, look!'

Her father crouched down beside me.

'Here, drink this,' he urged.

I recoiled from the fumes.

'It's warmed brandy, it'll help, I promise.'

I took a sip. It was the same drink Li-li had given me on my first visit and again it burnt my throat, but as it went down a delicious warmth spread all over my body. This time I didn't choke.

'She can't possibly leave,' Mr Lao murmured.

In alarm, I struggled to sit up. 'I must! Perhaps you could take me home in your carriage?'

'Yours is not a simple injury.' Mr Lao spoke with authority. 'Li-li, make sure Flora moves as little as possible. We'll get Dr Poliakoff to look at her in the morning.'

'Doc Poliakoff?'

My mind raced. Doc Poliakoff had attended to Grandpa Noah and Nano, and I knew for a fact that he'd never charged them. He had had more than his fair share of Grandpa Noah's home-brewed rice whiskey in the old days, and probably felt obliged to us. But he would surely charge a high fee.

'I have no insurance, no Dizcare…' I mumbled.

But Mr Lao waved my anxieties away. 'That's for me to worry about.' He sat at the foot of the sofa and made as if to pat me on the knee, but thought better of it. 'Li-li, I must go to my study for a while. I leave Flora in your capable hands.'

Li-li came and sat in the space he had vacated. I wanted to thank her, to thank them all, but try as I might, I couldn't keep my eyes open.

When I woke the next time, the first thing I focused on was the digigraph of the Rice King, frowning as always, which hung above the granite fireplace. Everybody in Nortland had the same digigraph, though not many as large as the one here. Nano had hated it when Grandpa Noah turned ours to face the wall – she worried that the Uzi guards would make a surprise inspection and find out. But, somehow, my grandfather had always had the wits to turn it back just in time. And by the time his wits had left him, he didn't care that Nano always displayed it facing out.

The two lurchers were sprawled on a soft white animal-skin rug, basking in the heat from the blazing fire. They thumped their tails when they saw that I was awake. Li-li came rushing over and held a hand to my forehead, just as Nano used to.

'Good evening! Welcome back.' Her tone was a little teasing, but kind. 'I have to feed you up – strict instructions from Papa.'

She carried over a platter of roast meats, cheese and grapes. 'There…' She handed me a plate. 'What would you like?'

I pointed to one of the meats.

'Yes, and…?'

I shook my head. I couldn't concentrate.

'Just give her some of each.'

I turned with a start. Yo-yo was sitting in another part of the room.

'Are you eating too?' I asked.

'Of course, and I've just told the skiv to let Papa know you're awake. He'll join us. Like one big – or not-so-big – happy family!'

I would have been in heaven if it hadn't been for the pain, but as we ate together, I silently thanked the rabbit hole for tripping me up. It was wonderful to be back at The Hall.

Unaccustomed to crisp cotton sheets, I woke in the middle of the night, my ankle throbbing. Li-li had insisted I share her room in case I needed something in the night. Muslin curtains weighted with shells fluttered around our four-poster beds. She turned over in her sleep. Through the draped mosquito net her face was smooth and unworried.

The soup! *Kit!* I thought suddenly, frightened for a moment that I might have spoken out loud.

I had to get home. I sat up and tentatively put my foot on the floor but an excruciating pain shot up my leg. My groan woke Li-li.

'What are you doing? Do you need to pee?'

As soon as she suggested it, my bladder felt as though it would burst.

'I... I think I'll need some help,' I said.

With Li-li supporting me I hopped to the bathroom next door. There was a proper bath, a shower and porcelain WC with a flushing system. Hot water came from the taps. I had heard about such things, but never experienced them. Did all privs and travs live in this sort of luxury?

'Thanks,' I said, as she helped me back to my bed.

Li-li gave me a quick hug.

'Sleep tight,' she whispered, once she was satisfied that she had tucked me in properly.

I slept undisturbed until dawn broke.

I climbed out of bed onto a white polar bear rug, the sad, flopping head still attached, eternally snarling, baring its yellow teeth. My ankle was only mildly painful and I made my way to the window without waking Li-li. I sat watching the mist rising from the distant water and creeping up through the bosky valley to surround the granite walls south of The Hall. I had plenty to worry about, but my main concern was for my boot. Mr Lao shouldn't have cut it off my foot like that. It couldn't be repaired now. How on earth was I to work without boots? Grandpa Noah's were too large and Nano's were too small, as were my mother's old shoes. I'd have to barter theirs for bigger ones for me.

Doc Poliakoff smelt of rice whiskey when he was shown into the sitting room that morning. He looked surprised to see me there.

'Faith! What have you done to yourself?'

'Flora, I'm Flora. Faith was my mother's name.'

'Oh yes, of course.' A little flustered, he examined my injury, then he plastered my leg up to the knee.

'You will need to rest this ankle for several weeks if the break is to mend properly,' he told me.

'It's not broken. That's not possible,' I said, swinging my feet down from the sofa. 'I have work to do.' He knew that better than anybody.

'You'll have to hop then,' he said, writing out a bill and handing it to Li-li's father. Mr Lao simply handed the doctor a roll of notes. After counting it carefully Doc Poliakoff pocketed it, and handed me a box of pills.

'Take two now and one every four hours. It'll help the discomfort.' He saluted Mr Lao, winked at me, and left.

'How can I repay you?' I said to Mr Lao once Doc Poliakoff had gone.

'Think nothing of it, child.' He put his hand on my shoulder.

I didn't feel like a child, but to Mr Lao I suppose I was. I watched as he realigned blue and white decorated pots on a high shelf. Perhaps he was the same age as my father would have been.

When he was happy with the arrangement Mr Lao excused himself, telling me he had work to do. I was alone again and I felt cross and frustrated. I even cried a little.

Several weeks? How was I to get home? Shell Shack was going to fall apart at the seams. So much for starting a business.

Kit.

Had he realised that I hadn't come back last night? Probably not. We had parted so badly. However, he must be told, if only to make sure that he fed Manga and the pigeons. And took the stockpot off the range. At least the fire would have died.

When Li-li returned I asked for a pencil and paper.

'What for?' she asked, as if surprised that a girl like me could read and write.

I stiffened. 'I must send my neighbour a note,' I said. 'There are things that need to be done at home.'

'Of course!' Li-li went to a desk by the window and brought me beautiful thick blue paper with a new pencil. She sat watching me as I wrote.

'Could Annie take this to him, do you think?' I asked, folding the letter in thirds. It seemed rude to ask for a seal – as if I didn't trust her not to read it.

'Where does your neighbour live?'

I explained where Kit's yurt was.

'I'll find him.'

'You? But Annie…'

'She'd only take advantage and make a home visit.' Li-li's decision, as ever, was final.

She left the room and returned after a few minutes dressed in her riding clothes. 'Don't do anything foolish like trying to get up,' she ordered. I watched as she smeared red shiny stuff on her lips, then she turned, fluttered her long fingers towards me, and blew a kiss.

'Tell Kit I'm sorry,' I called after her. I don't think she heard.

I dozed for Rice knows how long. It must have been the painkillers. When I woke, Yo-yo was sitting reading nearby. I hoped I hadn't been snoring.

'Does it hurt?'

I nodded, and he smiled sympathetically. Actually, it didn't, it felt numb now, but I rather liked the idea of Yo-yo feeling sorry for me.

'Play chess with me. It'll take your mind off the ankle.' He slid open the lid of a wooden box and spilled the carved bone pieces onto the chequered table.

I had played chess with Grandpa Noah, but I wasn't very good. I had always been more interested in the intricacy of the pieces, which he had carved from cuttlefish bones. Yo-yo and I played a couple of games and he won easily.

When I suggested a third, he looked bored.

'How's the telescope?' I wanted to get him talking, to ensure he'd stay a little longer.

He nodded. 'Nearly done. When you are able to get up the stairs to the tower you can look through it.'

'I'd like that.'

There was silence. In a moment of madness that almost made me giggle, I wondered if he might offer to pick me up and carry me there.

'I saw you looking at the books when you were here before,' said Yo-yo. 'What sort of thing do you like?'

'Oh, anything really,' I said airily.

He conjured a key from his pocket, unlocked one of the glass doors to the shelves, and returned with a large, beautifully bound volume. It was, he told me, about the seven man-made wonders of World. With our heads close together we gazed at illustrations of the Sydney Opera House, Oz; the City of London, Ing; Manhattan, Amerik; and Disneyworld, Amerik. All drowned in the Great Flood, Yo-yo told me. I had never heard of any of them. My favourite was a white building with a curving roof and beautiful arches – the Taj Mahal, Inja.

'This shining temple was built in memory of an emperor's favourite wife,' Yo-yo read. He turned to me. 'He loved her so.'

I gazed into his eyes. He was as beautiful as his sister.

'Have you travved much?' I asked, desperate to appear intelligent.

He nodded. 'Except when hostilities stop us. My father loves to trav, and he always takes us with him – but we never quite know where we're going next. You'd be amazed at how much war there is in World. Our plans are constantly being changed. You're lucky here,' he said. 'You have us to thank for peace in Nortland.'

Us? What was he talking about? Yo-yo put the book back on the shelf and returned with another – a bound collection of women's magazines from the 20th century.

'Oh, the clothes!' I was fascinated. We turned page after page of digigraphs of a world which had been swept away. They showed young women as tall as me, with naked arms and legs and bare midriffs, and skin that seemed impossibly smooth. I was suddenly embarrassed to be looking at them with Yo-yo. I glanced round at him.

'You like fashion, I think?' Looking amused, he added, 'Flora of the red petticoat.'

'I wish I had lived in those days. It must have been wonderful. What are these things?' I pointed to a colour digigraph of a young man holding a small tablet with pictures on it.

'Smartpad. You could talk to people and see them even it they were in another part of World. There were moving images and information for everyone who could afford to buy one.'

'Seriously?'

'The end of Oil did away with all that. The 21st century was a golden age of technology. All gone now, of course.'

'What's that white stuff?' I asked, pointing at a digigraph labelled 'Winter Wonderland'.

'That's snow – frozen water.'

'Snow.' The word meant nothing to me. 'It's beautiful.'

'Perhaps, but inconvenient. And cold.'

I had never been more aware of my ignorance of life, of World, of history. Why hadn't we seen books like these at school? I wondered if the Laos would allow me free range of their library while I stayed with them.

For some reason I thought of Kit and felt immediately guilty. Here I was in the lap of luxury while he toiled away. He would have received my note by now and would already be on his way to check that all was well at Shell Shack. I felt sad that I couldn't see him and sort things out between us.

My train of thought was broken by Yo-yo leaning across me and pointing out a digigraph of people with hair standing upright on their head, like spikes. I inhaled again the lemony scent of his skin. He was so different from Kit.

'Punks. Apparently they had their own music – punk rock. I wish I knew what it sounded like.' So did I. I liked the way they dressed in leather and safety pins. Their uniform was similar to the Uzis but amusing and light-hearted and they had sculptured coloured hair.

I couldn't stop sneaking looks at Yo-yo. Our eyes met and – although the feeling passed in a fraction of a moment – I wondered if he might kiss me. But just at the critical moment – or at least it would have been in *Pride and Prejudice* – Annie knocked on the door and came in with a tray of drinks. I smiled at her and asked her how she was, but Yo-yo interrupted, coldly telling her to leave the tray on a side table and get out. He was so rude, but Annie didn't seem bothered. He was treating me as if I was a priv like him.

Just as Annie left, Li-li returned, rosy-cheeked and energised after her trip to find Kit. She fussed about, checking that my leg was supported properly, making sure that I had my medication – and sending Yo-yo away, claiming that he had tired me.

Yo-yo blew me a kiss and retreated.

'Look at you! Flushed. Exhausted. Chess! Books indeed! You must rest.' Li-li drank her brother's drink, removed the books to a side table and helped me upstairs to her bedroom. 'Rest,' she insisted.

I awoke in the early hours to the unfamiliar sound of water gurgling through the pipes. I snuggled down into the softness of the bed, going over the events of the previous day in my mind. I realised with a start that I hadn't even asked Li-li about Kit.

In the morning Annie brought me my own clothes, clean and pressed, apart from the ruined stockings. Nano would never have discarded them, she would have darned them carefully, but Li-li wasn't the darning kind. I had been taught never to throw anything away. Annie might have rescued them from the bin. Perhaps she would make use of them? I didn't ask. Annie said nothing and refused to look me in the eye.

I put on the dress and wrapped one of Li-li's shawls around my shoulders. But I couldn't get the new stocking on over the plastered foot and ankle. Li-li must have risen early so while I waited for her to come and help me, I tested myself, gingerly tipping my weight onto my damaged leg but eventually I collapsed onto the bed. Doc was right, it would be some time before I could walk on my own.

Li-li arrived at last, wearing her riding outfit.

'Good morning!' she said brightly. 'You look very fetching in my shawl.'

'I forgot to ask last night... Did you see Kit?'

'Oh yes, I saw him – and smelled him!' She half-hid a grimace behind her hands.

I flinched. I knew I sometimes criticised Kit's personal hygiene myself, but I didn't like to hear it coming from somebody else.

'Has he gone to Shell Shack? Did he eat the stew?'

'Yes. He said he waited for you to come back but in the end, couldn't wait any longer. He ate it all!'

'Did you explain about my ankle?'

'Wasn't it in your note?'

'Oh, yes, of course.' I hoped that Kit's reading was good enough for him to have understood. I didn't want to suggest to Li-li that he might have needed any help. 'Did you see my dog?'

'No,' she said, carelessly. 'But your not-so-fragrant friend gave me these to give to you.' She held out a bunch of buttercups, their golden heads drooping. They had been without water too long. I felt irritated by Li-li and at the same time embarrassed by the humble, wilting flowers. While she was opening the curtains, I threw them into the brass bucket that stood by the fire.

CHAPTER EIGHT

I HAD NEVER, ever spent so long doing nothing. Nano always found something for me to do – cleaning, polishing, mending, darning, sorting. She would never have left me to lie around like this.

Li-li unpacked some of her doll-houses for us to play with. Moving furniture around and pretending to be the tiny dolls was fun at first. The small beds and tables, the miniature mugs and plates on a little wooden dresser, were fascinating, although I thought that I should have grown out of that kind of make-believe. But she went off on her pony most mornings and I didn't see much of her brother either, so I was often on my own.

I used the time to write in a beautiful journal bound in green leather that Li-li gave me – a gift to her from her father, but she'd never used it. The paper was in a different class from the home-made stuff we had rationed so carefully at Shell Shack. With Mr Lao's real ink, I intended to write a story. The perfect love story. But for some reason, I couldn't find a way to express all my crazy ideas on paper.

Waiting for inspiration to strike, I decided to set down Nano's recipes and some of the skills Grandpa Noah had taught me. I closed my eyes and imagined being with Nano in Shell Shack, played out her movements in my memory, recalled the ingredients she used and how she mixed them.

On the first page I wrote my name and address:

Flora Mandela
Shell Shack
Eden Spit
Eden County
Nortland
(temporarily of The Hall, North Spit)
24 June 2137

Then I drew a map of the whole Spit, showing Shell Shack, Kit's yurt, Spit Fort, the Wangs' place, MacFarm, the next door Bartermart, Spit School and the coastguard station, Doc Poliakoff's cottage and The Hall.

BASIC STOCK
Meat bones or fish bones
1 Onion
1 Carrot
Lemon juice
Herbs
Water
Salt
Pepper
Bring to boil and simmer.

To make soup -
Strain through clean rag and
Add potatoes, lentils, any green veggie until cooked.

Nano's recipes weren't just for food.

INK
To make ink boil half a cup of fresh berries,
pound and press through a clean rag to get
pulp-free juice. Add half a teaspoon of vinegar
(to hold colour) and half a teaspoon of salt
(preservative). Mix well.

Nano's candles were widely known for their quality, and people came from a fair distance to buy or barter them.

CANDLE-WAX
*Gather red Bayberries speckled with white spots
and boil in water. Remove skins. Boil down
to produce a greenish wax and melt down for
candle-making. (Fifteen pounds of berries to
yield one pound of wax).*

*I looked around at the Laos' beautiful
candlesticks with their tall, smooth candles.
There was no real need for them, they were simply
to decorate the place. The Hall had its own power
supply for the lights and lamps.
Grandpa Noah's skills mostly involved the
outdoors.*

TO CATCH MUTAN CODLING
*Set baited (with mussel meat) hooked lines
between wooden stakes on the seaward side of the
Spit. Gather when the tide is low.*

DIGGING FOR BAIT
*At low tide in the mouth of the estuary, dig where
you find the worm casts on the mud surface. Red
rag and lugworm can be caught here. Both are
good for fish bait.*

COCKLES
*At low tide, go onto the mudflats in the Ede
Estuary and search for the tiny blue sandy
volcanoes with a hole in the middle. Shovel up
the mud with your hands. The cockles live a
hand's depth down.*

To clean them, leave in fresh water to filter out

*the sand for several hours. Then cook in fresh
water. They are cooked when they open.*

Recipes and instructions were far easier than stories, I decided. And then, all of a sudden, I wrote –

I am in love. But who with? Li-li, Yo-yo, or their father?

The words seemed outrageous, but I read and reread them and hugged them to myself like some secret that has been folded smaller and smaller until it was small enough to fit inside my heart.

I closed the notebook. I must make sure that it was for my eyes alone.

Not that Li-li was very interested in anything I was doing. She seemed happy enough to see me when she returned from her riding expeditions, but she rarely asked me what I had done with my day and she never shared anything about her own exploits. I found myself drawing pictures of Shell Shack, with its walls made from rusting panels of 4x4 and driftwood, the sheet-metal roof, the Shell sign wired to the chimney. I sketched the turreted pigeon palace with doves flying over it, and the antique wheel-less trucks we used as sheds. I even drew a picture of the chicken run and the bee skep. I rubbed out Kit pushing a wheelbarrow. I was no good at people.

My drawing of Manga looked just like him. I pulled my finger back and forth across the top of his head, scratching the paper, missing him terribly.

At Spit School we had only had slates and chalks, no paper. We learned letters, numbers, darning, sewing, drawing and woodwork, skills we'd need helping our parents and grandparents on our smallholdings. We learned about how rice was grown, of course. Each day started with our chorused pledge of allegiance to the Rice King. During the mid-morning break we played skipping games and marbles in the outfield, and we played grab-ball. I was always in Kit's team, with Olaf de Kooning and his little brother,

Stafan. I loved grab-ball, loved the feeling of a really good kick, the exhilaration of running with the ball under my arm until I reached the tree, where I leapt as high as I could and popped it in the net. It was one of the few times being tall and gangly was an advantage. I was the best! Kit had a good throwing arm, but with his limp he had to leave the speedy bits of the game to others. I went to practise once a week until I was thirteen, coming back to Shell Shack full of stories. Thirteen was the leaving age for all of us. There was no education for povs like us beyond Spit School.

As my first week at The Hall turned into the second, I itched for something to happen. Yo-yo had never repeated his offer to find me books, and I didn't have the courage to ask. He spent most of the day in the tower with the telescope. I would have liked to spend time with Annie, but she was always busy elsewhere. If our paths crossed she would lower her eyes, almost cringing away from me.

One morning I asked her to sit with me for a while. She went and closed the door, then walked smartly up to where I was sitting, my foot elevated.

'Don't be any more ridiculous than you are,' she hissed. 'I have a *job*.'

Li-li's footsteps on the stairway told us she was on her way, so Annie shot off. I was left smarting at my old friend's words.

Even though we had spent time together when we were little, Annie and I had not got on so well as we grew up. She was interested in boys, I'd been more interested in fishing and rowing and skimboarding. She was jealous of my friendship with Kit, too.

The way Li-li shouted at Annie left me with an uncomfortable feeling inside.

'Don't go all pro-skiv on me,' Li-li told me once, catching my pained expression. 'She's slow-witted, that girl. Needs a telling. Says she's been to school, but there's no sign of it...'

I felt heat rise on my neck, but I said nothing.

Later that day, I asked Li-li if she would choose a book for me.

'Why on earth waste time reading?' She plumped up my cushions. 'Anyway, that dusty old doc is coming this afternoon, so you might be off home after supper. You seem to be getting about pretty well.'

I never knew where I was with Li-li. One minute she was treating me with affection – well, at least as much as she gave her dolls; the next, she was distant and bored-looking. Did she want me gone? And Yo-yo had paid me hardly any attention after the initial drama of my arrival. The high hopes I'd had were plummeting as each day passed.

Later that day I was on the window seat in the sitting room watching the clouds – there a hippo, like one of Grandpa's sculptures, there a pufferfish, there a galloping horse – when Doc Poliakoff arrived to check on my progress.

'I let myself in,' he said. 'There's nobody around.'

'Li-li's out,' I told him. 'I don't know where. Yo-yo and Mr Lao are upstairs.'

'Good. So how are you today, Missy?'

'Fine...' And then I shook my head and whispered, 'I don't think Grandpa Noah would approve of all this.' I gestured around us.

'Perhaps not.' Doc Poliakoff patted my knee, his face solemn. 'Perhaps not.' He moved my ankle from side to side. I tried not to wince.

'Courageous man, your father...' he said in a low voice.

'Courageous? I never thought...' I shrugged. 'I just miss him, his funny ways.'

'Not Noah, dear.' Doc kept his voice low. 'Your *father*. A remarkable, courageous man.'

'Oh...' I didn't know what to say. 'My father... he was courageous?'

'Very.' Doc glanced up and smiled.

'Did you know him then?' For the first time in my life I was discussing my father!

'Ssh, child. Yes, Flora, I knew Red very well.'

'Please tell me, what was he like?'

'Impatient for change. Didn't suffer fools. Impetuous.'

Impetuous. That word again.

'And my mother? Did you know her too?'

'Ah yes. Lovely young woman, Faith was. A terrible tragedy.

Your grandfather was never quite the same after she died. At least he and Nano had you to take their minds off what they'd lost.'

'I know nothing about my father. I only have one digigraph of him – standing by the boat he sailed off in. Why did you say he *was* brave – my father? Do you know – is he… is he dead?'

'Noah didn't tell you anything?' Doc Poliakoff's voice was barely audible.

'What do you mean?'

He continued gently attending to my ankle.

'Your grandfather was one of my closest friends, but that doesn't mean he wasn't…'

At that moment, Yo-yo marched into the room. Doc tapped me warningly on the hand.

Without any further words being exchanged, I understood that the conversation could not be continued, though I didn't understand exactly why.

'Yo-yo!' Doc Poliakoff said, standing up and offering an outstretched hand.

'Good evening,' Yo-yo greeted him. 'How's our house guest?'

'This young woman needs an occupation, you know,' the Doc said. 'She's not accustomed to idleness.'

'I came downstairs to teach her to beat me at chess,' Yo-yo said, smiling at me.

'Good, that's good… The ankle has some way to go, I'm afraid.' Doc covered it up again with the rug. 'You can't go home for another couple of weeks, Flora.'

I watched Yo-yo's face brighten. I couldn't stop myself smiling broadly. It took so little for my spirits to rise.

'I'm sure we can stretch out her recuperation even longer than that,' he said. 'Li-li won't be able to let her go. They're like sisters these days.'

He obviously hadn't been party to her suggestion that I might leave that afternoon.

Doc showed me some exercises. 'As soon as you feel able, start some gentle walking. I'd recommend that you use a stick. Don't overdo it, or you'll set yourself back.'

After dinner that evening, Yo-yo entertained us by playing the piano. None of the music was familiar to me. I didn't manage to pay full attention because the speed of his fingers skimming over the keys brought to mind the image of Kit tying fresh bait to his fishing lines. Li-li, who had announced earlier that she'd been terrified that Doc would pronounce me fit and mobile, danced for our entertainment. She was a wonderful acrobatic dancer. Lying there with my foot up, I wished I was supple and small-boned like her, not a tall stork.

That night, for the first time since the fall, I managed to hop to my bed on my own, with the help of the stout walking stick Yo-yo had found for me. I noticed with a thrill of excitement that there were some more dresses hanging up for me to choose from.

A few days later, Yo-yo appeared at my side carrying a bundle of rolled papers. It was rare for him to spend time away from the telescope so I was delighted.

'What are they?'

'Maps. I am a mapper, didn't I say?'

'Maps of Nortland?'

'Yes, and other places. It's one of the great things about travving by air. You see so much more from a kite.'

'It must be like being a bird.'

'I'll take you up one day.'

Kites rarely flew over Eden Spit. Nobody I knew had ever flown in one.

'That would be wonderful,' I said, so excited that my voice actually shook.

With our heads close together, we pored over the maps. Yo-yo mesmerised me with his talk about maps and map-making. He was so earnest, so passionate about the subject.

I thought I knew the Spit like the back of my hand, but its shape wasn't as I'd imagined it. It looked so fragile – a thin finger of land poking out between the sea and the bay. I had never before had this sense of where I was in relation to other places, most of which were a mystery to me.

Yo-yo also showed me some pre-Great Flood maps. So many

countries had been lost, drowned.

'Eden Spit has been flooded in the past,' he said, 'but it's always survived, with the precious rice fields.'

Hours passed before he rolled the maps carefully away.

'What happened? Why was there a Great Flood?' I asked him.

'You don't know?' He raised an eyebrow.

I felt resentful at my ignorance. Who had decided what we didn't need to learn at school? We had always been told by our teacher that at Spit School we were learning what we needed for life.

Yo-yo started to tell me about what had happened to World in the 21st century, the drastic warming which had taken place within the span of fifty years.

'The result? Drought in half of World, flooding in the other half.' Yo-yo was a good teacher. 'The Gulf Stream – that's a warm current that circulated in the oceans – it changed direction, then came many violent storms and huge waves. The ice caps – you remember the snow in those digigraphs I showed you? – well, ice caps were made of extremely thick snow and ice, and they melted. The balance of the elements that made up the air altered, poisoning huge areas, killing off vegetation and animals. People weren't quick to give up on whatever place they called home, even when the land was no longer able to sustain life. When enough of them had starved, mass population movements followed.'

I didn't understand most of what Yo-yo was telling me, but one thing I did know was how much I loved him talking to me like this, with such intensity, clouds of words pouring out of his mouth, making strange pictures form in my head.

A frown cut grooves in his forehead as he continued, 'But at the end of the 21st century there was a volcanic eruption on a small island in the Atlantic Ocean – remember we saw that on one of the old maps? – and a huge landslip occurred which caused a mega-wave far more massive than anything before. It engulfed lands on both sides of the ocean.'

I tried to take in the scale of what he was describing.

'Were many people killed?'

'Millions,' Yo-yo said in a flat voice. He had immersed himself so deeply in this story of the past that he really felt it. 'There was some warning – they had very intricate ways of monitoring the sea's movements in those days.'

'So why did so many die?'

'Some of them hadn't been evacuated high enough. Some didn't believe the warning, or it didn't reach them. There were people who stayed put because they thought it was the end of World, which had been predicted again and again – this time, they were almost right.'

History. A treasure trove people like me weren't supposed to know anything of, let alone think about. I recalled Nano's disdain for the subject. But hearing about the past like this made it all the more important to me now.

I started as Mr Lao suddenly broke into our conversation. He had entered unnoticed, and had apparently been there for some time.

'Yes, Yo-yo, and don't forget the mass exodus from Amerik, Afrik, Indo-Aje, China and Oz that happened in the late 21st century due to drought, disease and war. Complete nations on the move, ready to fight to the death to gain control of what good, profitable land was left.'

'My father is a historian, you know, in his spare time,' Yo-yo said respectfully.

'I don't have spare time. All my time is well spent, unlike the younger generation, who seem to have nothing better to do than go on jaunts.'

I didn't know if Mr Lao was serious and didn't really care. I was basking in the fact that both men were treating me like a priv adult, as if it was the most natural thing in World. All my feelings of loneliness and isolation faded. Shell Shack couldn't have felt further away. And for the moment I was happy to leave it there.

The Hurricane Weeks were definitely on their way but a few days later there was a little respite when the heat was bearable and it wasn't blowing a gale. Without asking, Yo-yo lifted me up from the sofa one morning, and in spite of my protests that I could walk perfectly well now with the help of my stick, carried me out to the garden and sat me on a carved wooden seat. He made me feel like a piece of the fine porcelain that the Laos displayed on their shelves. Until a few weeks ago I spent my days getting muddy and dirty, hands red-raw from hard work. I had come a long way.

An Uzi guard was approaching us across the parched lawn with a falcon gripping one gauntleted hand. When he reached us he transferred the gloves and bird to Yo-yo and marched away again.

The bird was alert, austere, proud. It reminded me of Mr Lao.

'Watch me fly this beauty,' Yo-yo said, sending the falcon to a distant pole, where it watched him intently, bobbing slightly. At his whistle it flew back to his gloved hand, which now held a dead mouse. The bird neatly tore the mouse apart and ate it.

Yo-yo turned to me with a look of triumph. 'Brilliantly trained. Isn't she magnificent?'

'How many falcons do you have?' I asked, nodding.

'Only two fully trained,' he replied. 'Others still under instruction.'

Trained for what? I wondered. With a flicker of nerves I hoped Kit was looking after the pigeons. Then banished the thought. Now wasn't the time.

His handsome face infused with delight and pride, Yo-yo perfectly fulfilled my mental picture of the dashing Mr Darcy. Yo-yo was arrogant, yes. But he admired me, I hoped. He had been so insistent that I see him with the falcon, had seemed to seek my approval.

'*It is a truth universally acknowledged that a single man in possession of a good fortune must be in want of a wife.*' Feeling like one of Jane Austen's characters, that was exactly what I wondered. Could this single man in possession of a good fortune be in want of a wife?

CHAPTER NINE

AS SO OFTEN happened during those weeks at The Hall, my happiness and optimism didn't last long.

I worried about why Kit hadn't come to visit me. What if he hadn't been able to read the notes I'd sent with Li-li – three so far, the third demanding a visit. He couldn't read very well, but surely he would have asked Li-li if he was unsure. And she would have told him about my ankle, that I was at The Hall and couldn't move, wouldn't she? So why hadn't he come?

Despite the way she gushed over me in front of her father and brother each morning at breakfast, I still hardly saw anything of Li-li. She spent hours bathing, dressing and making up her face, and then she was busy ordering the skivs around and organising the housekeeping. She usually went out after lunch and I noticed that she was returning later and later.

'It's nearly dark and blowing a gale. I don't want you out and about in such conditions,' her father told her one evening.

'Papa, I can't bear to be cooped up in this place. Flora rests in the afternoon.' Li-li yawned. 'But I am getting bored with Eden. When are we going on our next trav?'

I felt my heart jump at the thought that they would leave The Hall.

'No time soon,' Mr Lao replied. 'Halley's Comet won't be visible for a while. Flora seems to be very much awake in the afternoon. What more could you ask for?' Li-li's father threw her a stern look.

'When you are well enough, I'll teach you to ride,' Li-li turned to me with a dazzling smile. 'I promise.'

'I would love that,' I said, feeling convinced that it would never happen.

Later, I looked out at the night sky and recalled what I might have been doing at this time, had I been home at Shell Shack. I suddenly missed my book, the comfort of its well-thumbed pages. I knew long passages by heart, but that wasn't the same as holding it. How out of place it would look here, battered, water-stained, detritus from its latest hiding place clinging to its sticky jacket.

One day Manga appeared on the kitchen doorstep. Annie brought me the news.

'You'd better come and get him before the lurchers sniff him out.'

I limped into her domain. 'Oh, Manga, you clever boy!' He was deliriously happy to see me, leaping up and almost somersaulting in joy. For once Annie relaxed enough to laugh with me. How he had found me I don't know, but I was delighted to see him, dirty and skinny though he was. Annie put some scraps in a dish on the floor and he almost choked in his desperation to gobble them up.

'Best get him cleaned up,' she said, filling a sink with warm water, and together we scrubbed Manga. In the end he quite enjoyed the bath. It looked as if he had lost some teeth, which would explain why he was so hungry. His rat- and rabbit-catching days were definitely numbered.

'Looks and smells better, doesn't he?' Annie said. She was much more at ease here in the kitchen, without any of the Lao family around.

'Thank you,' I said.

But I was bitterly disappointed, even angry, that Kit hadn't looked after my dog as I'd asked. How could he neglect him so? Annie found Manga more scraps from the larder and he ate, wagging his tail and almost falling into the bowl in his excitement.

I sat down at the kitchen table. 'Annie, have you seen Kit recently?'

'You must be joking! I'm not even allowed to go home to see Ma.'

'You get time off, don't you?'

'One day a month. That's my lot. She's ill, can't cope with the kids. By the time I've walked the length of the Spit to get home, I have to start back again so that I'm not late.'

Mrs Wang had five boys and Annie, who was the eldest.

'How many of your brothers go to school?'

'None! Refuse, don't they. And she hasn't the energy to make them. Wu helps Pa with the crap cart, and the others help clean the Uzi barracks with Ma.'

Annie's father was the crap collector on Eden Spit, making a small living from cleaning out everyone's crapshacks. Annie probably had a better life here at The Hall than she had at home in their hovel, I thought. She was well fed and her uniform dress and apron were flattering. But not being allowed to see her family more than once a month? The way she was treated seemed very harsh.

Manga soon settled in at The Hall, but had to remain in the scullery. We were two of a kind, living a life of ease – fed regularly, a warm place to sleep. He kept clear of all the other dogs – scared of them, no doubt. As I was.

Annie explained that Mr Lao kept the two lurchers for hunting – although he had never to her knowledge gone hunting. The guard dogs kept in the caged enclosure were exercised with the lurchers and were only allowed to roam the grounds once everybody was indoors for the night. I often heard them baying. It was a terrifying sound but Li-li assured me that the Uzi guards who manned the gates had the dogs back in their cage at dawn. The aged spaniel mostly stayed by her master's side in the library. Manga tried to befriend her once when she visited the kitchen with Mr Lao, but she was totally unmoved by his playful bowing and nudging. He was, after all, a pov dog.

The weather warmed inexorably. It was hard to believe that I had ever not known Li-li and her family. Mr Lao presented me with more of his dead wife's clothes, which all fitted me so well. The dresses were cut low for my age – or so Nano would have said. I sometimes wanted to ask if his wife had worn denims, but

I couldn't really imagine Mr Lao married to anybody who wore denims. He said I was to keep the beautiful suede shoes they'd given me that first evening. I looked forward to wearing them when my ankle was healed.

For a while after the conversation with her father, Li-li was more attentive to me. When Doc had removed my plaster cast, although my leg looked very thin and had clearly lost a lot of muscle tone, he reassured me that with regular physiotherapy I should regain complete use of it in a few weeks. He had asked Li-li to massage my ankle and she took her responsibilities seriously, daily kneading the sole of my foot and ensuring that I was flexing it properly. She also massaged my hands with her creams and the welts and hard skin from life at Shell Shack were disappearing.

Although my ankle was much stronger, there was no chance yet of a riding lesson. Instead, Li-li unpacked the rest of her doll-houses – all seven. They were antiques, two Georgian, two Victorian, three from the 20th century. That was the order Li-li said them in. I asked her if that was the right order in history but she didn't see why it mattered.

My favourite was what Li-li called 'the Modernist house', though she hadn't a clue what that meant when I asked. It had curved white walls with metal-framed windows and there was a big rectangular bath on the flat roof. Li-li told me that the people who lived in such houses would swim 'in the pool', not in the sea. They must have had an army of skivs to carry the water to fill it! Or they might have had water delivered through pipes, as the Laos did in The Hall. Each doll-house had its own set of tiny occupants with moveable limbs and all sorts of odd clothes the likes of which I'd never seen. There was even a miniature dog and dog-shack in one of them.

'Have this. I'd like you to have it,' Li-li said one day. She passed me a tiny baby doll in a cradle the size of my thumb.

'Thank you,' I said, blushing with pleasure. 'What shall I call her?'

'What was your mother's name?'

'Faith.'

'So, she's Faith. Yes?'

'Yes!'

I hugged Li-li and she kissed my cheek. I pushed away all my doubts and felt myself lucky to have such a pretty and generous friend.

'Tell me about your red petticoat. Where did you get it?' Li-li asked me, brushing my thick curly hair with unusual vigour.

'It was my mother's. She loved pretty things.'

'Tell me about her.' Li-li put down the brush and rested her oval face on her cupped hands.

'There's a painting of her in Shell Shack, and a digigraph with my father. I'll show you when you visit.'

Li-Li flushed and turned away. Perhaps she had no intention of entering a pov dwelling?

'She looked a bit like me, but *she* was beautiful. All I know about her is what Nano told me. My grandfather didn't ever speak of her, it upset him too much. And there aren't any other people who really remember her…'

I recalled the half-conversation I'd had with Doc. His subsequent visits had been regular, but never without one of the Laos in attendance, so I'd never had the chance to pursue what he'd started. I sometimes wondered if I'd just imagined it.

'I can imagine what my mother looked like because of that one digigraph. And her clothes.' Too exotic for the seashore and Shell Shack, too delicate for feeding the chickens in – I had worn them anyway, to keep her alive; even her home-made gowns of antique polyester, which I liked to think still held her musky perfume. At school I had been laughed at, called names – pov, misfit, mutan – but I didn't care. I loved her gorgeous clothes, and mended them as they disintegrated under all the wear and tear, adding little touches of my own: patches, shell fragments, plastic beads found on the beach. I found myself telling Li-li about some of the work I'd done on my mother's clothes.

'She wanted to be an artist, like my grandfather.'

'Oh, yes, the animal sculptures man,' Li-li said thoughtfully. 'And the palace for the doves. I do so like that.'

How did she know our name for it?

'He was good at embroidery too,' I told her proudly. 'He did cross-stitch mottoes to hang on the walls.'

'How bizarre! A man doing embroidery!'

'Not really. He was once a sailor,' I said, leaving it at that. Sailors always knew how to look after themselves, he'd told me. Sewing, cooking, mending, making furniture. I had his HOME SWEET HOME embroidery hanging above my bed.

Li-li seemed preoccupied. Perhaps I was boring her.

'Could you bear to take Kit another message, please?' I asked.

'Of course, my darling, anything for you.' Li-li patted my smooth, well manicured hands.

Dear Kit,

I hope you are well and that all goes as well as possible with your father. Thanks for looking after things at Shell Shack. I am worried that you haven't been in touch with me. Do you know that Manga is here? Please do come and see me. My ankle is getting stronger, with the kind attention I am receiving in the Lao family and I should be able to come home soon, but I would love to see you, if you have time. I have permission from Mr Lao for you to come here. Best not bring Jess.

I miss you,
Flora x

PS Send your reply with Li-li.

Li-li tucked the letter into her pocket.

'Could you possibly take it tomorrow?'

'Sure. I'll make a special journey.' Her smile was a little strained.

'I don't want to put you out, Li-li.'

'It's not a problem.'

Next day, I waited patiently for her return. She came into the sitting room looking pink-cheeked after her ride, as usual. She threw down her crop and without a word went to the bathroom. When she reappeared she had never looked lovelier. Her colouring was heightened by the creamy colour of her soft goat-wool dress.

Her shining hair was night black, her eyes sparkled. I waited for her to say something.

'Well?'

'Well what?' She hurled herself onto the opposite sofa, stretched and yawned extravagantly. Only Li-li could yawn like that and remain poised and pretty.

'No note?'

'Note?

'From Kit,' I said, failing to disguise my impatience.

'Oh, Kit! He's busy, you know.'

'You did *give* him my note?'

'He's looking after your place, gardening and stuff.' She yawned again, revealing her even little teeth.

'He didn't give you a message for me?' I hated having to beg for news.

'He's... well. And busy.'

'Good.' I bit my tongue. Li-li was obviously enjoying every second of my discomfort.

'He doesn't smell as bad as he did.' She gave a sly smile and yawned yet again.

I couldn't help myself. 'Really?'

'Really. I told him he should bathe and he did.'

So, he'd wash for her and not for me! I was trying not to show my... my... it wasn't jealousy, was it?

'Well, that's good. Congratulations!' I tried to keep calm. Why was Li-li talking about him with such familiarity? Why hadn't he visited me? I had asked him. Outright.

Li-li was watching me.

I told myself I didn't care.

'You don't really want to go back to your shack, do you?' Li-li came over and put a slender arm round my shoulder.

'I miss home, that's all.'

'But you could come to our home. Once they've seen the comet we'll trav there.'

At the news that the Laos planned to leave Eden so soon, I was appalled to feel tears welling in my eyes.

'We live a long, long way away, on a green mountain covered

with trees and flowers. It's a beautiful white castle. We have streams of clean cold water. We have our own yoghurt with honey and almonds for breakfast. You'd love it there.'

Go to that wonderful country? To think my father lost his life trying to find a better place to live – and I'd just received this casual invitation. Of course, I knew that Li-li was teasing. But before I could stop myself, I took the bait.

'How can I? I have to earn a living, you know. Plant things, grow food, gather fruit. Pickle shallots for your father and people like him,' I reminded her sharply.

'Oh, but you could live with us always. Be like my sister. Wouldn't you like that?'

Was she serious? Did she mean it, after all?

'How old are you, Li-li?'

'How old do you think I am?'

'Fifteen?'

She shook her head and giggled. 'Wrong! Seventeen! How old are you?'

'Sixteen.'

It seemed impossible that she was older than me, this cosseted little person. She seemed such a child. Surprised at myself, I felt a pang of real pity.

I lay awake most of that night, tense and anxious. It was as if I didn't know any more what I wanted from life. In just a few weeks I had almost forgotten what it was like to dig and hoe, to carry heavy loads of wood, to saw and chop it until I almost dropped from tiredness, to battle with the kitchen range every day to keep it alight, to clean soot from the chimney, to freeze my fingers searching for cockles on the windswept mudflats.

My hands had softened; my nails were no longer chipped. Li-li had given me lotions and creams for my face and body. She had painted my lips red, drawn dark lines around my eyes, dyed my fair lashes black. Playing with me as if I was one of her dolls, she had washed my unruly hair in water scented with sweet herbs and then teased it into plaits and pleats.

I did not recognise myself, but I liked what I saw reflected in her mirrors. I preferred this version of myself to the old me.

It seemed impossible now that I could want to join Kit in a venture that meant a lifetime of hard physical work. Kit, who couldn't even be bothered to come and visit me. Who was always criticising me, always finding fault. Who couldn't be bothered to wash himself properly when I was about, but could somehow manage it for Miss Li-li. Was it my fate to live in a draughty driftwood shack, having to go out to the crapshack in the dark, scared of being bitten by funnel webs and red-backs?

Grandma's words echoed in my head. *'Stay on Eden Spit.'*

My brain was in turmoil.

'East, West, home's best,' I heard her say.

CHAPTER TEN

'FATHER IS TRYING to persuade Li-li to show some interest in the telescope. He despairs of her! So we can talk properly, now that she's not here to distract us.'

Yo-yo's sudden appearance in the sitting room with several rolled-up maps under his arm lifted my spirits. So what if Kit had forgotten me, I thought as Yo-yo perched beside me on the sofa and placed the maps on the low table beside us.

I felt ridiculously pleased at his presence. There was nothing I wanted better than to continue our previous conversation.

'I'd love to know what the Tescopec Mountains are like. Have you kited over them, Yo-yo?'

'Sure have. What are they like? You don't really want to know. Just huge masses of smashed metal and plastic – freezers, automobiles, washing machines, computers, televisions, all that ancient stuff. Rusting in a toxic fog.'

'It sounds terrible.'

'And there are forts, bristling with machine guns and anti-kite artillery. To protect us. And thousands of carrion crows and gulls fighting over scraps. From the kite you often see wild boars and wolves.'

'But what do they feed on?'

'Rats, scavs, toxics.'

His casual, matter of fact manner showed that he didn't share my horror at the thought of starving kids like little Barcode scavenging among the rubbish and scrap metal, so desperate for food they were prepared to expose themselves to such danger. I felt a stab of anxiety – what had happened to Barcode? I felt consumed with guilt that I hadn't given him a moment's thought since he'd run off that day. I hoped he was safe. I hoped somebody else was leaving scraps out for him.

'What are the machine guns for? Protecting us from what?' I asked Yo-yo.

'Well, we have to defend our territory, don't we? Everyone wants to get into Nortland. It's the rice-bowl of World.'

'Is it?'

'Yes, Flora, it is. They have to be starving, desperate or stupid to attempt the crossing. But they do. And they don't make it. Boat people, even if they manage to get through the reefs, can't get past the coastguards and armed forts. He stroked his chin, staring at me. 'But let's talk about something else. I can see that you are upset.'

He was right. I was shaking. I suddenly felt frightened for myself and for everyone I knew. Nano had been wrong. I should have been taught my history. I had become unhappy with my lot, but I might have been a scav, hiding from wolves and Uzi soldiers, the odds of survival stacked against me.

'We'll be migrating north soon. After we've viewed the comet.' Yo-yo's words, softly spoken as they were, fractured my train of thought.

'Li-li said that. You won't be here for the Big Heats?' I tried to keep my voice normal.

'No, we'll trav to our main home.'

'What's it like?'

'Newland. Have you heard of it?'

'No.'

He gave an awkward laugh and looked down at his hands. 'No, I don't imagine you have. It's even better guarded than Nortland. You need a special passport. Only Rice Lords and H2O oligarchs can get into Newland.'

'And travs? You are a trav, aren't you?'

'A trav!' He put his hand on my shoulder. He seemed to be

on the verge of dissolving into hilarity. He looked straight into my eyes, (which had the usual effect on me). 'Father is a Rice Lord. Didn't you realise? Lord Lao! He has control of Nortland, Sudenland and Westland.'

'I didn't realise.' I coloured in embarrassment.

'And my own job, mapping, is high priority. Making new maps is vital with World changing so much all the time. Countries are still being flooded, in other places it's deserts that encroach – like the Desert of Euro. You know how it is.'

No, I didn't.

Throughout my childhood I had seen parts of the Spit become islands for a while with the arrival of the rainy season. Sometimes we were cut off by channels the water had forced from the bay to the sea. Then sandbanks had grown between them and the Spit had elongated or widened. At the end of the rainy season, we often had to learn new paths and trails because the old ones had been rearranged by the rising waters. I had always assumed that this was how World worked. I had the barest inkling of why the way the water moulded and remoulded the landscape was quite so important to Yo-yo's mapping projects. Some of what I was learning didn't bear close examination, but I was totally gripped.

Yo-yo was building up momentum. Could he be trying to gain my admiration?

'I've travved everywhere that's survived climate change. There are some ancient cities left that don't contain too many crims, but travving's getting harder all the time. We stay in Uzi-guarded Travillas. Our own castle is very secure. It's surrounded by good riding and hunting country, forests and farms.'

The thought of my father quitting everything he knew to find a better way to live flashed through my mind again.

'We have swimming pools, tennis courts, a zoo, visiting circuses. In summer we enjoy mild, cool weather,' Yo-yo enthused. 'There's frost in winter, beautiful white, clean frost, and in the spring, cherry trees in blossom.'

'Is frost cold?' I ventured.

'Deliciously so.'

Newland sounded like heaven. Perhaps my father was there.

Perhaps Yo-yo knew Redvers Mandela?

'It's dangerous. There's always someone who wants what we've got. You lead such a sheltered life, Flora.' Yo-yo took my hand in his. 'You have no idea what dangers there are in World these days. Toxics and mutants. Carriers of new diseases. Outcasts.' His expression darkened. 'They turn cannibal on islands where there's nothing left to eat. And we're all living on islands, islands that are shrinking.'

I shivered and he put his arms around me. 'Don't worry, Flora, the Rice Families – and their favourites – will always flourish. We are natural rulers. Povs and debt slaves will always work for us. And we are well protected.'

Had he forgotten that I was a pov? I was repelled by his arrogance, yet at the same time hypnotised by his power.

'Are you cold?' he whispered. I ducked away as his face came closer but he pulled me back. 'Don't think about it. It's not your problem… beautiful Flora.' He started kissing my neck.

I had never been kissed before, except on the cheek by Grandpa Noah.

Never been kissed like this. I trembled and heat raced through my blood.

Yo-yo pressed closer, put a hand on my breast and caressed me through the velvet of my dress. I was breathless. I didn't know how to respond but I wanted his touch. He placed his mouth on mine and I found myself kissing him back. He laughed into my mouth, stroked my hair, my face, my throat.

Much later I pushed open the door to Li-li's bedroom and crept in. To my immense relief she didn't stir.

I burrowed under the covers and lay, still trembling, locked on the memory of what had just happened, going over every detail again and again until the sun began to rise.

CHAPTER ELEVEN

IT WAS AS if I had memorised every line of Yo-yo's muscled neck and arms, his face, his hair, the feel of him, his smell. There were times when I thought I might faint with desire. All I wanted was to be with him. I was constantly keyed up, analysing each sound I heard, willing it to be him.

Often I was not disappointed. Yo-Yo stole kisses at every opportunity. I knew he wanted more than that, and I wasn't finding it easy to hold back, but Nano had instilled in me the importance of keeping myself pure until I was married. But could Nano have had any idea what it was like to feel like this? I doubted it.

Just to be in the same room as Yo-yo made me tingle all over.

'Do you love me, Flora?' he asked a few days after we had first kissed.

'You know I do,' was my reply, pushing him away. I had never been so happy, or so confused.

'Do you love me?' I murmured in his ear as he drew me to him again.

'Mmmm. You are the most beautiful woman I have ever met.'

My mind raced ahead of me, whipping up ideas and images with crazy speed. If Lord Lao approved of me, might he allow his son to marry me?

'You are looking much better, Flora,' he said to me one day when we happened to meet in the library, where I spent most of my time gazing at the spines of the books.

'I am feeling better, thank you,' I smiled at him. 'I should go home soon,' I added.

'No, no. No need to leave us yet... Doc Poliakoff was definite about that. It's only five weeks since you arrived.'

On the far wall I noticed a painting of Eden Spit. I hadn't seen it there before but it looked familiar – not because I knew the place it showed so well, it was the whole manner of the painting that was somehow familiar... something about the strong brush strokes, the colour palette. I walked over and squinted at the signature in the bottom left-hand corner – *R.D.*

'Lord Lao, do you know the name of the painter of this landscape?'

'Charming, isn't it? I acquired it locally, from the farm.'

'From the Mackenzies?'

'Yes, that's the one, from the Mackenzies. A simple couple. I made them an offer they couldn't refuse.' The stiff moustache twitched nervously on one side, but

I could see that the recollection pleased him.

There was something about this man that scared me. I hoped that he would never make me an offer I couldn't refuse for the portrait of my mother. But the thought evaporated as soon as it arose. I would not be inviting Lord Lao to Shell Shack.

Lord Lao took a silver key from the pocket of his black silk waistcoat and unlocked one of the glass cabinets.

'Here, read this.' He handed me a book about art. 'You are obviously interested in painting. 'There is no value in books that remain closed, Flora. In fact, I would like you to read out loud to Li-li. Every evening if possible. I think she will find it easier to learn with you there, learning too.'

I didn't ask him if he had checked this arrangement with Li-li.'

'I should have thought of it before. Read anything you like, my dear. You'll find the Jane Austens over there.'

The key swung from a large ring, clinking softly against the metal tag that I suppose said 'BOOKS', in their language.

He handed me the key then swept out of the room, his yellow silk kimono swishing in his wake.

Did I hear right? Did he say Jane Austens, plural?

Within seconds I held a leather-bound volume in my hand.

I found my favourite perch on the window seat by the open window looking out onto the gardens, where palms blossomed and weaver birds twittered, and the heady perfume of lemon trees came wafting into the room. I made myself comfortable on apple-green velvet cushions.

About thirty years ago, Miss Maria Ward, of Huntingdon, with only seven thousand pounds, had the good luck to captivate Sir Thomas Bertram, of Mansfield Park...

Li-li and I had never quite overcome the difficult conversation about Kit and had given up trying to pretend to her father and brother that we were the best of friends. Lately she spent most of her time out riding. The Hurricane Weeks and Great Heats were late and she was making the most of the remaining fresh days. I was content. I had several Jane Austens to lose myself in. And with Li-li away from the Hall, Yo-yo and I had more opportunities to be alone together. Annie had taken over the job of massaging my ankle and the day after Doc's visit I took myself down to the kitchen for a session. The truth was that her hands, though calloused as mine used to be, were usually kinder than Li-li's.

'Let's have a look,' she said, loosening her corseted uniform. She was putting on weight. Still crunching on a pear I had brought her from the silver fruit bowl in the dining room, she lowered herself onto a little stool. I settled myself in front of her in the kitchen armchair and placed my foot in her lap. Annie chucked the pear core right across the room. It landed neatly in Manga's bowl.

'Good shot!' I said, thinking back to our grab-ball days with a pang of nostalgia.

'You're worked so hard here,' I said, finding it impossible to allude directly to how rudely the Laos addressed her.

'Don't worry about me. I get fed. It's a job.'

'Have you seen anything of Kit?' I asked.

Her expression was bitter. 'Told you... hardly allowed to leave here, am I?'

'Ow, not so hard, please,' I begged.

She stopped rotating the ankle and said in a low voice, 'These people are no better than you or me, Flora. Don't make the mistake of thinking that they are. You'd do well to watch yourself around...'

She broke off as the door banged open. Li-li swept into the kitchen.

'Any message from Kit?' I asked Li-li the same question every day when she returned.

'He's mended your roof.' Li-li undid her soft leather riding gloves and tossed her hat in Annie's direction. 'Clean it,' she ordered.

'No message?' I persisted.

'No,' Li-li said with slight smile. 'I'd have said.'

I felt disconcerted.

Li-li put her hands on her hips. 'Anything else, Flora?' she said, her eyes big and innocent.

'No...'

'In that case, I'll take myself off,' she replied and turned on her heel.

Annie continued rotating my ankle. 'Kit'll be doing his best by you,' she said softly.

I was reading in the library the following day, when Lord Lao came in.

'I hope you don't mind... You said...' I was covered in confusion.

'Of course I did!' he reassured me, twirling the waxed ends of his moustache. 'I'm delighted. Now... Flora Mandela, I have to go away for a week or so on business, and I very much hope you will still be here when I return. You are a calming influence on my children. They are too frivolous.'

'I really do appreciate your hospitality,' I said.

He shook his head. 'It's my pleasure.'

Yo-yo opened the door and smiled when he saw me.

'Remember,' said Lord Lao, shaking a stern finger at his son, 'No wild parties while I'm gone. I haven't forgotten what happened last time.'

I was intrigued.

He left later that day. I was walking almost normally by now. Doc's next visit would surely result in him saying that I was well enough to look after myself. In all honesty, there would soon be no reason for me not to go back to Shell Shack. But I so wanted to be at The Hall when Lord Lao returned.

Once his father was out of sight, Yo-yo strode back into The Hall as if he owned it. I limped along in his wake.

'Flora, would you like to attend a ball?' he cried, whisking me into his arms and twirling me round.

'A ball?' Into my head came a vision of muslin gowns with flounces, me with fresh flowers in my hair... then reality intervened.

'I don't know how to dance,' I confessed.

Yo-yo was not a man to leave a fly sticking in the ointment.

'I'll teach you,' he said with absolute confidence. 'You've had a tough time, Flora. You deserve a ball.'

'But my ankle?'

'We'll organise it for ten days' time. You'll be well enough by then.'

Ten days. By then I'd be well enough to be home, hoeing the vegetable furrows.

Li-li interrupted my dancing lesson, perspiring from her ride. 'What are you two plotting? I can see there's something going on. Tell me. *Now*!'

'We are going to have a ball. In honour of Flora.'

'Papa will be...'

'Papa isn't to know, you silly girl! We won't tell him.'

I remembered Lord Lao's earlier comment.

'What happened last time you had a party?'

'Oh, nothing much. A Travilla got trashed, that's all.'

Li-li laughed at the memory while Yo-yo put his finger to his lips. 'It was nothing. A bit of youthful exuberance.'

Preparations were set in motion. Extra staff arrived. Women and children I knew from the Spit – Olaf, Mrs Karim, Cher and her older brother, Sami – along with strangers from the town. I kept a low profile, watching the comings and goings, the food being delivered, the paper decorations hung. The main sitting room was cleared of carpets, and chairs were placed around the edges. Gaming tables were set up in the library.

I came across Olaf in the scullery, where he was polishing silverware.

He'd played marbles with me at school but it took a few minutes for him to place me.

'Flora? Flora Mandela?' He looked as if he'd seen a ghost. Did I really look so different? 'Sami said he'd seen you. What are you doing here?'

'Recovering from a broken ankle,' I explained.

'Oh yeah!' He sniggered and made a face. 'That's not what I hear.'

'What do you mean?'

'Kit says you're having it off with the Rice Lord's son.'

My stomach lurched. Olaf was blunt, but he wasn't stupid. 'Kit? He doesn't know what he's talking about,' I spluttered. 'And Olaf, don't you dare go spreading that rubbish.'

'Keep your hair on.' Olaf looked subdued. 'Who wouldn't want to worm your way into a family like this?' he muttered in an oddly deferential tone. 'Good luck to you, I say.'

I flounced out and made my way to my room, furious at the humiliation Kit's gossiping had subjected me to.

Li-li looked up from her seat in front of the mirror where she was painting her nails. 'What's the matter with you?' she asked, but didn't sound as if she really cared.

'Nothing. Nothing at all.'

I wanted peace and fresh air. I limped downstairs and out into the garden, where I hobbled around without the stick, too agitated to sit down. I tried to distract myself by telling myself that I had to get used to putting weight on the ankle if I was going to be able to dance. But I couldn't deny the pain. I sat on the steps and watched the clouds gather, but I couldn't identify any of the shapes.

How dare Kit imagine he knew anything about my life here? How dare he spread nasty rumours about me? But deep down I realised that Kit knew me better than anybody. He would know that I *was* attracted to Yo-yo. I was in love with him, there was no denying it. I was in love with the son of a Rice Lord. I felt bleak. What possible future could we have together?

Just then, Yo-yo strode out through the main door and came to sit down next to me.

'Why so sad?'

I blushed. 'I was thinking... I'll have to go home soon.'

'Look – over there – sheet lightning,' he said as if he hadn't heard me. 'The Hurricane Weeks are almost on us. They'll send you toxic with fever, and then you'll have to stay even longer.' Although he was teasing, there was something serious in his voice.

I reached out my hand, palm up to feel the first raindrops.

'You don't have to leave.' He lifted my hand to his lips and kissed it. But he didn't say anything more.

'Who is invited to the ball?' I asked, loath to let him go.

'Oh, the usual suspects: Uzi officers, their wives and mistresses, people I know from the town, some casino mates.'

'Casino?'

'Yes. Gambling is a hobby of mine. Not that Father knows, of course. I slide off after dinner when he's busy with his calculations, then sneak back in the early hours – down as a dog when things haven't gone well, high as a kite when they have.'

'But the guard dogs. Aren't they let loose in the grounds during the night?'

'Oh Flora, they're no problem. I've got one of the kitchen skivs – Annie – to make sure there's always raw meat in the pantry. That keeps the mutts happy. Anyway, they wouldn't harm me, they know me.' Yo-yo glanced up at the threatening sky and kissed me on the brow. 'Now come on, it's about to chuck it down. Time for another dancing lesson, I think.'

But we didn't go to the library where we usually practised. We went straight to Yo-yo's bedroom.

CHAPTER TWELVE

AS THE NIGHT of the ball drew nearer, The Hall took on an increasingly exotic air. Sumptuous floral decorations hung from the ceilings and sparkling silver bowls were piled high with fruit. Chalk was sprinkled on the polished floor of the largest room and the furniture pushed back against the walls or removed to other rooms.

Yo-yo and I had barely spoken since the night he had taken me to his room, probably because he was so busy.

Li-li was in her element.

'You must look your best,' she declared, discovering me curled up with *Mansfield Park*. 'You might catch somebody's eye.'

Three skivs arrived with armfuls of her mother's gowns. Li-li made me try them all on. I decked myself in a succession of embroidered silks, lush satins and velvets coloured like jewels, some of them sewn with sparkling stones. As I pirouetted in front of the mirror and Li-li delivered a hilarious commentary on my appearance we both dissolved in excited giggles, the tension between us gone once again. Too caught up in our impromptu fashion show for any soul-searching, I was just happy that we were friends, having fun.

My heart was set on a full-skirted sapphire blue silk dress with lace panels and a plunging neckline, but Li-li had different ideas.

'No...' she said. 'I want you to wear this for your first Lao ball.' She presented me with her choice.

My first Lao ball. Would there be others?

The night of the ball arrived and Li-li daubed my face with

powders, outlined my eyes in black and gold, applied red grease to my lips and helped me dress. We sat at an upstairs barred window and watched as the first guests arrived. There were a dozen or more carriages, some open, some covered. The women stepped out gingerly – all were wearing the highest of heels and elaborate feathered headdresses. Sequinned Ball gowns shimmered in a flash of lightning.

'We could go down now,' Li-li said after a while. 'It doesn't do to arrive too early. Even if it is in our house.'

A trio of musicians were playing at one end of the packed sitting room, their music almost drowned in the rising swell of conversation. Candles flamed on every mantelshelf and table. Almost immediately, Li-li left me 'to do the hostess thing' and I was left on my own, surrounded by noisy strangers.

My white silk dress, strapless and straight-cut, looked positively puritanical next to what other women were wearing. A pang of shame shot through me as, for a brief moment, I saw everything through Nano's eyes. She would have hated it. But I pushed her thoughts firmly from my mind. They didn't belong here, but I did, I told myself.

Still awkward and hoping it didn't show, I gravitated towards the gaming room, where I could see that Yo-yo presided.

'The tables are full,' he cried, ushering out a few would-be gamblers with the assurance that they would have their chance later. As he closed the door he caught sight of me. 'You look ravishing,' he declared. 'Doesn't she?' he said to one of the men he was evicting from the room.

He kissed me lightly on the ear lobe and promised he would be out to dance with me soon.

Li-li materialised by my side, grabbed my hand and pulled me over to a knot of handsome officers, where she made swift introductions before abandoning me again. Yearning for Yo-yo to come to me, I politely accepted their invitations to dance. Amazingly, my ankle didn't hurt at all.

The officers' accents were difficult to make out, especially with the noise level rising all the time. They were downing their drinks fast and it wasn't long before it showed in their voices. And the ball had hardly got under way.

I didn't recognise a single guest. The only people I knew were the skivs serving food and drink – the coastguards' wives, including Mrs de Kooning, my old schoolteacher. Most of them looked at me with open hostility. I tried to meet their eye, to let them know that I was still one of them, but they were all determined that I should have no contact. Eventually I gave up. Why shouldn't I grasp life and enjoy myself? Why should they spoil my night? I had every right. I took another glass of wine from the tray Mrs de Kooning was carrying, with only a nod of thanks. And that glass led to a third.

Unsure what else to do, I remained with the group of officers. Periodically one of them would head over to a side table to ask for a twist of the whitesnuff Yo-yo had laid out on the glass surfaces. When they came back their eyes looked odd and they talked even louder than before. It was offered to me several times but I refused. The drinks were making me feel quite different from usual. Myself, but more so. I was enjoying being me.

'Flora! Be my sweetheart!' rumbled one of the officers, pulling me onto his knee.

'*Au contraire*,' bellowed another, 'She's mine!' and whisked me back onto my feet again. I took it all in the spirit of fun and laughed along with them.

I remember noticing the candles in the candelabra were being replenished by the skivs and thinking how time must be rushing past, and no sign of Yo-yo. Next thing, I was dancing with a Chino officer, a charmer who steered me round the floor, attempting to kiss me. I had watched Li-li put a few officers in their place and followed her example. It was remarkably easy.

'No!' I said, lifting his chin and turning his head to his left. 'I'm dancing, not kissing.'

'You're a tease,' he moaned. 'Just one kiss?'

'No. I said no.'

And with that, we whirled and bobbed until the music finished, ending up back where we began, next to a Russ woman who turned out to be his partner.

Without a word, she rose to her feet and smacked him across

the face. To my horror, his face twisted into a snarl and he struck back at her, then grabbed her by the shoulders, lifted her in the air so that her high heels jerked off her feet, and started shaking her violently. She looked like a flimsy doll in his hands. As I retreated, stunned and shaking, an appreciative audience surged forward, applauding and cheering.

I felt sick. Where was Yo-yo? He said this ball was for me. Why wasn't he protecting me?

I fled to Li-li's room, hoping that Yo-yo would come to find me, but he didn't. After about twenty minutes the door burst open and Li-li almost fell through, giggling hysterically. To my horror, I saw that she was being followed by the same Chino soldier who had hit the Russ woman. They stared at me for a moment before she dragged him out, still giggling.

I opened a window. Lightning and the searchlights from the fort at the far end of the Spit lit the sky. The muslin curtains around the beds flapped wildly like the wings of white swans. Heavy rain continued to fall. For all the anticipation, the evening seemed endless.

In the end I went downstairs again and wandered around, scanning constantly for Yo-yo.

A fair-skinned young man with a shaved head and bristly chin grabbed my arm, squashing me to him and pulled me in among the whirling dancers. He was very tall and the gold braid of his uniform scratched my face. Somehow I managed to push him away. I wove through the dancers, my head buzzing. How could I have ever imagined that this night would play out like a scene from *Pride and Prejudice*.

I went out into the hallway, picked up a glass of what I thought was orange juice and gulped it down. The women around me seemed to be turning into parakeets the way they screeched and I wanted to scream to them all to be quiet. I put my hand flat against the wall to steady myself.

Suddenly the main door was thrown open and Lord Lao strode in, his hair and cloak soaked from the storm. I stared at him, my heart pounding.

'What is the meaning of this?' he boomed. The chatter died

down. Even those further away, who had not witnessed his return, realised that everything had changed. The musicians stopped playing, apart from the fiddler, who carried on for a few frenetic bars.

The door of the library opened and Yo-yo emerged into the tense silence, his jacket undone, cravat loosened. He looked around, confused.

I watched a nerve leap on his father's face, twisting one side of his mouth. Yo-yo stopped in his tracks.

'Get them all out. Now!'

Yo-yo's eyes narrowed but he obeyed his father.

Disgruntled, the party people gathered their tiger, mink and leopard skin cloaks and staggered off, holding each other up.

There was nothing grand about the evening now.

Li-li appeared at the top of the staircase, ran down to her father and took his arm.

'Father, it was only a bit of fun.'

He was immune to her pretty ways for once.

'You are improperly dressed, Li-li. Go to your room.'

I flinched as he approached me. His eyes swept me from my head to my toes and back again. 'And you, Flora, I'm very disappointed in you. Go with Li-li. And tomorrow you will return my wife's dress, if you please. You are not worthy of it.'

CHAPTER THIRTEEN

TWO DAYS LATER, all the finery and decorations dismantled and the extra staff dismissed, the atmosphere in The Hall seemed a little calmer. I had suggested that I should go home the morning after the ball. But Lord Lao had dismissed the idea with a wave of his hand. 'There is no reason for you to run away, Flora. The fault is not yours, though you were foolish to go along with the idea.'

That afternoon, as I was about to enter the library, I heard two voices behind the closed door. I was about to turn back down the corridor when the sound of my own name stopped me in my tracks.

'Yes, Flora is attractive. Very. And she is a pov.'

'She means so much to me...' There was a pleading tone in Yo-yo's voice.

'She is a pov, will never be anything other than that. And the son of a Rice Lord does not marry below his station. Or at least, not that far.'

'The high privs need new blood, Papa.'

'You did not hear me? You must and will marry a high priv, insolent boy. Whatever you like to imagine, you know nothing of World, nothing of the need to preserve the bloodline.'

'But Papa, I am so... attracted to Flora.'

Lord Lao gave a dry laugh. 'Privs marry privs,' he said as if he was talking to a toddler. 'That's the way we maintain our power. Attraction doesn't come into it.'

'Papa...' Yo yo sounded desperate.

'Listen Yo-yo, you'll do as you are told. Do you want to lose status? Become an outcast? Make a fool out of me? You'll marry who I tell you to marry. I will not have you sidetracked by an infatuation with an insignificant little pov. Forget her.'

The words ripped through me. *An insignificant little pov.* For weeks now I had been telling myself that I was in some way being introduced into the Laos' world, that these people valued me for who I was.

There was no audible reply from Yo-yo.

'We've spent enough time on all this nonsense. News has reached me that the paddy fields' workforce has been infiltrated by insurgents and the most recent intelligence indicates that the situation is far worse than I thought. Nortland is under threat. B&NG is under threat. I've been away setting up systems to sort things out. Quelling that threat should be your absolute priority, young man. The product of the paddy fields represents a crucial part of your inheritance. Li-li's inheritance too. And here you are, mooning about a girl who is nothing more than a passing entertainment. It's time you understood the terms of engagement. She can offer you nothing. Nothing!'

I crept away, devastated.

Fortunately Li-li was out riding so I had our room to myself. I stood looking out of the window, chilled to the marrow.

What had I missed? How had the discussion begun? Had Yo-yo been asking permission to marry me? Yes. That's what must have started it, I was sure. On the one hand it felt like a revelation. Yo-yo wanted to marry me. I folded my arms across my stomach and sank onto my knees. Oh, I loved him so. But on the other, it felt like a defeat. Did he love me enough to go against his father's wishes? I thought of Shell Shack, my miserable poverty. No. I could not go back there, to that life. Not now that I knew what was possible. I was going to fight for what was within my reach.

Yo-yo loved me, I was certain of that now. Why else would he have risked his father's fury? I would do everything in my power to win over the Rice Lord.

Lord Lao behaved coolly towards me for a day or two, but he did not ask me to leave. My ankle had not benefited from the ball. It was swollen and I was limping again. Doc Poliakoff was called. He gave the puffy joint a perfunctory squeeze and assured me that there was nothing amiss that elevation and rest wouldn't heal. Once again, we weren't alone together. Li-li hung around, playing the nurse. And anyway, I was in no rush to prompt him to return to what he'd been saying about my father. My future was suddenly far more important to me than my father's past.

Yo-yo was avoiding me, or kept busy elsewhere, but I told myself that until he had everything settled, he didn't want to raise my hopes. Li-li, as usual, was off each day, who knows where. Meeting her Uzi officer maybe, or one of her brother's gambling buddies?

I decided I must not fade into the background. I had nothing to be ashamed of. In the library I found a book about a figure in history Lord Lao had once commented on, a Russ leader called Joseph Stalin. I offered to read it out to him after dinner, a few pages every night. He agreed without hesitation. And so every evening I would take off from where I had left the story – Lord Lao sitting with his feet up on a footstool, eyes closed, concentrating, his faithful spaniel, Mao, by his side. The story was a grim one, but he liked it.

'How come you read so well?' he asked me one evening, when the only illumination in the darkening room was the orange beam from the searchlight at the other end of the Spit. There was no reason not to explain how my grandfather taught me to read from the reject book, *Pride and Prejudice*, from the Great Flood Library.

'Oh, yes, the Library – we demolished it. And not before time. Do you still have that book?' he asked.

'No,' I lied.

'Just as well. Burned in the purges, I suppose?'

I shrugged, not knowing what he was talking about but knowing I shouldn't have had access to literature.

'Or any other reading matter?'

'Your books are the first I've seen since I was a child.' It struck me that I had mentioned to Li-Li that I still had the book, and I went hot and cold with anxiety. I was no good at lying.

'Hmm,' he grunted. I didn't know whether he believed me. 'Li-

li doesn't enjoy reading to me,' he complained. 'She stumbles over words so much that I lose patience. What a useless creature she has turned out to be.'

'She's lovely though...' The words sounded false in my mouth.

'Being ornamental is all she's good for. Whereas you... you have such a quaint and unusual way of talking. And intelligence... I suppose it must have been the exposure to the subtleties of Jane Austen. You have absorbed knowledge most povs never have access to.'

I warmed to his flattery. I was winning round Lord Lao.

After two long days of thick fog, there came a clear, fine day. To my delight, Yo-yo sought me out and announced that he had a surprise for me. He was carrying a hooded cloak, thick mittens, a hat and a scarf. 'Dress warmly,' he commanded, as I pulled the garments on. I followed him out of The Hall.

On the high field was one of the Laos' smaller, two-seater kites, bright orange, set up and held by three Uzi guards. Without a word he handed my stick to one of the guards, helped me into the kite, strapped me in and slipped in next to me. Once he was ready, he instructed the three men to let go.

Gradually, as the ropes were untied, the wind lifted us into the air. The sensation of flying was like nothing I had ever experienced before. My stomach seemed to leave its proper place and dropped briefly. But as we rose above the fields and Hall, I was so amazed by the scene below and for miles around that I forgot my nerves and could only gaze, thrilled beyond words. The Hall was small beneath us now, the panorama below opening up like one of Yoyo's maps. I could see the spires and towers of the drowned town of Sainsburyness, like a quivering mirage beneath the smooth sea to the east. Pelicans flew underneath us. It was so strange seeing them from above.

'See your shack?' Yo-yo shouted above the noise of wind in the sails.

'Yes, and the orchard – it looks so small, like a toy.' My words blew away on the wind. I spoke louder. 'May I fly the kite?'

'If you like. It's a bit tricky. When you take over the controls, just keep your eye on the horizon. Fly flat, don't tilt the wings too much, or we'll stall.'

I shoved the lever up and down to see what happened and soon had the hang of it. Yo-yo's gloved hand covered mine, making minor adjustments where my movements were too jerky or extreme.

'You're a natural pilot, Flora,' he told me.

The debt-slave quarters were beneath us now, high-walled and surrounded by wire. I wanted away from them.

'Can we look at the mountains?' I asked.

'Another day. You're blue with cold. Here, I'll take the controls again.'

I hadn't noticed how cold I was until he said it. I was shivering, and my eyes streamed from the icy wind. He passed me a bizarre contraption of metal and glass.

'Look through them,' he said, gesturing. 'They're special vision enhancers.'

I found the eye pieces.

'But everything is so far away!'

'No, the other end!' he laughed at me.

I turned the vision enhancers round and started at the apparent closeness of the scene below. But once my eyes adjusted it was fascinating. I could see people moving about. The black uniforms of the guards stood out against the bright green of the rice plants – I had never realised that the paddy fields were so heavily guarded. The debt-slave kids were herded together. They looked so small. A sudden movement caught my eye. Something was happening in the middle of a row. At first I couldn't understand what I was seeing, then I realised it was a soldier clubbing a young woman on the head with the butt of his Uzi.

I turned to Yo-yo, sickened, but he was oblivious, concentrating on flying the kite.

I trained the vision enhancers back on the scene in the paddy. The woman was on the ground and the Uzi soldier was kicking her now. Then a man broke from a row of workers and lunged towards her, but the guard instantly smashed him in the face with the gun. And then I saw a brief spurt of flame, saw the body jerk for what seemed like an age, then become still.

I lowered the vision enhancers, too horrified to speak and too cowardly to look again. Yo-yo, apparently unaware of the vile drama that had unfolded below, was preparing for landing.

My mind reeled at what I'd seen. The barbarity of it. And those were Lord Lao's paddy fields. Lord Lao's workers. Lord Lao – intelligent, cultured, charming Lord Lao. Surely he couldn't know what was going on down there. But then I remembered the conversation I had overheard, his cold, domineering manner, the reference to insurgents in the rice fields. Was this how Lord Lao ran his business?

We landed smoothly on the hill behind The Hall, the men came running to hold the kite and tether it when we disembarked.

Yo-yo climbed out and lifted me over the side in a whirling movement.

'Enjoy your first kite flight?' he asked cheerfully. 'Perfect flying conditions.'

CHAPTER FOURTEEN

I SPENT THE next couple of days in my bed, alone, not knowing how to behave, what to think. The sick feeling in the pit of my stomach would not go away. I desperately needed advice from someone wise, like Nano or Grandpa Noah – or Kit.

I told Li-li that I'd caught a chill on the flight and she was happy enough to leave me to my own devices. Again, Yo-yo made no attempt to talk to me. And even if he had, I couldn't have explained that I had eavesdropped on his conversation, or described the scene in the rice field.

I made myself get up and exercise my leg, up and down by the bedroom windows. I needed to be fit. I wanted to go back home. I had had enough of The Hall.

I asked Li-li to explain to her father that I wasn't well enough to read to him. The last thing I wanted to do was to read about Joseph Stalin. He was no hero of mine. He stood by as people were killed. He ordered the deaths of untold numbers of people. I shivered at the thought of how much Lord Lao esteemed this awful man. But I kept going round in circles in my head.

I wanted to believe that the Laos knew nothing of what was going on in the paddy fields. Lord Lao might not deliver the blows, but as Rice Lord, he was responsible – but did he know about it? Should I say anything?

I wondered if Doc Poliakoff patched up the slaves after their beatings. Was he aware of the killing?

I wanted to un-see what I had seen from that kite.

'I have decided, Lord Lao,' I announced at breakfast the next morning, 'that I must return to Shell Shack. My ankle is almost mended.' I held my voice steady, a treacherous part of me hoping he would wave away my decision and persuade me to stay.

'Before you go, you must see the telescope,' was his smooth response.

He showed no sign of regret at my impending departure. Yo-yo's face was a mask.

I climbed the winding stairs to the tower, the father in front, the son behind. Even after all my soul searching, I desperately wanted Yo-yo to be the man I wanted him to be.

The tower was a circular stone room with windows all around and above. A huge telescope sat on a brass tripod.

'Look through here,' Lord Lao pointed to an eyepiece on the side. As I did so, he started to explain that it worked with mirrors, but his voice faded into a background drone.

What I saw through the telescope was a revelation – in full daylight, Moon, and then Saturn with its many grey-brown and white rings of dust.

'I had no idea that the stars and planets were so beautiful,' I said with awe in my voice. 'At school we were taught that they were lumps of hurtling rock.'

Yo-yo laughed quietly. 'There's rather more to them than that,' he said.

'Are there people living on the planets? Has anyone ever travved there to find out?'

'Oh yes,' replied Yo-yo. 'In the 20th century men were sent to Moon and beyond, but nothing came of it. There are some old papers and moving digigraphs that suggest they landed, although some googlers say the digigraphs are forgeries. And since then World has suffered so many calamities that mankind can no longer afford space travel.'

'It was too late to find another world for the survivors to go to,' his father added. 'We were stuck with what we have now – desert and disease and toxic wastelands.' The tic by his mouth began to twitch.

'And where is the comet?' I asked.

'Not visible yet,' he said.

'I must be getting back to Shell Shack,' I said. 'I can't thank you enough for your hospitality.'

'Do keep that gown,' Lord Lao said, 'it suits you. The shoes also.' He turned back to the telescope. I was dismissed.

I followed Yo-yo down the spiral staircase.

My brain hurt with all that I was still trying to assimilate: the brutality in the paddy fields, Yo-yo's conversation with his father, the way brother and sister changed in their manner towards me without warning. I wanted to say something but found no words.

What was I afraid of? I loved him. I was sure of that. I so wanted Yo-yo to beg me to stay.

Outside my room, Yo-yo paused and said, 'I'll arrange for the trap to be at the front door in an hour.' He gave a brief smile and strode off down the corridor.

I shed angry tears as I packed my clothes into a holdall. What a fool I'd been! Nobody here was going to offer me a lifeline. I had spent all this time in a fantasy. The Laos were casual and utterly unfeeling about letting me return to an existence they despised. Then I thought of Nano and Grandpa Noah, working their fingers to the bone at Shell Shack. Nano would have been ashamed of me, of the way I'd embraced empty luxuries. The abundance of everything – warmth, clothing, food, company – had been in such contrast to the world I was about to return to. It was as if I just couldn't help it.

At the front door, Yo-yo shook my hand. That's all he did, shake my hand. And step back.

'You have been the perfect house-guest,' said Lord Lao, stepping forward and kissing me on both cheeks. 'Li-li will accompany you home.'

No invitation to come again.

I was angry with myself for being a coward. I was angry with Yo-yo for not standing up to his father. I was angry with Kit for neglecting me.

If this was what growing up was all about, I wished I had remained a child.

CHAPTER FIFTEEN

AN UZI SOLDIER drove the trap. At the last moment, Lord Lao had pressed on me a bundle of his dead wife's clothes and enough rice to keep me going for several weeks. Manga sat on my lap, no doubt upset at leaving the kitchen, which must have been titbit heaven for him.

As we rode away I felt empty inside and had to swallow hard to prevent myself from weeping. The two handsome men standing side by side were almost identical from a distance, except that Yo-yo was taller by half a head. I waved and watched as he stood there long after his father had gone inside. As we reached the last of the lush hills that surrounded The Hall, I turned away from him to look through my tears at the barren windswept Eden Spit.

Li-li hardly spoke on the journey and I was glad of her silence.

I tried to push away all thoughts of Yo-yo, but ifs and buts cascaded through my mind. Of course he didn't love me. I had imagined it. Why would he want to share his life with a pov with a chipped tooth and scarred chin? I berated myself, on the one hand for dreaming a ridiculous dream and on the other for not pursuing it successfully.

Face it, I told myself, he had not asked me to be his wife. He was the son of a Rice Lord, there was no future for us. Yet I could still feel his lips on my throat.

Perhaps Nano would have told me to go back, confront him, force him to admit his feelings. But Grandpa Noah would have spat on that idea. He would have called the Laos fascist slave killers. He would have been totally against me having anything to do with them.

The horse, its shaggy mane blowing over its eyes, slowed as we reached the sandy path along the middle of the peninsula. Only the few, scattered dwellings and the ugly fort and barracks at the end of the Spit punctuated the featureless landscape. On one side was the crashing sea, on the other the brimming brown water of the bay. We turned through the water meadow onto my small piece of Eden.

Manga leapt down before we got to Shell Shack. Jess barked in greeting and the two dogs yelped and pranced around each other.

Kit was in the vegetable plot, digging up potatoes. I could see at once that the rows of vegetables had been hoed of all weeds and were thriving. The orchard was tidy, the path had been raked clear of leaves and there were chickens in the coop. As I climbed down, Kit went over to the pump to wash his hands. He dried them on his trousers and came and hugged me.

'You're back,' he said gruffly.

'Home, yes,' I said.

He looked clean. He even smelled clean!

We went inside Shell Shack and he closed the door behind us. Then he leaned behind me, drew Li-li to him as if it was the most natural thing, and kissed her full on the lips.

A stew was cooking on the stove, the dishes were clean and the floor was swept. There were sunflowers in a jug on the table, which was laid for two.

'I don't understand. Kit, have you done all this?'

'Don't you like it?' Li-li butted in. 'It's a surprise for you. We did it together.'

'You... and Kit?'

I knew I had no right, but I felt betrayed. Li-li'd been playing the pov, living my life. I was filled with envy, anger and misery, all at once. And then I thought about Yo-yo and me and felt even more confused.

Li-li looked cross. 'What about the chickens? Don't you like them?'

I forced a smile.

'One piece of bad news, Flora,' she added. 'Your feral cat got the pigeons.'

'Oh no, not Grandpa's pigeons!'

'Well, they were barely alive. Cat did you a favour, putting them out of their misery.'

But they were Grandpa's. There was no point in saying it aloud. Kit and Li-li were wrapped up in the cosy world they'd made here, in my home. They wouldn't understand. I could hardly bring myself to speak to them. Not that they seemed to notice. They chatted away together ten to the dozen as I stomped around putting away my things.

I couldn't reclaim my territory soon enough from Li-li, the usurper. When she finally announced that she was leaving, I barely concealed my relief.

'Flora, don't tell Papa about me and Kit,' she whispered as she kissed my cheek.

Kit helped Li-li into the carriage and kissed her goodbye, while I strained to catch their parting words.

I never wanted to see her again.

Kit and I sat in silence over our meal. Only when we had both cleared our plates of the rabbit stew did I bring myself to ask: 'Why didn't you send a message, Kit? Why didn't you come and see me?'

'For one thing, my dad died, Flora. Didn't Li-li say?'

'Oh, Kit, I didn't know, no, she didn't tell me.'

'Just after your accident, it was.'

I was stunned. 'What happened?'

A strange look came over Kit's face.

'Hanged himself.'

'No!'

'He couldn't... he'd no hope. He'd been threatening to do it for ages. But I never thought he actually would.'

'Poor man. Poor you.' I went round the table to him, put my hands around his drooping head and pressed my lips to his hair. It smelled of wood smoke.

'Kit? Are you and Li-li...?'

'She's a sweet girl. And so lonely. There's no future in it, I know that.' I said nothing. He changed the subject. 'Do you like the chickens? Li-li chose them for their looks.'

'Li-li?'

'Yeah. She paid for them.' Kit sounded defensive. 'She has more dees than she knows what to do with, that one.'

I closed my eyes. 'And what about Manga? He arrived at The Hall in a terrible state.'

'Ran off, didn't he? Couldn't find him.'

'At least *he* found *me*.' I was hurt and couldn't hide it. 'What about Barcode? Have you been looking out for him?'

'Course not! Flora, I've warned you again and again about him.'

'He's just a little boy...'

'Well, you might have had spare scraps at The Hall, but there were none to spare here. As usual.' Kit's voice was harder than I'd ever heard it.

'All right. There's something else – why did you tell everyone that I was having a relationship with Yo-yo?'

'I didn't need to. Everybody knows. Stafan overheard him boasting about you at that dance at the Hall.' A pained look crossed his face. 'Flora, I wasn't sure you'd ever come back.' His dark eyes met mine and I looked down. 'You are... going with Li-li's brother, aren't you?' he asked.

I didn't answer.

'What's the matter with you, Flora?'

'I've changed! What's wrong with that? We've both changed.'

After Kit left, I wandered round noticing all the repairs and improvements he'd done, but rather than feeling grateful I just kept picturing him there with Li-li. No doubt they used Shell Shack because he realised his posh little friend wouldn't be up for slumming it in his smelly old yurt. I felt a blush of shame creep over my face. Keeping clear of the yurt would have had something to do with the way his dad died. Kit must have found him.

I lay awake, my mind churning, all night long. Where had Kit and Li-li slept? In my grandparents' bed? I felt sick at the thought.

As the sun rose, I sat in bed with Grandpa's patchwork quilt around my shoulders, the journal I'd brought from The Hall in my lap. Lord Lao had given me a large bottle of ink and a good pen. I wrote for hours. I wanted to set down everything that had happened to me in the months since my grandparents died. I covered page after page after page in writing, as tiny as I could make it, to conserve space.

The process of setting things down on paper forced me to face up to some hard truths about my own behaviour. I had taken it for granted that Kit would always be at my beck and call. I had turned down his offer of a closer relationship, so I was hardly in a position to complain about him and Li-li, especially considering my own feelings for Yo-yo.

I didn't want to write about the Laos. If I wrote down what I knew, what I'd seen, it would be so damning that I couldn't justify seeing them again. And I did want to see Yo-yo. Despite everything.

Equally sure was the fact that I wanted nothing from Li-li.

I felt in my pocket for the tiny doll she'd named Faith and chucked it onto the pile of kindling beside the range.

CHAPTER SIXTEEN

THE NEW COCKEREL woke me next morning with his loud call. As soon as I was washed and dressed in my old overalls, I raked out the ashes from the range and removed them to the compost heap. I inspected the orchard, breathing in the delicious scent of orange blossom, then I walked around my smallholding, noting the neat heaps of firewood and sea-coal Kit had left. Not only had he mended the roof and plugged holes in the walls of Shell Shack, he had filled the gaps in the shed walls, too.

I let the chickens out to run in the yard, where they immediately started to peck and feed. They were beautiful, I had to admit, even though Li-li had chosen them. Glossy black feathers tumbled over their claws and spread over their necks. They were far more handsome than the plain brown hens I had grown up with. They were like the Laos – exotic and glamorous and strange. At first they were nervous of me, but when they realised that I was now the source of their feed, they gradually came closer, until they were eating out of my hand.

It was while I was feeding them that the Lao family arrived at Shell Shack.

I couldn't believe my eyes.

'So this is your small kingdom, Flora!' Lord Lao dismounted, opened the gate and walked in. Yo-yo and Li-li followed.

'Please come in. I'll make a pot of mint tea.' Flustered, I fell back on the hospitality taught me by Nano.

'No, we won't bother you. I've come to see the sculptures. My daughter tells me they are most unusual and extraordinary.'

'My grandfather's work, you mean?'

'Yes. May I look around?'

I showed him the driftwood and recycled metal creatures – an elephant, a zebra, and other extinct mammals. A peacock with metal rods as tail feathers. Lord Lao was impressed, I could tell. I tried to catch Yo-yo's eye, but he was looking everywhere except at me.

'Would you be prepared to sell any of them, Flora?' Lord Lao twisted the ends of his waxed moustache.

'Sell?' The possibility had never occurred to me before Li-li's throwaway comment. No one had ever shown an interest in buying the work, although they'd taken digigraphs of them, and paid for the privilege. But I thought of the dees at Lord Lao's disposal and what I could do with them.

He could see my hesitation. 'Name your price,' he said.

'I don't know. I hadn't thought anyone would want them.' Except me.

'They have artistic merit and a naïve charm. Your grandfather was a talented sculptor. I would like to buy as many as you care to sell.'

I was beginning to feel panicky, imagining the place without the sculptures. It was as if I was selling Grandpa Noah along with them.

'Let me think about it,' I said.

'That's very sensible, Flora.' Lord Lao tilted his head, smiling. 'Let me know when you've made your decision.'

'I should give them to you, really, to repay you for the Dizcare.'

'Nonsense. It was my pleasure.'

Li-li rolled her eyes. 'I want the pretty dove palace, Papa.' she begged.

'The Hall's dovecot *is* falling down. Add it to the list, Flora.'

No. 'The dovecot isn't for sale,' I said, looking stonily at his daughter.

'Very well. Let me know which of the sculptures you're prepared to part with. Then I'll make you an offer.' Lord Lao climbed on his horse and with a brief wave, set off.

Yo-yo and Li-li followed without a word.

Who had too much pride and who was prejudiced, I thought? I was no Elizabeth Bennett, that was for certain.

My book! I hadn't seen it since my return. Where was it? Where had I left it? I prayed that Li-li hadn't spotted it on one of her 'visits'. She might have thrown it out. Kit knew how important it was. I hoped he had hidden it, but where? I rushed inside and searched all over. Then I tried the pigeon palace, the loft, the sheds, the barn. Nothing.

Tears came. This time I curled up on my bed and let them flow. I cried for everything that I had lost. How contented I had been as a child in this poor place! Thank Rice Nano and Grandpa Noah had protected me from people like the Laos.

Gradually the painful sobs that racked my body subsided. Nano and Grandpa Noah had loved me. Nano fed me good home-grown vegetables and fruit, grown as a result of her hard labour, her sweat, her muscles, her long days, her anxiety, and her strength. She gave me rules to live by. She had been my fortress against the crims, the scavs, and all that was wrong and sad.

'*One day, Flora, you'll be able to make your own decisions, to stand on your own two feet,*' she'd often said, especially when I complained that she was over-vigilant.

'You died too soon,' I whispered into my pillow. 'You didn't stay long enough. I'm nowhere near ready.' I had let her down. '*Stay – don't leave Eden,*' she'd said. And at the first opportunity I had tried to do just that. I had allowed myself to be tempted and seduced by the dream of life as a priv, life with the son of a Rice Lord. I had made a deliberate effort to get Yo-yo to marry me and take me away from Eden.

And I thought of Grandpa Noah, who had put heart and soul into building this little shack. In spite of his gammy leg, his poor eyesight, the bullet that remained in his skull and probably caused his brain damage, he had carried me on his shoulders, taken me fishing, told me stories, taught me to read, encouraged me to be strong and fearless. Grandpa was my hero. My gentle hero. I hadn't even been able to look after his precious pigeons. '*Pigeons are vital to the Cause, Flora, never forget that.*' Even when he was at his most confused, he had tended to those birds. Nano resented them, resented the way he'd disappear for hours, waiting for them to return from their far-flung flights. I hoped that any man I eventually lived with would be as kind and good as Grandpa Noah.

CHAPTER SEVENTEEN

MY BOOK! I must find my book, was my first thought when I woke with a start. Perhaps Kit had hidden it in the pigeon palace. After my chores, I re-read what I'd written in my journal. Not all of it made the sense it had when I wrote it, but it helped settle my scattered thoughts. I hadn't realised until now how much Nano and Grandpa had given me. When I got out of bed and washed at the pump in the garden, I felt renewed and contented with my lot – well, more so than I had when I first came back to Shell Shack. I promised myself that I would try harder to be the person they had known and loved, not the person I had let myself become under the influence of the Laos – lazy, indolent, wanting comfort and riches; with '*ideas above my station*', Nano would have said. But, oh, how my hands had suffered since I had returned to Shell Shack.

Thanks to Kit, and Li-li, I admitted to myself, Shell Shack looked much as it had when I was a child. I needed to keep it that way. It was time to clean out the pigeon palace, a job I'd avoided at all costs. Now, I wanted to do it. Find the book. Perhaps I'd find a way to buy new pigeons.

With Manga scrambling close behind, I climbed the ladder, a cloth tied over my mouth and nose to diminish the stink of droppings. After sweeping all the soiled straw out onto the ground, I set about cleaning the three nesting boxes. Rats had chewed through the wood in places but the damage wasn't so bad. It was while I was peering through one of these gaps that I saw it – not the book – but a large metal key, hung on a hook in a dark corner. I reached over, unhooked it and popped it into the pocket of my apron, determined not to be distracted from the job in hand. It was only later, once I'd washed the dust and filth of the pigeon palace out of my hair that I returned to the locked chest under my grandparents' bed. Could this be its key?

Trembling slightly I put it into the lock of the chest. It was stiff and at first nothing happened, but I wiggled it back and forth and eventually I heard a click. I lifted the lid.

What did I expect to find? It certainly wasn't treasure. A mouldy sailor suit. Grandpa's medals, wrapped in a blue shirt. But underneath, a pile of old papers; and underneath that, a cardboard folder, wormed and dusty and grey. In the folder I found a bundle of envelopes tied with a ribbon and a small tin, its hinges rusted over. The tin was difficult to open, but when I banged it on the floor the lid sprang off, spilling out the contents: small grey metal capsules about as long as my thumb, with folding tabs on the sides. I eased a few of them open. Inside each one was a tiny piece of paper with numbers and letters written on it, reminding me of the antique vehicle registration plates that were sometimes swept up by the tide.

DOV79H2.

I had no idea what they were or what they meant.

Manga sat by me, sniffing at the letters and wagging his tail.

'Okay boy, let me read you a love letter,' I said to him and he whined.

This is the last message.

I had started at the wrong end. I turned the bundle over and carefully opened the bottom one. It was stained and torn and nibbled by insects:

Made contact. It won't be easy. Plans have to be made, allies gathered. You might not hear from me for a while. Be strong. OUR CAUSE IS JUST.

Instead of a signature there was a tick, a little like the ones Mrs de Kooning used to make on my slate when she was pleased with me. But bigger. I felt my heart beating faster. The Cause? What cause?

Plans developing. Won't say more than that. What you don't know you can't divulge under pressure.

And the tick signature again. Except that now, when I looked at it, it might have been a bird.

I didn't read the entire pile of letters, just a few here and there, each one note-like, mysterious, inconclusive, with dangerous words –

sabotage... conflict... liberation... occupying forces...intelligence gathering... invasion... fascist regime, death to the Rice Lords... Nortland Resistance... riots... Freedom Fighters...Free Forces...

All had been sent by the same person, who signed off with a tick – or was it a bird?

The last letter was dated just before Grandpa Noah died.

DOVs gathering. Strike at any time. Air, sea, land. Be ready. DEATH OR VICTORY!

What did it all mean? My brain couldn't take it all in. The pile of old printed papers were of a similar size as the magazines I'd seen at The Hall, but without glossy colour or thick covers. They were headed *The Spit Speaker*. The headlines jumped out at me.

DEVASTATING FLOODS

NORTLAND DECLARED DISASTER AREA

EXODUS TO HIGH GROUND

NORTLAND OCCUPIED BY B&NG FORCES

INDO/AJE JUNTA SAYS
WE TAKE NO PRISONERS

OPPOSITION QUASHED

THOUSANDS KILLED

THE EDITOR AND STAFF REGRET TO ANNOUNCE THAT THIS IS THE
LAST ISSUE OF THE SPIT SPEAKER. MAY GOD BE WITH US ALL.

The last issue was dated February 2121 – the year that I was born. I sat there, my head bowed. Manga licked my hands, whining quietly. I stroked his wiry fur. 'It's all right, boy, it's all right.' But of course it wasn't all right. I went back to the newspaper headings, and read the smaller print that followed them. Nortland had been invaded and occupied by the Indo-Aje. We were ruled by the Rice Lords. *Rice Shites* was the epithet Grandpa had used, under his breath at first, but as he'd become more disorientated he'd sometimes yelled it out. Nano had shushed him, distracted him with her cakes and fruit. 'If the Uzi soldiers hear that...' she'd say.

Why hadn't my grandparents told me? Did Kit know about this? Who did know? Yo-yo's words came back to me – '*The Rice Families and their favourites will always survive. We are natural rulers.*' I shivered. I'd considered myself a favourite then. It was all right for me.

I looked again at the tiny cylindrical canisters in the tin, tried to work out how they might relate to the papers. What could they be? I put one in my pocket to show to Kit, when I got a chance. If he ever bothered to come to Shell Shack again. I burned with jealousy and hatred for Li-li. How could she! How could *he*! I needed Kit's support, his help. More now than ever before. But things had changed. There was a knot inside my stomach, an acid lump burning a hole. I wanted revenge, but on whom, I wasn't really sure.

I put everything back in the chest and tried to shove it back into its hiding place but it was hard. The chest was remarkably heavy for something with a few old clothes and papers in it. The little cylinders weighed next to nothing. And that was what decided me to take a second look. Once again, I removed the overalls, the tin and the file of papers and letters and beneath them I touched a lip of metal, a handle of some sort. I yanked at it.

Nothing.

I then realised that it was attached to a sliding door of sorts. I moved it across, easing it as gently as I could, and a panel opened to reveal a hidden compartment. I put my hand into the hole and drew out something heavy wrapped in a blanket. My fingers touched cold metal. I knew before I had extricated it what it was – an Uzi sub-machine gun. With my heart in my mouth I unpacked a second rifle, and six huge magazines of cartridges, the kind the Uzi soldiers attached to their saddles. My haul looked totally out of place lying on the floor of Shell Shack. This was no longer my place of safety. Stunned, I wrapped everything up once again and just before I replaced them in the bottom of the chest I found something else.

A letter.

It was addressed to my mother.

Dear Faith,

I know your time is near and I wish you luck with the birth of your child. But Faith, I must remind you of what we talked about. Your father is behind us, and your husband, as you know.

Have you had time to think about what I told you? My dear friend, we need you to commit to local resistance. I believe you feel as I do, that we must fight back. We cannot enjoy the fruits of freedom while our countrymen suffer slavery, starvation, privation. We are the lucky ones. We cannot turn a blind eye to those who weren't as fortunate. The invaders and their armies cannot be allowed to occupy our beloved land any longer. It is up to ordinary people like you and me to Deliver Our Victory. If you reply with a simple YES, I will send the pigeons. Your grandfather knows what to do. When the time comes wear the DOV *uniform, so our fighters will recognise you as one of us.*

> *I salute you,*
> *Your friend and ally in the Cause,*
> *Rosa Dov*
> *Commander in Chief, Nortland Division June 2121*

PS *I have remembered something your Grandfather said to me once: 'The only thing necessary for the triumph of evil is for good men to do nothing.'*

The naval uniform – I had thought it was an old battledress of Grandpa's, but when I unfolded it I could see that it was a set of white waterproof overalls embroidered in black with the letters DOV. There was also a red scarf and a red cap with the same letters stencilled in black.

'*When the time comes.*'

What time? What did she mean? Was there a plan to take back Nortland from the occupying forces? I was still reeling from the idea that we had been – were still – occupied. This must be why Grandpa Noah was so against the Uzi soldiers and B&NG. And also why Nano would never discuss the past and always said history was of no interest to her. But perhaps that wasn't quite the case. Perhaps it was because history was dangerous.

My mind whirled. Who was my mother's friend, Rosa? I walked over to the framed portrait of my mother and stared at it, willing her to give me some answers. Her eyes met mine, just as they always had, calm and wise. But the silence in the room was deafening. Just as I was about to turn away my eyes caught a mark in the bottom left-hand corner.

The mark was a signature: *R.D.*

Rosa Dov.

CHAPTER EIGHTEEN

I PACKED EVERYTHING away and went outside to think. I had to talk to Kit. The night was dark, but I knew the various shades of black as well as I knew my own hand. There was the hedge, there the oak, there the darker line where sea met sky. I lit a storm lamp on the lowest setting and set off, walking swiftly along the sandy path, the waves crashing on one side, the bay waves lapping on the other. An on-shore breeze blew the hair over my face. I strode out, Manga yapping at the waves and running ahead to chase blown foam. There was no moon, but enough starlight to bounce off the sea and light my way. As I reached the lower dunes, the searchlights from the fort flashed across the landscape, making our shadows huge, showing us the way.

A light voice rose from the scrubland to my left.

'Flora Mandela... Flora Mandela...'

Manga woofed and started turning somersaults in his excitement as Barcode suddenly appeared beside us. The small boy bent to stroke the dog and I bent to hug him. Unlike Kit, he smelt no better. But I didn't mind. As we walked along together in the dark, Barcode clasped my hand.

Questions were still skidding through my mind about the trove of papers I'd discovered. Had my mother been convinced by the artist's arguments? Had she become a member of the Resistance? A DOV? Had she answered Yes? Were the pigeons I thought were Grandpa's pigeons actually Rosa Dov's? Where was Rosa Dov now? Was she still alive? If so, she would have answers.

I was like a fly caught in a spider's web, unable to get free. No, worse than that – it was as if I had been born in the web. The web was my home. I had been born of a fly that had been trapped, and I, being newborn, did not know that it was a trap. I had thought of my life as normal – as life should be.

Nano had often told me how lucky I was. What I had witnessed that day from Yo-yo's kite – violence, cheap lives, powerlessness – all went to show I was one of the lucky ones, luckier than I had ever realised. I had never suffered at the hands of the Rice Lords. *Count your blessings.*

As we got close to Kit's place Barcode ran off. Everything was in darkness and there was no sign of Kit. I lifted the flap of the yurt and peered inside.

The smell of blood met my nostrils, so strong I could taste it. My storm lamp was so dim that I walked into cold feathers – a brace of pheasants hanging from a hook, blood dripping from their heads onto the earth floor. The place was in chaos – wolf skins thrown into heaps, Kit's few belongings scattered and broken.

Manga wouldn't stop growling. He didn't like the wolf skins. I tucked him under my arm and he quietened. But I knew from the tension in his body that I wasn't safe. I slipped out onto the path on the peninsula. Over and above the sound of waves and wind I heard the regular thump of marching men. I blew out the lamp and slid back down the bank, whispering to Manga not to bark. I could feel the growl gathering in his throat. On the path there were about a hundred Uzi soldiers in camouflage gear with guns on their backs, headed for Eden Spit Barracks. They all looked the same under their helmets, like giant killer ants. At the back, half carried between two of them, was the limp figure of a man. Manga stiffened. He had seen what I'd seen.

The man struggling to keep up, bruised and beaten, was Kit.

After a sleepless night, I rose early and went back to the yurt. Barcode joined me again and this time he didn't run away. In the cold light of day I saw what I had missed in the dark.

Jess, lying dead on the dirt floor. Torn apart.

Manga sniffed her, whining, his small tail tucked under his

back legs. Barcode sobbed and gripped my hand tighter. There was nothing I could do. All this was the work of people who cared nothing for people like Kit. Or for people like me.

It was the work of our rulers. The Rice Lords.

I marched Barcode and Manga back to Shell Shack and fed them both with leftover stew. Barcode grabbed his bowl and disappeared, as if I might take it from him again. There was no point in telling him what to do. He'd stayed safe so far without any help from me, after all.

I took my boat and rowed to the cove. On my way from the sea up towards The Hall I could see orange kites in the hangars – many more than before. Huge kites that could carry many men, troop carriers. Adrenalin pumped my legs onwards. I was not afraid. *'The only thing we have to fear is fear itself.'* I came to the razor-wire boundary fence and showed my identity card to the bored guard. He stared at my breasts. I drew my coat closer to cover myself.

It seemed like a lifetime since I'd stood here with my basket of pickles and beans. I rang the bell at the heavy door of The Hall. No one came. I rang again, and again.

Annie answered, looking flustered and red-faced, her clothes awry.

'Oh, it's you!' she said, flustered. 'What do you want?'

'I am here to see Lord Lao.'

She led me down the passageway, past the portraits and marble columns, over zebra and tiger skins and silk rugs. The horned heads of extinct animals stared down at us from the walls. I felt sickened that I had ever hoped that this museum of ill-gotten gains might one day be my home.

A door opened and Yo-yo stood there, his shirt undone, bare chest gleaming with sweat. He said nothing. Annie shrugged her shoulders at him and showed me into the library.

'Flora of the red petticoat! Have you decided to sell the sculptures?' Lord Lao rose from his chair and advanced towards me, arms outstretched.

'No, I've come to find out why you've arrested Kit Patel.' I stood back from his embrace.

'Patel?'

'The boy with the withered leg.' It was Li-li who spoke. She swivelled her large leather chair around to face me. In her hand was their leather bound copy of *Pride and Prejudice*.

'You mean the thief?' said her father. His welcoming smile was replaced by the nervous tic by his mouth.

So, Kit had been arrested and beaten because of poaching.

'What's a brace of pheasants to you?' I spat.

'Nothing, of course. It's the principle of the thing. Let him get away with game birds and who knows what he'll take next, eh?' The lurchers lazily swished their tails by the crackling fire.

Li-li twisted her chair back to face the fire.

'What will happen to him?'

'What usually happens to thieves on my territory: he'll be shot like a common scav.' A vein stood out on Lord Lao's forehead. I was truly scared of him. But I had come here with a purpose.

'I'll pay for his release with the sculptures,' I blurted. 'All of them... and the dovecot.'

He was smiling, but not with his eyes.

'Oh yes, Papa, please. Let me have the pigeon palace.' Li-li jumped out of the chair and took her father's arm. 'Please?'

Lord Lao chuckled at the beseeching look on his daughter's pretty face. 'Very well, I will release him. In exchange for the dovecot and the other sculptures.'

'Only if you release him now,' I said quickly. Kit wouldn't live long enough if they held on to him.

'Later, later. Dear girl, your histrionics are spoiling a rather enjoyable afternoon with my daughter. She's been reading to me.'

'Now!' I demanded. I was trying so hard not to cry.

I prayed that Lord Lao would agree. Kit's life was far more precious to me than my grandfather's art.

He stared at me, nodded briefly and rang a bell. An Uzi soldier came in. Lord Lao barked an order in his own language. The soldier saluted and left the room.

I took a last covetous glance at the books, the books I once believed held all life's secrets. I despised the Rice Lord and his family.

The one person who disgusted me more was myself.

CHAPTER NINETEEN

I HELPED CARRY Kit into Shell Shack. He dragged his leg more than usual, groaning at every step. His arm was bleeding, his face swollen and bruised, and his nose broken. He looked dreadfully frail.

I wanted to spit at the Uzis who had tossed him out of the wagon at my gate. They took a couple of the sculptures away without saying a word to me. After cleaning Kit up and bandaging his wounds, I made us a broth of potatoes and leeks. He ate with difficulty. His jaw was swollen and they had knocked out several of his teeth.

'How did they catch you?'

'Dunno. Probably Li-li...'

'Li-li?'

'Yeah. Bored with me, I expect. We had a bit of a... falling out.'

I wanted to kill her.

I made him as comfortable as possible in my grandparents' bed. Neither of us mentioned Jess.

Next day, I left Kit in bed and went to the yurt to burn the remains of his dog. There wasn't much left after the rats had had their fill. A scuttling movement by the blood-soaked animal skins suggested that they were ready for a second helping. To my amazement, it was Kit's ferret that emerged. Although she stank worse than ever, I took her back to Shell Shack and when I placed her on Kit's chest he almost smiled.

Over the next few days Kit's bruises bloomed like storm clouds of green, yellow and purple over his arms and face. He wouldn't let me look at his leg and he didn't want to talk about what the soldiers had done to him. Mostly he stayed in bed and ate nothing but soup. Barcode kept away, though I did glimpse him playing with Manga in the dunes when I went to gather some cockles.

When Lord Lao's kite skivs and a couple of guards came to dismantle the pigeon palace and remove the rest of the driftwood and metal sculptures, I wept. They obviously felt awkward, and I was touched at the care they took.

The garden and orchard looked bare without the animal shapes. The bare yellow patches where they had stood accused me. I couldn't help feeling that I'd betrayed the memory of my grandfather by bartering his life's work, especially his beloved pigeon house.

Every few hours I bathed Kit's wounds and changed the dressings, using some of my mother's cotton shirts and skirts as bandages. He was morose and in a lot of pain.

I tried to draw him out by speaking to him of our childhood – reminding him of how we had board-skimmed in the estuary, how he had taught me to skin a rabbit.

'Do you remember when I put a peg on my nose to keep out the smell?' I didn't really expect a response. 'Were you there when I fell out of the tree? Didn't I howl? Manga was still a young dog then. Remember how Cat used to chase him?'

Nothing.

I wanted to talk to him about the cache of documents I'd found, wanted to ask if he knew that our lives were a sham. But it wasn't the right time. It didn't seem the right time to bring up Li-li's name either.

Then I thought of Doc Poliakoff. Perhaps he would help. I would have to owe him, but I still had the few dees I'd earned from the Laos.

I walked the four miles to his place on the hill behind the Mackenzies'. It was a modest, mud-brick cottage, with a willow thatch roof. The sunflowers in the small garden made it look cheerful. He answered the door, his bag already in his hand and his jacket on. When I told him what had happened, he swore, apologised, took me firmly by the arm and drove me in his small, horse-drawn trap back to Shell Shack.

'Where are your grandfather's sculptures?' He looked stunned as he surveyed the flattened empty patches where they had been.

'I bartered them to the Laos.' I lowered my eyes.

He grunted as he washed his hands at the pump.

His intake of breath when he started to examine Kit told me that I'd done the right thing. I made tea for us all, letting the kettle boil and whistle on the range for longer than was necessary to block out some of Kit's moans.

'Can I help?' I asked, but without pulling back the curtain that cut the bed off from the rest of the room.

'No Missy, I'll deal with this. Terrible, terrible!'

Eventually Doc came out from behind the curtain and closed it behind him. I could hear Kit's quiet sobs. The sound gave me a tight feeling in my throat.

'He'll live, Faith.' Doc said to me, smiling grimly.

'Flora. I'm Flora.'

'Sorry, child, but you do look so like your mother.'

'Do I?' Once more, I was ridiculously pleased.

'And I'm getting old,' he admitted. He looked at his watch. 'Let Kit be for a while. I've given him a strong painkiller. He needs to rest. Can you cope? I'll leave some ointment and clean dressings. No time for tea.' He waved the proffered mug away. 'I must be off.'

'I'd like to talk to you about something,' I said. I didn't want to waste the opportunity. And after all, it was Doc who had mentioned my mother in the first place.

'Yes, of course, but it must wait for another time. I have a vital operation to perform. In the slave quarters, you know. Should really have gone there first.' He sighed heavily and washed his hands again. When I got the chance, I would tell him what I'd seen from the Laos' kite.

'What do I owe you?'

'Nothing, nothing at all. Shocking business. Look after each other,' he said, distracted. 'I'll try and come back, if I can. There's so much...' He stopped himself and smiled at me. 'Try and stay safe.'

I watched him chivvy his horse into a trot and he disappeared along the road in a cloud of sand.

'He wouldn't take any payment! Can you believe it?' I said to Kit when I gave him the mug of tea. He took some tiny sips, but still he didn't respond. I couldn't imagine what he'd had to endure at the fort. He had been injured in more ways than one, I was sure.

'Doc says you need to rest now.'

Kit rolled away from me, burying his head in the pillow. I drew the curtain across and crept out to feed the chickens. It was too much to bear, seeing him laid so low.

My dear friend remained subdued as the days passed. He looked strained and thinner than he had ever been, and Kit had always been a skinny lad. I cooked him soothing soups and mussel stews, and generally followed Doc's instructions. But there were some things he refused to let me help with. He didn't like me to see his withered leg. After a week, his injuries more or less healed, he decided to move back to the yurt. I tried to make him stay, but he simply refused. He was so stubborn! I was terrified he would go back to poaching and be arrested again, but there was no point in having that conversation. I couldn't save him a second time. There were no more sculptures to barter with.

Within half an hour of his departure I was missing him. I even missed his ferret. I worked on the vegetable patch, determined not to let things slip once again.

Later that day Yo-yo rode up on his stallion, its flanks purple with sweat. I was sitting outside, a mug of tea cradled in my hand, looking at the clouds with Manga, wishing that Kit hadn't left.

I was horrified to feel my heart gallop. What was it about Yo-yo? In his presence I lost all common sense. It was if he was some sort of drug that I couldn't do without.

'Come. Come with me.' He leaped off the horse, leaving its reins loose.

I rose to my feet, speechless. Immediately, he grabbed me and kissed me hard. The mug clattered to the ground.

'I love you, I love you,' he kept saying, his breath hot on my face.

Yo-yo had never said those words before. Despite all I now knew, my body tingled with longing.

'Flora, I want you so much. I've missed you. Come with me.'

My resolve to have nothing more to do with the Rice Lord's family dissolved. Maybe if I became his wife I could change Yo-yo. I knew his sweet side. Maybe he could become a force for good in Nortland.

I ignored how Manga's ears had flattened when he saw Yo-yo, how he'd growled his lowest growl.

Without protest I allowed Yo-yo to lift me onto the saddle. He swung himself up in front of me and as the horse galloped away from Shell Shack, I clung to him, my head against his back, the wind sweeping my hair free of its combs and pins. All I knew was that he would leave me here... unless...

We dismounted in a deep dune valley, sheltered from the strong wind. He held me to him and kissed me on the lips, pushing his tongue into my mouth. He slid his hands under my red petticoat.

'Yo-yo, do you truly love me?'

'Yes, yes. I love you.'

His fingers were warm on my thigh. I allowed him to caress me. It was as if my flesh was melting. We sank down together on the marram grass, his cloak under us.

'I love you. Let me make love to you...' He was breathing heavily.

'If you love me, Yo-yo, you will tell your father to stop...'

His lips covered mine, but I wrenched away.

'No, Yo-yo. Promise to make your father stop the killing. The rice slaves...'

'It seems you are not as intelligent as I thought, Flora,' he said, pressing me back onto the grass. 'My father will do exactly as he wishes. And so will I.'

'No! Stop!' But I couldn't stop him. He tore at my underclothes. He did exactly as he wanted with me.

I struggled as hard as I could and managed to twist away from under his suffocating weight.

He hit me hard across the face.

In a complete panic, I bit hard on one of his ears. I almost vomited at the taste of his blood in my mouth. He yelped and rolled away, clutching at the side of his head, then he staggered off.

'Pov bitch,' I heard him say as he mounted his horse and galloped off.

Three black swans flew close overhead, their wings whistling.

I don't know how long I lay there. Then I heard a voice crying out my name over and over. 'Flora Mandela, Flora Mandela.' It was Barcode, looking as terrified as I felt.

Small and skinny though he was, he helped me across the dunes back to Shell Shack. Every time I sank to the ground, overwhelmed by anger and humiliation, he wiped away my tears. His filthy little hands were gentle and kind. As darkness fell, we arrived back home.

I bathed myself, over and over. I felt I would never be clean again. I didn't have the strength to climb up the ladder to my own bed and so I got into Nano's.

Barcode tried to feed me with cold rice, but I was too upset to eat. He sat beside the bed and stroked my hair. 'Bad man, bad man…' he kept saying, pulling out his knife and making stabbing actions in the air. 'Barcode kill bad man.' As I drifted into oblivion, he was still mumbling away to himself, a fierce expression on his little face.

Kit came to the shack a couple of days later. He looked almost back to his old self, but my bruises were ripe.

'What's happened? And what's he doing here?'

Barcode had scarpered.

I told Kit about the attack.

'But why… how could you have gone with him?'

'I… I… I'm sorry, I don't know.'

Without saying another word, Kit opened the door to go.

'No, please wait. Listen, there's more.'

I told him everything. About what I'd witnessed from the kite, about what I'd read in the hidden newspapers. I showed him the chest and its contents. I read out some of the papers and the letter Rosa Dov had written to my mother. I told him all I knew about everything.

Kit looked almost scared. 'Will you be all right on your own?'

'Why? Oh Kit, please don't go. We need to talk about this. Did you know about the invasion?' I wept again. Everything was ruined.

'I need to think.'

As long as that was all he was going to do.

Barcode came back almost as soon as Kit had gone. He sat on the floor close to me, looking anxious. I was getting fond of him. And he needed me.

CHAPTER TWENTY

DAWN CAME SLOWLY, the sad cries of curlews drifting over the sea-flats. Bruised and sore, I forced myself to make a start. I had to work: feed and clean out the chickens, dig, plant, water, gather, store. All the usual chores. I left a bowl of water and soap by the barn, with a towel. But he just drank the water and tried to eat the bar of soap. I saw him spit it out.

I found myself panicking at the thought of losing Barcode too. I took him to the dunes to play with Manga, who had come home sometime during the night. Like Barcode, he needed some proper fun. I heard the boy blowing a blade of grass between his thumbs to make a shrill sound, and watched as Manga jumped at his hands, trying to catch the peculiar noise.

'Flora Mandela!' Barcode called, like a parrot. 'Flora Mandela.'

'Barcode!' I called back after a while, 'Come home and eat.' I beckoned him back to Shell Shack where I had rice cakes baking. He sniffed the air like a dog. I held one out to him. He snatched it from my fingers and dropped it, shaking his hand and gazing at it in astonishment. He had never had hot food. I picked up the rice cake and blew on it to cool it. He took it again and bit into it, his face blossoming into a beatific smile. I showed him that there were more. He snatched one and ran.

Perhaps I could teach Barcode Nort, teach him to read. I could raise him, he could help with the farm. I'd hide him from the Uzis. That's what I wanted to believe was possible. Yet I was aware that all this thought of a normal life was foolishness. When and if the revolution began, and the idea still sounded utterly ridiculous in my head, there would be injuries, deaths. The Uzi soldiers weren't going to lie down and give up their arms, just like that. The fighting might go on for months. Years.

Still no Kit. What was he up to? During the night I had had visions of him turning up at The Hall and gunning Yo-yo down. I walked to the yurt, anxious about what I might find. It was empty. At least there were no dead duck or pheasants hanging from the roof to condemn Kit as a thief.

But where was he? I had a wild thought that he might have run away to join the revolutionaries. Perhaps he knew who Rosa Dov was. Perhaps I'd given him all the information he needed to go and join up. Join the Cause.

I knew what I knew. But it was all so hard to understand. As I walked back across the narrowest part of the Spit I took in the loveliness of the place. The barren beauty of the sand-dunes and sea-fields, the wind flowing through the yellow grass. The big sky. As Nano had so often said, I was fortunate that this was the place of my birth. Why rock the boat? I wondered whether that had been my mother's response to Rosa's pleas for help.

When a few days later Kit came back to Shell Shack, he looked bashful. I hugged him and he handed me a bunch of daisies, a basket of blackberries – and the book!

'Where have you been? Thought you'd given up on me.' I unwrapped the precious book from its sandy plastic bag and wiped it clean. I put the flowers in a cola of water.

'I needed to talk to people, to find out more about things. We can't know what we now know and do nothing, Flora.'

I nodded.

'So that's what I've been up to. For now it's best we bide our time.'

The look in his eye told me that he wasn't ready to explain. I changed the subject.

'The book – why did you take it away? If you'd been caught with it, as well as the pheasants…'

'After Li-li… after we'd split up, I thought Li-li might use it as evidence to get you into trouble one day.'

It was the first time Li-li's name had been raised in a while, and it was almost a relief to remember that not just me, but both of us had been seduced by glamour. Led into temptation. And instead of something that would come between us and destroy our friendship, I suddenly saw it as something shared that might even strengthen our bond.

'I'm sorry,' Kit said. 'I've been thinking about what you said about the invasion and the revolution and all that. I did know a bit about it, from Dad. I never knew whether he was talking sense or not. It looks like Nortland is in trouble, Flora.'

We sat and ate the blackberries that he had brought. Barcode appeared but darted behind the big barn when he saw that Kit was there.

'That kid'll get shot.' He sighed.

'Not if no one tells the Uzis.'

'Someone's bound to see him and tell.'

'He's stayed safe this long,' I could see Barcode peeking around the corner of the barn. 'Kit, he practically carried me home after Yo-yo… He looked after me. He's a good little lad, really he is.'

Kit shook his head.

'Barcode – come here, come on,' I called. Barcode didn't approach us, but he hung around, blowing through his grass and making a crude music with it, before running away into the dunes.

Kit turned and looked at me. 'I think I ought to move in with you for the time being, in case he comes back.'

'I've told you, he's harmless.'

'No. In case Yo-yo comes back.'

Yo-yo? I felt cold at the thought.' Kit, that would be wonderful. You can even bring your ferret.'

He looked at me with his crooked grin. 'It's a deal, then.' We hugged. 'I'll go and get some stuff – I don't have much.'

Kit was gone no more than an hour, returning with a bundle of belongings which he stowed under Nano and Grandpa Noah's bed. The ferret belted around the place, delighted to be back. Manga wasn't too happy, though. He turned his back on the room, curled up in his basket.

'Actually,' said Kit after a while, 'even *I* can smell her. I'll put the ferret in the shed for now.'

I wasn't sorry. Just a few minutes in the creature's presence made me nauseated.

Kit and I made a good team. We worked well together. As the days passed it dawned on me that I was happy for the first time in months. Every so often, something would remind me of the uncertainty of our existence and my insides would clench, but by keeping busy I held worry at bay. Kit took his turn cooking and although I found some of the consequences of his poaching hard to stomach, he made the most wonderful broth from the meat stock, which soothed my nervous stomach.

We were together in the orchard, painting the tree trunks with a tarry liquid to stop the ants climbing up and burrowing into the fruit, when I saw a figure stumbling across the water meadows. The wind blew my hair into my eyes and at first I couldn't make out who it was. Then I recognised her. I ran to her.

'Annie! What's happened?'

'Thrown out.' She was panting, bent double.

'By the Laos? Why?'

'Can't you guess?' As she straightened up, she gestured to her plump belly.

I didn't know what to say. 'Was it... an Uzi soldier?'

'No! Who knows! Probably the son. Maybe the father.'

I couldn't take it in.

'And my mother's thrown me out too.' Annie sank to her knees in despair.

'Come on inside, Annie. You look done in.'

As I helped her to her feet, I noticed that her face was bruised. I called to Kit to carry on with what he was doing while we went indoors. I didn't want him reacting to more grim details about the way the Laos treated people.

By the range, with a cup of mint tea in her hands, Annie recovered herself a little.

'I know how you were soft on the son,' she said. 'Even the

father was nice to me at first. When I told them I was pregnant, Lord Lousy made me give back the uniform and told me to get out.'

I bathed her eye with witch-hazel.

'Did he hit you?'

'No, that was Ma.'

'The Laos...' I trailed off. The memory returned of a dishevelled Yo-yo, his shirt unbuttoned. It was clear to me now. I had interrupted them. And then I remembered the baby her mother had lost recently, and thought how terrible Annie must feel, carrying a child that no one wanted.

'You can stay here if you like,' I said.

'Thanks. Tonight would be good. While I think what to do.' She was still breathless.

'You don't mind sharing with me?' I asked.

She looked surprised. I suppose she assumed that Kit and I were sleeping together.

Annie spent half the night throwing up in the crap-shack. Next morning, she sat pale and wan across the table from me. Kit was already working outside.

'Have an apple. It's the only thing that'll do when you've been sick,' I said to her.

'I tried to get rid of it, but it won't go. Stubborn little beggar.'

I winced. 'How many months gone are you?'

'Dunno. Five?'

Too late for a termination, even with the dees for that.

'Do you want to tell me about it?'

'Tell you what?' Annie laughed humourlessly. 'That they used me and threw me away when I was no more use to them? We're all in the same boat here, aren't we? Eden Spit trav attractions.'

'What do you mean?' I was rattled by her odd turn of phrase.

'Eden Council had a meeting at The Hall not so long ago. I was serving. They talked about us on the Spit as if we weren't real people. In the trav leaflet we're described as "relics" and "colourful local characters". Tame povs, that's what we are, Flora. Our shacks, MacFarm, your orchard and veggie plot, Kit's yurt –

they're only allowed to be there for the sake of privs and travs who want to experience how World used to be. We're part of a "living museum". People keep their heads down and their mouths shut if they know what's good for them.'

'That's ridiculous,' I whispered.

'And now the travs are staying away. You don't get them lining up to take a digigraph like they used to. Flora Mandela, you always were a dreamer. Wise up.'

'Where is this trav leaflet then?' I asked.

'They're at The Hall, just lying around. I'm surprised you never saw one. It has a map of Eden Spit showing Shell Shack, Kit's yurt, MacFarm and the Bartermart and the coastguard station, all with star ratings. Even our place. Shell Shack was top attraction, but with the sculptures gone, you'll lose your ranking. Your orchard gets a special mention – the oranges are a rare type.' Annie's voice rose. 'Can't you see, we're only here so that we can be gawped at.'

Surely Nano would have told me, I thought.

'Flora, we are prisoners as much as the rice workers are. Can't leave the Spit, can we? Can't even go to Spitsea, we have to sell everything at the Bartermart. Remember the travs coming there to watch us trade? We might as well be in a cage.'

I shuddered. I needed time to think about what she'd said. I changed the subject. 'What will you do now, Annie? What about the baby?'

'Dunno. There's a soldier sweet on me. Maybe he'll think it's his. Look, I'd better go. Ma will have calmed down by now. Thanks for letting me stay.'

At the door Annie gave me a quick hug and set off into the soft rain.

Nothing was as it seemed any more. My life was no longer simple. It was almost as if my life wasn't, in fact, mine.

A large V of pelicans split the sky like a tick sign, like the signature on the letters in the chest.

CHAPTER TWENTY-ONE

POUNDING RAIN AND gale-force winds kept me in most of the following day. I had been sick in the early hours, and had only just reached the crapshack in time. I felt faint and sweaty, too. Maybe I had malaria again? I often suffered at the onset of the hurricane weeks. There had been an outbreak of dengue fever a few years before, but I was sure it wasn't that, I didn't feel ill enough.

I went around the shack with a fly swat killing as many mosquitoes as I could, quite glad of the excuse to stay inside. I wanted to re-read the papers in the chest. Kit was putting in stakes for new fences to make good the boundaries.

I made myself a nest on a cushion on the floor and took the copies of the *Spit Speaker* out of the chest. I was beginning to put together the jigsaw of what was a terrifying history of events. I spent hours reading and re-reading them, until it was too dark to see and Manga chewed at my socks for me to let him out.

I read how democratic Nortland had been invaded by the rice armies of Indo-Aje twenty years ago – four years before I was born. Our army had fought back. Many thousands had died at the hands of B&NG, which until then I'd only of thought of as a business, not a political power.

One of the articles described the effects of climate change, which had been going on since the end of the 20th century – the flooding, droughts, mud-slides, earthquakes, tsunamis and volcanic eruptions. And the wars that flared up over oil, water, rice and land. The Water War that Grandpa Noah and Kit's dad had fought in when they were young men had only been one of many.

When Kit came in for supper, I told him everything I'd learned.

'Kit – the rice slaves aren't crims or debtors. They are climate refugees.'

The injured and flood-stricken who came to Nortland looking for safety had been forced to work for nothing more than a bowlful of rice each day and were killed if they tried to escape.

And Annie was right: Eden Spit was designated a trav-zone, a living rural museum, and those born on the Spit were live attractions.

'Eden is to be a designated Site of Scientific and Environmental Interest and Trav Zone, with traditional subsistence farming,' I read aloud.

Like me, Kit was flabbergasted. 'What can we do, Flora?'

I handed him the tin.

'Have a look in there. And listen to this,' I read to him from one of the last issues of *The Spit Speaker*: 'All Nortland food outside of Eden and other Trav-zones will be factory produced by B&NG.'

And then I read out a pronouncement from on high:

The indigenous people of Nortland
will no longer have the vote
BY ORDER OF THE RICE KING

I wondered what a vote was. What did it mean? Kit had no idea either. I thought about it. It must have something to do with choosing who was to run the government. And we didn't have it. So, we had no power to change things. Unless we fought back physically and in that way got rid of the regime. I was beginning to understand what Grandpa Noah meant when he burst out with *fascist bastards.*

But how could I, a sixteen-year-old girl stuck on the Spit, do anything?

Kit was fingering the odd metal canisters in the tin.

'These go on carrier pigeon bands. That's what they are,' he said. 'Dad talked about using pigeons to send messages in the Water War. These fit around the birds leg and fasten... so.' He showed me, using his finger as a substitute pigeon's leg.

My eyes widened. Had Grandpa Noah used his fusty old pigeons to take messages?

'Remember those rice wine meetings in the pigeon palace your Nano disapproved of so much? Well, perhaps...' Kit was onto it as well.

'But, there are no pigeons left now,' I said, feeling very sad. How I wished my grandparents had told me what was going on. But I could see why Nano had preferred to keep me in ignorance, she'd only been trying to protect me.

Kit and I batted ideas and revelations back and forth, our voices low, aware that this was a conversation which sparkled with danger.

'All we can do is wait,' said Kit. 'That's what I've been told.'

'Who told you?'

He said nothing.

'Why won't you tell me?'

'It isn't safe, Flora. It's best you don't know. Anyway, all the information I have is second-hand.'

'Doc? The Mackenzies?' I tried to force him into telling me, but he shook his head.

'We have to be patient.'

'I think Grandpa Noah tried to tell me,' I said, 'but Nano hushed him up. He wanted me to know, I'm sure of it.' I felt as if I was going to burst with frustration.

'She did what she thought was best,' Kit told me, stroking my hair. But I couldn't stand it. Ever since Yo-yo's attack I couldn't stand anyone touching me. I pushed Kit's hand away.

CHAPTER TWENTY-TWO

JOHN MACKENZIE HAD been a regular visitor in the old days. A close friend of my grandfather, one of the group that spent hours with him in the pigeon palace. I determined, whatever Kit said, to talk to him about the resistance movement.

Still shivery the following morning and feeling slightly nauseous, I pulled on my best coat – the Japanese embroidered silk with fluted sleeves – and set off. Across the sea-fields, along the causeway, past the warren, along by the side of the railway line I went, carrying a basket of oranges, their glossy leaves covering them, and three jars of marmalade. If I was wrong about the Mackenzies and they were not involved I could simply say that I needed to barter for lardo.

The last time I had seen John and Gina had been at Nano's funeral. That was the last time I'd worn this coat too. As we had stood around the flaming pyre, they had taken my hands, kissed me on each cheek, and told me they were sorry for my loss.

'If you ever need help, child, you know where to come,' John had said. 'Your grandparents were fine people. Fine people.' He had put something into my hand and closed my fingers around it, 'For later.' I had put it into my pocket and, in my grief, forgotten all about it.

I stuck my hand in the pocket. It was still there – a coarse piece of paper that had been folded small. I unwrapped it, taking great care. Finally I was able to make out some writing.

Dear Flora,
We will do everything in our power to help you
when the time comes. Take care of the pigeons.
Sincerely, John and Gina Mackenzie

Because I knew what I now knew, I realised that the message said more than it seemed to say. It told me that the Mackenzies knew about Grandfather Noah's involvement with the resistance movement, the DOVs. But it also sounded as if they thought that I knew about it. And I had known nothing. They must think me a complete fool, or worse – a coward. I read it again. *When the time comes!*

In the distance I glimpsed Barcode running along the beach. He leapt behind a dune as a sail bogie swept by at speed along the metal tracks, loaded with boxes of ammunition for the barracks. The tall man at the helm wasn't the usual driver. He waved. I turned away. There would be no more pleasantries now for the milit, of the kind Nano had encouraged.

Distant thuds of gunfire reverberated under my feet. Uzi soldiers, practising. I'd heard that noise, felt those thuds almost daily for most of my life.

MacFarm was up a steep hill, and I was breathless by the time I got there. Just inside the five-barred gate was a small graveyard with three wooden crosses. The Mackenzie children's bodies had been burned on pyres, like my grandparents and my mother. The crosses were to commemorate their short lives. Each was carved: Rose's with a rose; Daisy's with a daisy; Lewis's with a boat; John's with a sunrise. There were wild flowers in colas in front of each cross. A lump came to my throat for my own losses. I wished I had a marker for my mother and Nano and Grandpa Noah. And some sort of relic of my father. I should have thought of it before. Maybe it wasn't too late.

Gina Mackenzie walked from the house to where I stood and put a hand on my drooping shoulder.

'Your grandfather carved the crosses for us, did you know that, Flora, dear? John junior was a little tinker – my baby. Always smiling.' Her face crumpled briefly before she recovered herself.

'I'm sorry.'

Any words were inadequate in the face of such loss.

'It's been a long, long time. Come in, Flora. How you've grown! A young woman, you are.' John Mackenzie welcomed me into the kitchen and pulled out a chair for me. He drew the curtains across the windows, 'to keep that sun at bay', and pulled his chair up close to mine.

'It's wonderful to see you,' he said warmly.

When Nano died, Gina, like the coastguard wives and Mrs Wang, had brought me casseroles to reheat, but I hadn't let her in. Nano had never been friendly to Gina, I don't know why. Perhaps her attitude had rubbed off on me. But now I thought, if I had accepted her support, how different things might have been.

'People said you were staying at The Hall. Were you... skivving?' Gina asked, pouring a cup of lemon verbena tea.

I flushed at the thought of people talking about me. 'No... it's a long story. I'm just glad to be home now.'

It seemed that I had a bad reputation. Would I ever live it down?

'As long as you're well,' she said carefully. 'You're certainly blooming.'

'I've only just found your note.'

'Our note?' The couple looked at each other.

I pushed it across the table towards them. 'Yes, about the pigeons. I'm sorry, they're all dead.' The explanation came out in a rush, how the birds had grieved for my grandparents and eventually all died in the Cat's jaws. I was finding it difficult not to break down.

'We thought that maybe you weren't interested in being – you know – with us,' John said. Gina took her husband's hand. 'Shame about the birds, rare they are,' he went on, 'But they would probably have ended up being killed by the Rice Lord's falcons.'

'Are you... did you...? Are you DOVS?' I whispered.

They both nodded.

I burst into tears. Gina held me close and I sobbed out of relief that I had found allies, but also for my missing father, my dead mother and my grandparents, even for the dead pigeons. I sobbed for Kit's dog, and for Kit. And also, I suppose, for myself, for my lost innocence.

'My grandfather was a DOV, wasn't he?'

'Yes, and your father,' John said.

'My father?'

'Oh yes, Red went for help before you were born,' his wife put in.

'So… he might still be alive?'

'We don't know, Flora. There's been no news for a while.' John shook his head. 'Best not raise your hopes.'

'Did you know him well?'

'Went to school with him. We were both keen on Faith at one time,' he said.

'John!' Gina cuffed him gently. 'You don't have to remind me. I know I'm second best.'

John slipped an arm around her waist. 'Oh, I didn't do so badly.'

'What was he like?' I asked.

'Red? Tall. Good-looking. Very intelligent. Flora, you should know that your father was a force for the good.'

'He was brave, he was. He printed and distributed a news-sheet, the *The Spit Speaker*, long after independent newspapers were banned,' Gina added. We used to help him sometimes, hiding copies with the vegetable boxes. The Uzi soldiers couldn't be bothered checking, so it wasn't a terrible risk. Red avoided arrest by the skin of his teeth many times. There's still a price on his head.'

The Spit Speaker! My own father's news-sheet! When I told the Mackenzies I had a pile of them they were excited. And worried for me.

'You don't want to let them fall into the wrong hands,' Gina advised.

I thought of the digigraph of my father: his confident pose, his direct look. Courageous, not afraid to face whatever life threw at him.

'What about Rosa Dov, the painter. Who was she?'

'Oh my dear! Wherever did you hear that name?' Gina's face had flushed with pride.

'Rosa is my sister. She's still working for the cause – and fighting.'

'Fighting?'

'In the dust desert of Euro and Freeland. Gathering forces. If it hadn't been for the children...' Her eyes welled with tears.

'Shh, honey.' John held her gently.

I needed to know everything.

'Is she fighting... with my father?'

'Oh, dear, you didn't know?'

'Know what?'

'Red married your mother because...' Gina looked flustered, 'he made her pregnant. But when it came to it, she wouldn't support his resistance activities. I'm afraid he went off with Rosa.'

This must be why Nano had been so antagonistic towards the Mackenzies.

'No, I didn't know,' I said in a flat voice. 'Nano never told me.'

'My sister!' She tutted. 'I was in the dark myself. Knew nothing until it was a done thing. Faith's best friend, she was, for a while.'

'Some best friend!'

'Your mother was no angel, either, Flora, though I shouldn't speak ill of the dead. She was always headstrong. She had a thing about Red, but he was dead keen on Rosa. And he talked her into the Cause, you know. After Noah talked him into it. It was all Noah's doing.'

'How do you mean?'

'It was Noah who was the main mover of things. The main dissident, before he lost his mind, poor man. He and my John, and Red, and Bill Poliakoff – and then there was Jan de Kooning. I kept out of it. What you don't know doesn't hurt you.'

'But you're a member of Dov, aren't you, Gina? You don't disapprove of them?

'Of course not. They are our only chance of independence.'

Independence of thought. A free mind. That was what I needed now. When we're young we do things because our parents, or grandparents, or teachers, approve. We soak up their values. Nano had been wrong to hide the truth about the state of things, but she had taught me the difference between right and wrong – or that there *was* a difference. And now I would make up my own mind about what to think and what to do.

'Someone mentioned the "Freeland" earlier – what is that?'

'Freeland is an isolated pocket of World not ruled by B&NG and the Rice Lords,' John explained. 'We are depending on Freelanders to help us liberate Nortland when the time comes.'

My mind was jumping with questions.

'Do you still hear from your sister?' I asked Gina. 'Would she know if my father is alive?'

'Things are more difficult than you can imagine,' Gina replied. 'Wars are probably going on all over, though we are given no information. As I told Kit, we have to wait until we get a signal, or a message. Who knows how we'll hear. But we will.'

So this was where Kit had come for his information.

'How can I help? I want to be a part of the resistance movement.'

I hadn't known that I was going to say that, but now it seemed so obvious. The Mackenzies sat looking at me. It was hard to tell if they were more pleased or alarmed.

'It's a shame about the pigeons,' Gina said pensively. 'They were our main means of communication.'

'Never mind the pigeons,' John interrupted. 'You're right, Flora. We've got to do something. We could start with the fort. If we make life difficult for the Uzi soldiers, they'd have a job putting down any uprising.'

'John, think before you come out with something you'll regret,' Gina warned.

'First we could sabotage the digicams along the bogie track to the fort.'

'The digicams? But they keep us safe from crims,' I said automatically. 'Don't they?'

'That's what they want us to believe. In fact they are watching us to make sure we keep in our place. Virtually nothing we do is private.'

So all those times I thought I was alone, enjoying the sea air and the wild landscape of the Spit, my every movement had been watched. I had loved a freedom that didn't really exist.

'The digicams – leave them to me.'

'Don't tell us what you plan. If we know… we could tell them under duress,' John warned.

'You mean, if they torture you?'

'They've been sniffing around, asking questions. They know something's up. By the way, Flora, it would be better for all of us if you could remain on friendly terms with the Laos,' John added.

I froze. I couldn't bring myself to tell them about what Yo-yo had done to me.

'You could be a spy in the enemy's camp,' John continued. 'Perhaps they have maps. Maps were banned years ago in Eden. And we need them now.'

They do have maps, I thought, but did not say. The germ of an idea came to me. As I left I noticed that a new sign headed with a crude stencil of a skull and crossbones had been pinned to the gate-post.

CURFEW
ANYONE CAUGHT OUTSIDE AFTER 1900 HOURS
AND BEFORE DAWN WILL BE SHOT

BY ORDER OF B&NG

CHAPTER TWENTY-THREE

WE ARGUED.

'You don't need to learn how to use an Uzi, you can have my shotgun.'

'Kit, I want to learn. Show me, please.' I was determined.

'It's not the weapon for a girl.'

'I'm as strong as you!' I was furious. 'And Nano and Grandpa must have known that eventually I'd find them!'

He shook his head. Rice, he could be so stubborn!

'All right, I'll teach myself. It can't be that difficult. If Uzi soldiers can do it – and if you can do it, so can I!' I stalked off with the gun over my shoulder. That did the trick. He followed me.

We went to the steep sand hills on the bay side of the Spit, as far from the sight and sound of the fort and barracks as we could get. It was the most secluded place on the peninsula, away from the bogie track and the sand road. Away from the digicams. I tried not to think about the last time I was here.

Among the marram grass and the high dunes, Kit taught me how to load and fire the Uzi.

I was almost deafened by the blasts, but after stuffing lint in my ears and pulling my hat down, the noise became tolerable. If any soldier heard, he would probably assume it was milit target practice. It was risky, but I needed to learn how to defend myself, and to fight.

'You're a natural,' Kit admitted.

'You reckon?'

'Yeah. You and me, we'll be a mini army.'

It was the first time I had seen him really smile since his beating. He'd been angry that I'd gone to the Mackenzies, but in a strange way he seemed relieved.

'Kit, could you help me climb the poles to get at the digicams?'

'Why not shoot them out? After all, you're a crack shot now.'

I didn't know whether he was joking or not. 'No, they'd know we've got weapons on the Spit and search everywhere.'

'Then how can we do it?'

'Easy.'

The night was moonless and starless. Manga was locked inside Shell Shack. I didn't want him barking and giving us away. Only the orange beam from the fort lit the scene as it passed over every few seconds. We crept along, keeping low, always ducking down before the searchlight exposed us. Coming to a digicam pole we heard a sudden sharp crack and the sound of breaking glass.

What was that?

Barcode appeared out of the blackness like a little ghost. We all ducked again as the light swung towards us.

He was holding something. He thrust several small, square plastic and metal tablets into my hands and pointed to the pole.

'What are they, Kit? He's got a collection of them.'

'Looks like digicam parts,' he said.

'Digicams. Barcode kill digicams,' Barcode said triumphantly.

'Looks like he got here before us,' Kit said, admiration in his voice.

Night birds called to each other.

Then I heard them. Four soldiers, marching along, the crunch of sand under their boots.

I fell flat to the ground and Kit followed suit.

As they drew near, there came the unmistakable high piping of Grandpa's tin whistle. It was years since I'd heard it and for a mad moment I wondered if it was him. The whistling stopped and was replaced by a call of, 'Barcode, Barcode, Barcode,' as the little boy ran away into the night, his crazy laughter blowing on the wind. A few seconds later, from another direction, the piercing whistling began again. As searchlight swept over, I saw the Uzis running after him, shooting randomly. They all disappeared into the darkness.

Kit hugged me to him. 'Brave little kid. Probably saved our lives.'

Barcode had led them away from us, as Grandpa had once shown me a mother duck doing when her nestlings were threatened by a black-backed gull.

'You don't think they'll get him, do you?'

'I hope not.' Kit hugged me again.

When we made it back to Shell Shack, Grandpa's tin whistle was lying on the mat by the front door.

The next day we went to MacFarm.

'These digichips are useless,' John said, examining what Barcode had given me. 'Look, they're corroded. There are half a dozen of them here – and you say the boy had more? I reckon it's safe to assume none of the digicams work.'

I felt we could relax for a while. I needed to rest after all the tension of the previous weeks. I was ridiculously tired and listless. My appetite was poor and although I was grateful to him, Kit's cooking wasn't terribly appealing.

'It's no wonder you're weary,' he said, eating his way through my portion of mushroom stew as well as his own. 'You've had a rough time.'

I suppose I had.

Mending my clothes, I came across one of Nano's floral patterned dresses and made Barcode a pair of shorts and a jacket, which I left next to a bowl of water with soap and a towel by the barn. Then I cooked a load of onions and left the door open so he could smell them sizzling. Onions I could deal with. The smell of apples and onions didn't upset my delicate stomach. Barcode came to the door, his nostrils quivering. But he hadn't washed or put the clothes on.

I shook my head and pointed at the bucket.

'Wash! Clothes!'

A powerful frown crumpled his little face. 'No!' he said.

He knew the word No!

I laughed. 'Wash, then food.' I mimed washing my face, then eating. He definitely knew the word for food!

Finally he did as I asked. Underneath the grime, he proved to be a yellow brown colour. Lighter than I had thought he was. Part Afrik, probably, like me, but paler. His ribs stared like a skinned rabbit's. He pulled on the shorts and grinned broadly.

'The jacket too,' I said, and helped him on with it. I was about to feed his dirty rags into the range when I heard something clinking in the trouser pocket. I shook out yet more digicam parts.

Barcode grabbed them from me and threw them onto the floor, arranging them and rearranging them, as if they were chess pieces. I remembered the collection of tiny pink shells I had loved when I was little.

Kit and Barcode eyed each other suspiciously over the dining table and I smiled to myself as I served them a mussel and onion broth. I had made an effort at making rye bread. It wasn't up to Nano's standard, but it was warm and filling, good dunked in the peppery broth. For a while, there was no sound except the slurping of soup and mussel meat, the clink of discarded shells, and occasionally shells being crunched with sharp little teeth.

I was wearing one of my favourite dresses – apple-green polyester, faded and patched, but still lovely. I must still be growing – it felt tighter than I remembered.

Barcode squatted on a stool, bony knees up by his chin. He licked his fingers, looking blissful.

'He looks like a girl in that flowery stuff,' Kit said, as if Barcode couldn't understand.

'Kit, he likes it.' The floral suit did look rather bizarre but it was an improvement on its predecessor.

'Where you from then?' Kit asked Barcode, speaking loudly, as if the child was deaf.

'Leave him, Kit. He doesn't know.'

Barcode blinked and looked at us. 'TESC-OPEC. Barcode TESC-OPEC,' he informed us.

'The toxic mountains?' Kit looked stunned. 'How did you get here?'

The boy shook his head and went silent.

'That's a long way to trav on his own, isn't it?' I said.

'Maybe he wasn't on his own,' said Kit thoughtfully.

What was Barcode's history? Had he lost his parents too? I felt sad that he couldn't tell us.

Barcode climbed down and began to look around the shack. He reached up to touch the doll's head, the ship in a cola, the painting of my mother, the framed mottoes that Grandpa Noah had stitched: *HOME SWEET HOME. IGNORANCE IS BLISS.*

'Don't touch anything,' Kit warned him.

'He's all right.' I smiled. 'Let him look.'

Kit fetched Grandpa's tin whistle and waggled it at Barcode. 'This is what you saved our lives with,' he said.

Barcode looked nervous, but when Kit began to play a jig he sat at his feet, mesmerised. I applauded at the end of the tune and Barcode leapt up and down, clapping and laughing.

'Here, you have a go,' Kit thrust the tin whistle at him. 'We know you can whistle a tune.' Barcode put it to his lips and blew into it, delighted at the noise it made. We clapped and he was even more pleased. Manga yapped and wagged his tail. We were like a family, I thought.

The time had come for me to go back to The Hall. Of course, Kit didn't want me to go, but there was no stopping me even though I dreaded seeing Yo-yo.

I would not let fear dictate my actions. I would overcome it, do what had to be done. It would be worth it if I could gather some useful information for the DOVs. I was no one's skiv in my heart, I was me, Flora Mandela. In my head, I could hear Grandpa Noah cheering me on: '*Go on Flora, you can do it.*'

I washed, dressed in a loose blue cotton dress and threw a voluminous cloak over the top. Carrying a basket of eggs and oranges over my arm, I took the path around the bay. I felt nervous but determined. Manga trotted along, no doubt hoping for another juicy bone from the Laos' kitchen. I hadn't a plan as such, but I knew what I needed to do.

As I reached the slope that ran up to The Hall, I saw Yo-yo and his father riding together with two uniformed men in the direction of the rice-fields, the lurchers speeding along beside them. Good! Having them out of the way was a bit of luck, and I needed luck on my side.

At the checkpoint the guard examined my identity card and the contents of the basket, tried to see down the front of my dress and nodded me through. He wagged his finger at me, indicating that I could not take Manga in with me.

It wasn't worth protesting. 'Good dog. Stay!' Manga sat, obedient, his liquid brown eyes fixed on me.

As I walked towards The Hall my heart missed a beat. Grandpa's pigeon palace had been repainted and rebuilt on the front lawn. I counted seven white doves perched on top. It was good to see that it had been returned to its former glory, though regret at its loss bit deep.

I hurried to the door of the private wing and rang the bell. The skiv who answered was not from Eden Spit. I recalled seeing her at the ball, but she didn't recognise me out of the finery.

'I've come with eggs and fruit. And I need to see Lord Lao.'

'His Lordship's not here. He's hunting scavs with a couple of Uzi generals.' She took the basket. Her eyes swept me up and down, as if suggesting that I might be one of the hunted scavs.

'I'll wait. He asked me to.'

She obviously had no orders to forbid me entrance, for she showed me into the porch, indicating a bench. When she had gone I hurried to the library and closed the door behind me. Oh, the lovely smell of all those books that I would never read!

I found the maps stored in a plan chest, pulled out the documents I wanted, rolled them up and had just tucked them under my cloak when Li-li walked into the room.

'You! What are you doing here?' Her dark eyes flashed.

'Brought fruit and eggs.' My mouth was dry.

'Were you commanded to bring them?'

'Yes,' I lied. 'And your father wants to speak to me.'

'Really? He didn't mention it.' Her snub nose screwed up and she pursed her lips. She looked like a bad-tempered Pekinese dog. How could I ever have thought she was beautiful?

'Li-li, I suppose you know about Kit?'

'He was lucky not to be shot.'

'Did you ever really care about him?'

'A crip and a pov?'

Caution deserted me and I slapped her face. The documents nearly fell from my cloak.

'That's treason,' she held her hand to her cheek.

'I do not answer to you.' I pulled the door shut behind me.

I walked steadily down the corridor and let myself out. Li-li hadn't raised the alarm. Why? Maybe she thought that I would reveal her relationship with Kit.

When I reached the checkpoint, Manga wasn't there. 'Where's my dog?' I asked. The guard shrugged. Presumably he didn't speak Nort. And he didn't care about my dog either.

I whistled and called, but Manga did not appear. It was unlike him – he was always so obedient. I worried that he might have found his way back to the kitchen, but I didn't want to prolong my presence around The Hall, so I began to run downhill, calling on Manga as I ran. Then I saw him – he was chasing something. Thank goodness. He heard my whistle and reluctantly ceased his chase and came scampering towards me. Barcode was close behind him, carrying what looked like a dead rabbit. He waved at me, calling, 'Flora Mandela! Flora Mandela!'

Then I saw them: the four horsemen, the lurchers bounding in front, in pursuit of scavs.

Barcode!

I stared in horror as the pack of dogs caught Barcode. He went down, screaming. Then they rolled Manga over. The terrier stood back up on his three short legs and snarled, baring his teeth. I ran at them, screaming and hurling stones, but it was over in a moment.

The dogs ran off, muzzles dripping red, leaving the savaged remains of my brave dog and the little boy. I sank to my knees and watched as the pink roses on his shorts and top were joined by the brown roses of Barcode's blood.

The men ignored me and rode away, calling in their dogs. Half a dozen carrion crows circled and swooped down.

CHAPTER TWENTY-FOUR

KIT AND I burnt the remains of Barcode and Manga on a pyre by the shore, and under my mother's apple tree I planted the end of an old oar in the ground. Carved into the blade was the motto: Barcode and Manga RIP. I kept the little boy's knife.

Kit could not console me. I was heartbroken – Manga had been the last connection I had with my childhood and my grandparents. And I had grown so fond of Barcode. I would never know now what his history was. He had survived Rice knows what to reach Eden, only to meet this dreadful end. I could not believe that anyone could be so vicious as to deliberately hunt down and kill a child.

How I hated Lord Lao and his son! I lay curled up on my bed, sick and dizzy, and I couldn't stop weeping.

'We need to carry on,' said Kit gently, 'in their memory.' He rubbed my aching shoulders. Waves of nausea swept over me. I knew he was right, but I had never felt as hopeless as I did then. The horror of what I'd seen kept revisiting me, no matter how hard I screwed my eyes tight shut. I couldn't stop shivering.

Kit kept talking to me, quietly reminding me that we had to look forward. We had to be strong. Wrapping a blanket around my shoulders, he unrolled the stolen maps of Nortland.

'You need to help me read these.'

He insisted that we look at them together and I taught him what Yo-yo had taught me about the markings and the signs.

'I've never seen one of these before,' said Kit, reading the contours of land he knew well. 'I could mark the places I've trapped the best rabbits.'

It was no use. All I could think about was that the reason he'd never seen maps before was that they were banned. Anger roared within me.

'I have to get them to the Mackenzies,' I said, gathering them up. From between two of the charts, a leaflet fluttered to the floor. It was illustrated with a simple map of Eden Spit, showing the position of the Travilla.

It was all as Annie had described.

ROMANTIC EDEN SPIT – A LIVING MUSEUM

Trav to idyllic Eden Spit and experience life as it used to be.

Kite trips to view smallholdings run exactly as they were in the past.

Digigraph the Spit natives in colourful costume. Relics of the olden days.

Enjoy the flavor of Non GeeEm fruit and vegetables.

Bird watching, walking, private cove and beach.

The Hall Travilla now refurbished and open for business.

Sea and Ede Bay views. Hot water in all rooms.

Exclusive private wing available – terms on request.

CHAPTER TWENTY-FIVE

KIT ACCOMPANIED ME across the fields and up the hill towards MacFarm. He wouldn't let me out of his sight.

The Mackenzies were still astonished by what we had discovered about the digicams.

'They were put there to intimidate us,' said John. 'They tricked us.'

'At least it means they aren't as aware of our movements as we thought. That's good news. It frees us to do more, don't you see?' Gina always wanted to see the best in circumstances.

'I suppose so. Perhaps they don't suspect us. Assume we're no threat. Just a couple of old fuddy-duddies.' He hugged her to him.

'Speak for yourself, old man.' She pushed him away, laughing.

I closed my eyes.

'What is it, Flora, dear? Are you all right?'

'Fine, just tired, that's all. And my dog... my dog has... died.' I caught Kit's eye. *Don't tell them*, my look said. I couldn't bear to say anything about Barcode.

Gina touched my shoulder but I shrugged her off. I didn't want any sympathy. It only made me more sorry for myself. 'I'm okay, really,' I said.

'But you brought the maps! You clever girl!' John found a large pad of tracing paper and started copying them with swift, sure strokes of the pencil.

I explained how I'd found them, without mentioning Li-li's appearance in the library.

'How will you get them back?'

'I don't know. I'll find a way.'

But I wasn't so sure. My back ached, I felt ill and feverish. I stood to go and felt my legs buckle. I managed to crouch down before the blackness overcame me.

'You fainted, dear.' When I came to, Gina was holding smelling salts under my nose. She held my head down between my knees. 'You've been overdoing things.'

'Are you feeling well enough to get these back?' John looked anxious. The maps were in a roll in his hand.

'I don't think she should go back to The Hall, really I don't.' Gina frowned at her husband.

'She'll have to. It's vital they don't realise the maps are missing.'

John was right, I knew. There was no room for sentiment here. I had responsibilities to the Cause. But my head was muddled and I began to cry.

'I can't...' I wailed. 'I don't know how...'

Kit interrupted. 'John's got an idea.'

I swallowed hard.

In the discussion that followed, Kit argued against me going back to The Hall. But now that John had outlined what needed to be done, I wouldn't be swayed.

'I know you're worried about me, Kit. But this is the obvious thing to do. John's right.'

'But it's so dangerous. What if Yo-yo decides to hurt you again?'

'He won't,' I said, with more conviction than I felt. 'And if I *can* get a job there, it would be such a good way of overhearing stuff that we need to know. That the DOVs need to know.'

'I don't see...'

'There is nobody else. Only I can do this. The Laos don't realise I know what I know. And things seem to be moving fast – it probably won't take more than a few days at the most.'

'I hate the idea of you being there,' said Kit. But in the end he promised to look after everything while I was away.

Dressed in my oldest clothes, but clean and decent, my hair tamed under a black cotton scarf, I knocked at the barterers' entrance at the back of The Hall. The soldiers had let me through with no problem.

A skiv in a cook's apron opened the door. I didn't recognise him. And more to the point, he didn't recognise me. He was in a hurry.

'Yeah?'

'Have you any skiv work, please?'

'Done it before?'

'All my life.'

'Age?'

'Sixteen.'

I was in.

'Big night tonight,' he grumbled. 'Top brass from B&NG and two Uzi generals.'

I made impressed noises and counted the plates heating by the vast range. Assuming Yo-yo and Li-li were dining too, Lord Lao was entertaining six guests.

I was set to scrubbing the worktops and floors.

The meat and veggies from Mac Meat Mart and MacFarm were delivered by John Mackenzie, who beamed as he handed over the heavy trugs for me to empty. When I returned them to him, I passed him a note I'd scribbled about the expected guests, avoiding his eye so that we didn't raise any suspicions.

A dead swan was delivered to the kitchen. It was my job to pluck and clean it and prepare it according to the cook's instructions. It seemed a different age when I had last sat and plucked fowl. I'd moaned and groaned but those slain hens were nothing compared to the enormous bird I had to deal with now. Three times I had to go outside to vomit in the bushes. There was no time to think about my next move; I was too busy in the kitchen, trying not to be ill. Now wasn't the time to think about how to replace the maps. I had hidden them behind the offal bucket. No one but me was going to poke around there.

'Will you need a serving skiv for upstairs?' I suggested, once the swan was roasting in the hot oven.

'No. Lord Lao wants only good-looking skivs up there,' he sneered. 'You will not do.' I'd hoped to listen in on some of the dinner-table conversation. But I could use the time to replace the maps.

When the food had gone upstairs, the head kitchen skiv set me task after task – cleaning silver, polishing glasses and pressing a pile of tablecloths and napkins. I was exhausted. And I still needed to get into the library.

'Is there anything else I can do before I go home?' I asked, having finished the washing up.

'Home? You can't go home. Skivs board in,' he sniffed.

'I can't tonight. I have to go home to collect my things. I'll stay tomorrow.' I touched the man's arm, smiled and pushed my hair behind my ear. I desperately wanted him to agree to my plan.

'Go on then,' he said. He even smiled at me. 'You've worked well today. Be back at 6 a.m.'

I pulled the back door behind me and scuttled around to the front. The lights in the dining room were off. The guests must have left.

The front door was locked, as I expected. I rang the bell and hid in the bushes next to the porch. The door was opened by a male skiv.

'Who's there?'

While his head was turned, I threw a stone into the bushes on the far side of the porch. The skiv looked round suspiciously and went out to the bushes. Behind his back, I slipped in the open door, my heart pounding so hard I was surprised that it wasn't audible to everyone.

I had nearly reached my destination when I heard Lord Lao barking out an order at the other end of the corridor. I hid behind one of the marble pillars and a cold sweat drenched me as he walked to the library door and went inside.

What was I to do? I couldn't stay put forever. He might be in there for hours.

The male skiv who had opened the front door strode past, swearing to himself under his breath. I shrank into the shadow of the pillar and stood, still as a statue, holding my breath. I was terrified. It would mean certain death to be caught with the maps. I pictured Barcode's body. Was that to be my fate?

The thought of Barcode and Manga filled me with a vengeful anger.

I would not be intimidated by the Laos. I breathed deeply and slowly. I would brazen it out. Hadn't they always encouraged me to make use of the library?

The skiv had disappeared. I pulled my headscarf off, shook my hair free of its pins and knocked firmly. My stomach was doing cartwheels, but I concentrated on keeping my face calm. A dog woofed.

'Who is it?'

'Flora Mandela, sir.' There was no reply, just swift footsteps. The library door opened and Lord Lao stood there, a look of slight surprise creasing his face.

'This is an unexpected delight, my dear, come in.' Smooth as ever. 'It's rather late for a visit, isn't it?'

Smooth as ever.

'I've come to return your son's maps.'

'Maps?'

I handed the documents over. 'Yes, Yo-yo forgot to take them back. He was showing them to me when he came to visit me at my shack.'

'Was he now?' His mouth had the familiar twitch. He took the charts from me and turned away.

'Come in. No doubt you found them very interesting?' His voice had a dangerous edge to it.

'It was fun to look at my own piece of Eden. My home.'

He turned. 'I'm sorry about your terrier, Flora, I know you were fond of it. But you shouldn't have allowed it to play with a scav. You know what happens to scavs in this district, and it's for everybody's good.'

I kept my head bent so that he couldn't read my face. I didn't trust myself to speak.

'I know how it is to be fond of an animal.' Lord Lao idly pulled the ears of the spaniel by his side. 'You are looking peaky, Flora. Let me look at you.'

I composed myself, looked up and smiled, determined not to show any fear.

'I'm well, really I am, thank you.'

'I believe you and my son are no longer... what shall I say? Betrothed? No, it had never reached that point, had it?'

I clenched my teeth at his patronising tone.

'It would not have worked, believe me,' he continued. 'Yo-yo has a destiny to fulfil. You do understand?'

I looked him straight in the eye. 'Of course, my Lord.' I was now the one reassuring him. Adrenalin flooded my veins. I had infiltrated the enemy camp. I had got the maps back safely. He didn't suspect me.

'My Lord, I need to work. There isn't the trade at Shell Shack any more. I've been taken on as temp kitchen skiv. I hope you don't object? I'll go if you do.'

'Of course not, Flora. You'll be a welcome addition to the staff. I will speak to the head house skiv, let him know that we know you.'

'Thank you, Lord Lao. Now I must go,' I said, bowing slightly.

He looked so like his son, the same proud profile, the same lustrous black hair, except for the grey at the temples.

'Goodbye, Flora.' Without even waiting for me to leave the room, he returned to his book. I don't think he gave me another thought. I had been nothing more than a blip in the plans he had for his son. I was not worth worrying about and was certainly not to be suspected of terrorism – I was just Flora Mandela, insignificant pov.

I walked out of the front door, down past the sentry guard, where I collected my staff pass, past the hated guard dogs howling in their cage, down the wooded hillside, and along the sand to the safety of Shell Shack. My heart thudded hard with every moonlit step. But I was triumphant.

The horror of Barcode's killing kept coming back whenever I fell asleep. Such a harmless scrap of life, a survivor. So funny and quick, and motherless. To them he was a thing, not a human being. Hunted for fun. Killed for no reason.

All the tears I had held back for everything that had happened, everything that I had lost, came flooding now.

I went to the Mackenzies before dawn. Gina took one look at

my face – blotchy and swollen from the night's grief – and held me while I sobbed. It all came out. I told her how I had tricked Barcode into washing, how he had looked after me when I had been attacked by Yo-yo. How he kept to the barn. How he ate live snails and had offered me one. How Manga had liked him. How he was company for me. How he was beginning to feel safe with me and Kit. The penny whistle, the grass whistle he blew. My fear that I had caused him to be less vigilant by 'taming' him, that the coloured clothes had made him a vivid target.

'And why didn't Nano tell me the truth about the way things are?' I ended up. 'Why? I feel like my whole life has been a lie.'

'She wanted to protect you from the truth. Keep you innocent. Keep you her baby. She'd lost Faith, her only daughter, lost Noah to his war injuries – she didn't want to lose you. You were always headstrong, you know, when you were little.'

'Was I?' I was somehow pleased at that. I had always thought of myself as rather a mouse.

'A handful, yes. Running wild with Kit. Off skim-boarding, or off in your boat, More like a boy than a girl. She was terrified that you'd run off and join the cause if you found out about it. She never said as much, but I knew that she feared for you. Wanted nothing more than you staying out of trouble.'

'Huh! I couldn't have got into more trouble if I'd tried.'

'You mean the baby?' She whispered.

I nodded. Did everyone know? Was it that obvious?

'We all make mistakes, Flora.' John gave me a mug of hot tea with something stronger in it.

It took me a while to calm down, but when I did they listened, impressed, as I described the previous evening and how I not only had a job at The Hall, but also the blessing of Lord Lao. A job as a skiv there was the perfect excuse if anybody questioned me about being out during the curfew.

'You've done wonderfully,' said John, 'but you must be careful and not appear to be listening or taking in anything that's said.'

I nodded. That was obvious.

'She won't be alone, remember,' said Gina.

'Why? Who else will be there?'

'Best you don't know.'

'Why not?'

'If you knew you could give them away. Like this it's safest. For you both.'

' I must go. The sun's coming up.'

CHAPTER TWENTY-SIX

IT WAS INEVITABLE that I would meet up with Li-li or Yo-yo before too long and I had my story ready.

It was Li-li I saw first. I practically fell over her in the passageway a few days later. I was exhausted, the perspiration from the day's chores hung around me. She was wearing a gold shirt over black silk trousers. Her black hair was piled on top of her small imperious head. Over her arm was a black velvet cloak lined with yellow satin.

'You! What are you doing here?'

'Skivving. Need the dees.' I scurried off, my mop in my hand.

'You can skiv for me then,' she called after me.

I pretended to hesitate, then turned and walked back towards her. I didn't want to appear keen on the idea. 'I'm kept busy in the kitchen.'

'I'll talk to the head cook skiv.'

'I'm serving at dinner tonight. He needs all of us.'

'Good. After that, you can skiv for me. My clothes need pressing and packing. We're leaving soon.'

Leaving? Before the comet appeared? That was information worth knowing.

She threw her cloak at me. 'You can hang that up for starters.'

I bowed my head as she strode off. 'Of course, Ma'am.' Did she notice the sarcasm in my voice? I didn't care.

She paused and turned on her heel, walking back towards me.

'How's the pov crip anyway?' Her voice was low.

'Not missing you.'

She gave a tinkling laugh. 'Where's your red petticoat now?'

Everything was ready for the important weekend guests. Rooms had been cleaned, wooden floors buffed, beds aired, cobwebs swept away, glasses polished, wine chilled. Promoted, I received the guests' cloaks and hats as they came in the entrance hall. Most of the men were middle-aged or old, dressed in B&NG uniforms with many clinking medals. Their partners were much younger, women dressed in glittering, feather-trimmed gowns, diamonds dripping from their ears and throats and arms. The only person I recognised was Doc Poliakoff. He wore a too-tight black suit and white shirt with a yellow cummerbund and a black bow-tie. He looked hot and uncomfortable. 'Skivving here?'

'Needs must,' I murmured and smiled at him. His scruffy eyebrows lifted.

'You're still looking unwell. How's the Patel boy?'

'Kit's recovering. He's fine. We're fine,' I assured him. 'Perhaps you'll visit?'

'I must join the others,' he said awkwardly. A woman was waiting for him in the hallway, small and trim in a straight black dress and very short dark hair. I'd never seen her before.

Lord Lao didn't acknowledge me, which is what I expected. Yo-yo couldn't conceal his shock at my presence. His father must have neglected to tell him that I was now working at The Hall. I ignored him, forcing myself not to think about the attack, about Annie, about Barcode and Manga. Once again, nausea threatened, but I fought it and kept in my place.

In the sparkling light of the candles and cut glass chandeliers, the tapestries glowed midnight blue and blood red. The furniture was ornately carved with dragons, birds and flowers. The silk rugs that covered the floor made me want to tread barefoot over the richly patterned drift. While staying at The Hall I'd often indulged the impulse, but this time I was here as a skiv and I stood ready to attend to the needs of the guests.

Lord Lao was busy introducing his generals to the officials. I tried to remember their names. One of my new responsibilities was to refill the glasses during the meal. 'Never let a glass fall empty,' I was told. Except for Lord Lao's. He was not drinking as much as his guests and waved me away whenever I offered him a top-up.

Li-li led the women into the lounge after the sweet course, leaving the men to their port. I had been instructed to remain in the dining room. The men lit up their water pipes and got down to the important part of the evening – talk and smoking.

The conversation was all about the disruption of life in Nortland. There was insurrection in the rice fields, rioting in the towns. Rebels were fighting back. My ears were pinned back, but my eyes revealed nothing.

An evil looking man with six stars on his epaulettes and purple tattoos on his head slurred, 'My troops are moving into the towns. We'll be back in control soon. Cut down the bastards. Ha!'

'That's right,' agreed another brute. 'We've moved out a large squad from the fort already.' Medals clattered as he gesticulated.

'Dismiss the local coastguards,' declared a general sitting to Lord Lao's right. 'One at least is a suspected rebel.'

They all nodded. It was agreed.

The Doc looked nearly asleep in his chair. Next to him sat Yo-yo. I filled his glass, taking some pleasure in noticing the nasty scab on the upper part of his ear where I had bitten him.

Without warning, he grabbed me and bent my face to his.

'See this?' he whispered, touching his right ear. 'Don't think I've forgotten, my sweet.'

If blood can go cold, mine did at that moment. However brave I was pretending to be to Kit and the Mackenzies, I feared Yo-yo.

Lord Lao had noticed.

'Leave us now, Flora,' he said, frowning. 'Attend the women.'

I left the room with a curtsey, went to the cloakroom and vomited. I rinsed out my mouth and sloshed water onto my face. Revived a little, I took a tray of drinks into the drawing room. Most of the women were inebriated, and telling crude stories about their men.

'We'll soon move out of this godforsaken place, back to a civilised land, where we have swimming pools and more drinking water than we need. And there are no mosquitoes or cockroaches or backward locals,' announced Li-li, waving her glass and spilling some of the wine on the carpet. 'And you can clean that up immediately.' She kicked at my leg with her red, pointed shoes.

It was two in the morning before I was allowed to stop working. I had been allocated Annie's old room. At least there was a shower cubicle. I removed my uniform with relief. There was no lock on the door, so I jammed a heavy chair up against it.

The window overlooked the back yard. The men were still drinking and playing cards in the dining room, and occasionally one would go into the yard to relieve himself in the bushes.

I lay and memorised what I'd heard about troop movements and coastguards and was dozing off when I heard people talking just under my window.

'Tell me...' A woman's voice, polite, low.

The man's reply was muffled. But then, as clear as if he had been in the room beside me, I heard him say, 'We will overcome.'

When all sounds of partying were over and the only noises were of creaking wooden boards, mice scuttling behind the walls, and the cockroaches scratching under my bed, I dressed in my own clothes and made my way to the back door. The guard was snoring heavily. I slipped out, and ran down the hill and onto the Spit. The dogs must have been elsewhere, thank Rice. I was terrified of being chased by them. I knew the sand dunes like my own hand but even so it took an hour to reach the coastguard cottages.

'Good heavens, what brings you here at this hour, Flora? The curfew!' Mr de Kooning was in his nightclothes and embarrassed when he answered my frantic knocking. 'Come in, come in dear. It's been so long since we've seen you...'

'You're in danger.' I cut him off, told him what I'd heard at the dinner.

He rubbed his chin. 'Thank you child, you'd better get back before they discover you're missing.'

'What will you do?'

'I'll think of something.'

'Good luck.'

'Thank you Flora, but be on your way. Go!'

CHAPTER TWENTY-SEVEN

LI-LI KEPT A close watch on me. She took special delight in my discomfort, relishing her power.

'Be quick, fetch me my green cashmere,' she shouted the next morning and when I failed to find it, she slapped me. I was never quick enough. Especially after only an hour's sleep.

Later, she threw a bundle of creased dresses at me. 'Mend these.'

It gave me great satisfaction to sew up the sleeves of some of her prettiest dresses. She wouldn't know until she unpacked them, far away from the Spit and me. I cut holes in her fine underwear before packing them too, smiling to myself.

All morning she made my life a misery, chivvying me, nagging me, making me pack and repack the doll-houses, and insisting that I bathe the lurchers.

'Get one of the others to bathe them. I'm a house skiv, not a dog handler.'

I think my calm, steady glare annoyed her more than anything. No way was I going to bathe those dogs. She flounced off, swearing to herself.

The few hung-over guests who had spent the night at The Hall, left eventually, their carriages rumbling down the driveway at a slow pace to protect their passengers' sore heads.

Finally, when she had run out of ways to persecute me, Li-li took off on her pony. I couldn't help checking to make sure that she wasn't heading in the direction of Shell Shack.

Immediately she was out of sight I painted smudges all over my face, chest and arms with her rouge and ate a chilli pepper I'd taken from the pantry, which brought me out in real hives, and presented myself to the cook skiv. He threw up his arms in horror, pronounce me toxic, and dismissed me.

'Out! Off you go! We will have no sickness in my kitchen!'

Gina's tip had worked perfectly. I ran down the hill towards the Spit but instead of turning towards Shell Shack, I made my way up towards the Mackenzies. I had so much to tell them. I was sick on the way and wished I hadn't eaten the chilli pepper.

As I reached the farm I saw a bedraggled group of people pushing a large hand-cart along the path from the Spit. It was Mr and Mrs De Kooning and the boys, Olaf and Stefan. The other coastguard family, the Karims, followed close behind, the little ones crying. Cher Karim was dragging her ancient bike, which kept sinking into the sand. I stood and waved at them, wondering what was going on.

'Flora!' Young Stefan ran to me, his eyes bright. 'We're going away.'

Mr de Kooning said, 'The order to leave came this morning.' His eyes told of fear, of inevitability.

I could see that Stefan was glad to be leaving, but his older brother looked miserable.

'I'm sorry,' I said, as they approached. A basket of chickens and a couple of bundles of clothes were the only possessions on the cart.

'Everything has to come to an end,' Mr de Kooning said, giving me a knowing look.

His wife was not so stoical.

'No notice at all. We had to leave everything, *everything* – even my cooking pots!' She was weeping with frustration. 'It was our home, Flora. Mind they don't take yours too.' Mr de Kooning took her hand, partly to comfort her, partly to keep her moving.

When we reached MacFarm gate I embraced them all. 'Good luck, friends,' I said. 'I hope we meet again.'

'I hope so too,' replied Mr de Kooning. 'Thank you, Flora.

Thank you so much.'

I let myself through the farm gate. It was when I reached the first barn that I heard the screaming.

I ran back round to the corner and saw that as they had reached the fork in the path, at the sentry post where the road to the town began, a group of mounted Uzi soldiers had appeared and started beating them with their guns. I hid behind the barn wall and put my hands over my ears to keep out the screams. Then actual gun shots rang out. I forced myself to look again.

It was a horrific sight. In a matter of seconds all but one of the party of travellers were dead. Cher Karim was running up the hill towards me as if in slow motion, one arm held out wide, the other pushing her beloved bike, her mouth an anguished O. A soldier turned, took careful aim, and shot her in the back. She crumpled like a rag doll. Her bike tumbled onto on its side, the wheels turning slowly.

I crouched down unseen while the soldiers loaded the cart with the bodies and took them away.

I don't know how long it was before John Mackenzie, rushing from the farm to find out what was going on, found me and helped me indoors.

Gina put me to bed with a hot drink and lots of blankets. I shook uncontrollably for ages. When eventually I fell asleep I dreamt of being chased by Uzi soldiers onto the beach, where I became entangled in rolls of razor-wire. I woke, screaming.

'Why did they do it?' I sobbed to Gina. 'Innocent people. Children.'

'De Kooning was one of us,' she said.

'I know. I warned them last night. Why were they all killed?'

'If one is guilty, they all are. That's the B&NG view.'

'But the children?' I sobbed.

'I'm sorry you had to see that, Flora.'

They called Doc, troubled by the red lumps that now covered my face and limbs and chest, as well as by my general state of hysteria. I explained to him about my allergy to chillies. He examined me carefully, gave me an injection and I slept deeply for hours.

Kit was at my bedside when I woke.

'You're looking better,' he said, brushing a strand of damp hair from my face. 'I came straight away. I heard what happened.'

My mouth felt dry and I drank the water he handed me, then pushed back the bedclothes and stood up gingerly. But I didn't feel sick and the hives were fading. Perhaps I should offer to return to The Hall in case there was more information for me to gather? The head skiv would have me back when my lumps had gone. But I had no need to go back to the headquarters of the enemy.

'Look up there,' Kit said. I joined him at the window. Six huge orange kites were flying north above us. 'Good riddance!' He spat out the words.

'Have the Laos really gone?' I couldn't believe it.

'I should have killed him,' Kit murmured, as if to himself. I took his clenched fist in mine.

John Mackenzie knocked on the door and came in.

'How are you?'

'They've left.'

'I know.'

'What will happen now?' I wanted to be sure those deaths were not in vain. 'Who will rule when we get rid of the B&NG regime?' I asked him.

John raised his eyebrows, surprised by my directness. 'Well,' he said, 'there'll be votes, local councils, a co-operative government, like it used to be before the invasion. Democracy again.'

CHAPTER TWENTY-EIGHT

KIT AND I returned to Shell Shack the next morning. I was relieved that the Laos had left Eden, but Yo-yo's threat of revenge still rang in my ears.

There were soldiers everywhere, helmeted and faceless. More razor-wire appeared along the coastline, as if an invasion might soon come from the sea. I blew my top when I realised that my boat was on the wrong side of the barricade. Uzi soldiers moved into the coastguard cottages.

The curfew was extended and we knew it would be enforced with summary violence. Our movements were limited even more than before.

We were surrounded by enemies. Tension filled the air. Surely something would happen soon? Where were the DOVs?

Kit abandoned the yurt. It made sense for him to move into Shell Shack, and for the arrangement to be public. All he brought from his old home was a large wolf skull, which we hung like a crown over the digigraph of the Rice King. It suited him.

Nausea overcame me most evenings.

Yes, I was pregnant. I admitted it to myself. I couldn't bear the thought that this child was not the result of love, but of the attack in the dunes. I couldn't get up the courage to tell Kit yet, though he would have to know, eventually. *Kit, I think I'm pregnant. Kit, I'm going to have a baby. Yo-yo's child. Kit, I have some bad news. Kit, I have some good news.* How could I tell him?

I'd spent my remaining dees on supplies from the Mackenzies'

Bartermart – fruit canes, vegetable seedlings, new netting and boots. The beautiful suede shoes the Laos had given me were wrecked. It was a shame, but as I pushed them into the fire in the range I felt liberated, as if I was finally saying goodbye.

But then, in my head, Nano's finger was raised at me, and I grabbed them out of the fire before they had caught. '*Waste not, want not*', she would have said. Perhaps one day the shoes would come in useful. Or I could keep them to remind me to guard against vanity.

We had enough grain for the chickens, rice and salt for us, and whatever we could grow or forage. But with the beach now out of bounds, we could no longer gather shellfish. Inhabitants of Eden Spit had always had the right to forage on the mudflats and the shore. Our limited rights were being removed.

After hoeing, I set off, walking above the razor-wire, searching for edible plants, sea-kale and sea carrot, perhaps some snails. Frustrated at the sight of a whole mudflat of luscious green samphire on the inaccessible side, I heard in the distance the squeaky metal wheels of the flat-bed bogie truck loaded with the usual boxes of ammunition coming along the tracks, the brown sail filling in the wind. The Uzi guard at the helm. He waved and beckoned. I looked around. No one else was in sight. He waved again. It wasn't simply a greeting. He lowered the sail, slowing the bogie, dropped a basket over the side and pointed at it. He also shouted something, but the words flew away on the wind. He hoisted the sail and the bogie sped up and away towards the fort to make its delivery.

Intrigued, I ran over to the basket. It seemed to shift slightly on the uneven ground. As I got closer I could see that it contained something live. I peered through the woven willow and saw a pink-blue pigeon, its bright red eye surrounded by white, with a lumpy white cere, like a canker, above its beak. It was exactly like the birds we had lost to Cat's jaws, only this one looked very healthy. It purred and gurgled, peeping at me with its head on one side.

Keeping as well-hidden as I could, I carried the basket back to Shell Shack. I had never liked handling the pigeons, but Kit had no such qualms.

'Look.' He unclipped a capsule from the bird's leg. It was identical to the ones on the tin. 'Yes... I was right,' he said, easing the tiny strip of paper out of its hiding place while I fed the pigeon some grain.

'What does it say?'

'Dunno.'

I took it. Kit looked at me expectantly.

Note troop movements.
DOV invasion imminent.

So the tall bogie driver was one of us – a DOV! In my tiniest, neatest writing, I wrote down what we knew about the Uzi garrison, slipped the note back into the capsule and Kit clipped it to the bird's ring. The pigeon hung around for a while, preening and sipping water. Then it fluttered up onto the roof, stood on the Shell sign, looking about as if deciding which way to go. With a slight shifting of feathers, it crouched, then rose, took off up and away from the wind. After a short while it veered in a half circle and flew almost into the strong wind.

Don't let the falcons get it, I prayed. Kit grabbed my hand and held it tightly. We watched the pigeon until we could no longer see it.

For a while we were elated at the news that the DOVs were coming.

'Remember,' John Mackenzie said, 'keep everything normal. Just behave as you always have.'

Days went by, weeks went by, and nothing happened.

'Do you think the pigeon got there?' I asked Kit.

'Where?'

'Wherever he was supposed to go,' I snapped.

Was our information of any use at all? Why didn't they come?

My pregnancy was making me irritable, though the nausea had gone. My mood could swing from elation to despair in a day. How would I cope? Why did it have to happen to me? Why couldn't the baby have been Kit's and not Yo-yo's? How could I have been so naive? I wanted to turn back the clock, make the right decisions. It was too late. I had to make do with what life had given me. Make the most of it.

We hardly spoke to each other, except over meals, and then it was difficult finding things to talk about. Kit looked haunted and he was spending more time back at the yurt – doing the annual re-digging of the trench and run-off in case of flooding, I supposed.

'I thought you were leaving the yurt to rot?' I said as he set off once again one morning.

'It's important that we keep things normal, Flora,' he retorted. 'I'm keeping it neat, ready for the travs. We mustn't raise any suspicions, remember?'

I watched him trudge off.

What was normal, after all?

And if there was going to be a revolution, when was it going to start?

What was happening? Had all the risks I'd taken at The Hall led to nothing?

Kit was still at his yurt when the Uzi search party came to Shell Shack. In anticipation of a visitation, I'd buried the book, wrapped up in plastic.

The soldiers had never searched like this in the past. If they had, they would have found the metal chest, which Kit had buried in one of the veggie beds.

They poked around everywhere, even raking through the ashes in the cold range. I was body-searched. I cringed from the soldier's hot hands but when he fondled my breasts I said nothing, turning away from the smell of his breath.

Not long afterwards, they left.

If I thought I had my emotions under control, I was wrong. When Kit returned, he was carrying a bunch of buttercups. I burst into tears. He dropped the flowers on the table and came to me and held me close swaying me to and fro. 'Shh,' he said, 'I'll take care of you.' He kissed my hair.

'Oh Kit, I'm pregnant. It's Yo-yo's...' I sobbed.

'I know. Shh. I don't care whose it is. It's your baby, and I love you.'

' Kit, Kit, I love you too. Are you... are you sure? Have you got over Li-li?' I whispered.

'Yeah, just feel stupid about all that now.' He put a finger under my chin and lifted my face to his. 'It's you I've always loved. You know that.'

His scabbed hands closed over mine. He brought my hands to his lips.

'Yes, Flora, I love you,' he repeated.

That night we shared a bed for the first time. We lay quiet in each other's arms in Nano and Grandpa Noah's big bed, the framed cross-stitched motto, *Life is What You Make It,* hanging above our heads with all the other hand stitched mottoes that Grandpa Noah had nailed on the walls to hide blemishes and holes. Kit stroked my hair, my face, my throat, and kissed my forehead. As he traced the old scar on my chin, he kept saying, 'I love you, Flora, my flower.'

In the weeks that followed, I didn't want anything to spoil this feeling of loving and being loved. When Kit had nightmares, which he often did, I was there with a cooling cloth on his brow, soothing him. He still had flashbacks – not that he would speak of the Maxsec. He sometimes had a fierceness in his eyes, as if he had been brutalised by what had happened to him there. But he was always gentle with me.

I felt now that I could ask him more about his relationship with Li-li.

'Kit, did you, were you... in love with Li-li?

'I felt sorry for her.'

'Sorry!' I practically shrieked at him. 'How could you feel sorry for her?'

'Not at first.'

I felt bitterness rise in my throat.

'You know, Flora, she's not at all what you think.'

'A spoilt bitch?'

He let go my hand. 'Don't be like that. Listen. She was unhappy when I first met her. Spoilt, yes, but not happy. Working here, in your shack, she was a different person. I think she was jealous of you.'

'Li-li – jealous of me?' I was incredulous.

'I think she liked the simple life.'

'It's not simple – it's bloody hard.' I looked at my hands, that even in the short time since I had been back at Shell Shack, had reverted to their ruined state.

'And do you know, I found her reading your book, once,' Kit went on.

'My book?'

'Yeah, she found it in your bedding. She wasn't snooping, just tidying.' He could see that I was scared. 'I'd forgotten about it. She couldn't read fast, like you, but she wanted to read it. Said she hadn't read any books before. She was ashamed that she couldn't spell or read well and she was afraid of her father's anger.'

'But...'

'I think she wanted to be like you.'

I blushed. Perhaps he was right about Li-li. Perhaps I should have tried harder to like her. Kit seemed to understand her, why couldn't I?

'She told me that she hated travving all the time. She's scared of flying. She loved this place, your shack, the dovecot, the sculptures, everything.'

'Is that why she wanted to rob me of it all?' I turned away, confused.

Kit sighed. 'Listen, Flora, just try to understand. She's mixed up, she doesn't have your solid background. She's young for her age.'

'But she had you beaten up, arrested.'

'Yeah,' he shrugged.

Shame swept over me. I was ashamed of my harsh judgment of Li-li. How could she have been otherwise? Her father had dominated her by giving her everything she wanted – everything material, that is. And she was motherless, but unlike me, she had no Nano figure to keep her steady.

Maybe I was the lucky one. Maybe she was right.

In that second of insight, I let go of my hatred and decided that never to judge people so swiftly again.

I saw myself in the mirror – blooming, rosy cheeked, fuller in the face. Part of me was full of joy that Kit and I loved each other.

Part of me was racked with guilt and dismay at all the bad things that had happened. It was weird being so happy and so sad at the same time.

Most of all, I felt a great protectiveness for the child that grew inside me.

I was forever watching the skies, not for interesting clouds any more, but for signs of a DOV invasion. I was unsettled, itching for action.

When the DOVs came we would be ready to help overthrow the Rice Lords, I told myself. The B&NG regime would fall. The rice slaves would be freed. We would be liberated.

Kit and I discussed the future over supper one night.

'Who will rule? How will we choose our leaders?' It was becoming an obsession with me.

Kit was dubious about democracy.

'I could be a leader. You could if you wanted.' I prodded him in the chest.

'Don't be daft.' He lifted the chopsticks full of salted herby rice into his mouth.

'It's not daft. Anyone who cares could be a leader,' I said. I was bursting with plans to help make Nortland a prosperous, independent country. I saw myself standing on a platform, the crowd applauding my every word. I'd seen digigraphs of such events in some of the magazines I'd read at The Hall. Later, I washed the dishes at the pump and laughed at myself.

Kit's health was improving. We got on with life. After he had mended the mosquito nets we weren't so bothered by the insects. They'd been sucking my blood for years and I'd never been fazed by the odd attack of malaria. But Kit hated them. They liked him more than they liked me.

There were no more travs to gawp at us and buy produce. That was a relief. But, there were no more dees either.

Apart from the milit, all traffic on the Spit had been halted. We weren't allowed off and no one was allowed on. We were simply told. That was how it was. This was how it had been in Eden for as long as Kit and I could remember, but now we wanted answers, and we noticed when they weren't forthcoming.

So much had changed.

Between the fruit and veggies and the chickens there was just about enough to eat, even though we no longer had access to shellfish. I had to admit that the chickens – Li-li's chickens – *were* good layers. There was a new crop of maize and yams, and Kit still took his ferret out to catch rabbits.

'Repeat after me,' he would tease: '*Kit's smelly little ferret puts food on our table.*'

My appetite had returned and I spent the evenings letting out all my clothes. With Kit doing more than his share of the hard work, I had time to write. My journal was filling up with details of our daily life, and with memories, the good ones: helping Grandpa Noah decorate the walls with shells and coloured glass; sitting in the apple tree singing songs I'd learned at school; watching the geese return to Ede Estuary each winter to feed on the mudflats. I also wrote of Kit. How thoughtful he was, carrying heavy logs in, bringing water from the pump and lugging the sea-coal bucket inside. Our fuel heap was dwindling because we could no longer get to the coal on the beach. He cleaned out the range each morning and swept the chimney every Monday morning. He worked all hours to keep things going. There were days when we only had a bowl of rice and salt, or a porridge of maize and rye. Soup was a luxury.

One stormy night we had just gone to bed when we heard the thud of boots. We peered out and saw black helmets gleaming in the starlight.

CHAPTER TWENTY-NINE

THE NORTH WIND gathered strength and it started to rain heavily. Finally the hurricane weeks were upon us.

For days I had been fed up, frustrated by the lack of action. Moody. Kit had left in a big sulk earlier. We'd had a row.

About nothing.

He'd come in without taking off his boots, walked across my clean floor and deposited the ferret cage on the table.

'Boots! Boots!' I screamed.

He froze, as if we were back at school playing Grandmother's Footsteps.

'And get that stinking ferret out of here! Now! Go back to your yurt if you want to live like a pig.'

Embarrassed by my outburst, I left him to his own devices and crossed the fields to the end of the Spit where the Wangs lived.

The ground vibrated beneath my feet as I made my way down the path. Shell Shack had sometimes been threatened by rising tides but we weren't as close to the sea as the Wangs were. They were used to floods. But this was surely something else. The seas looked huge. Great rolling waves were thundering towards the shore as if something was driving them along. Close to the Wangs, Spit Fort and barracks were splattered with sea spray. The search light that drifted regularly over the Spit at night, wasn't on yet.

The Wangs' home was made out of three connected rusty containers propped on short concrete and cobble stilts. When I pushed the door open I found that they had moved all their belongings to the upper deck. The smaller kids were leaping around on the bunks, shrieking. Annie's mother was trying to get her fretful two-year-old to breast-feed. She nodded her thanks for the bag of oranges I'd brought. Annie, wrapped in a voluminous pinny, was cooking a huge rice dish. She stopped stirring, pushed back her greasy hair and gave me a wry grin.

'Perhaps I'll come live with you when this baby arrives,' she said over the racket. Get away from this mob, eh?'

I smiled. 'You're welcome any time.' I lowered my voice. 'You do know what happened to the coastguards, don't you, Annie?'

'Yeah. Come outside, I need some air.' Annie took the pan off the heat, shouted at one of the kids, and ushered me outside to a rusting metal step under the shelter of a sloped roof. The fort was a little higher on the hill, right at the end of the promontory.

The wind was howling across the sea, blowing spray backwards. Enormous waves broke on the distant drowned spires of Sainsburyness. Annie took a small bag of herb tobacco from her apron pocket, and sliding a thin paper strip from a packet, deftly made a roll-up.

'Want one?'

'No thanks.' I felt ill at the thought. 'Are there fewer soldiers than usual, or is it just my imagination?' I gestured towards the fort, trying to sound casual. I had noticed on the way that it was quiet. No marching, no firing exercises. Only two guards at the checkpoint. Some of the Uzis must have been deployed to the towns, I imagined. 'They're still coming and going all the time. Some new, younger than ever.'

'We saw a load of them the other night. Do you know any of them?'

'One or two are okay. Some of them give us rice and a smoke if I'm nice to them.' She looked hard at her roll-up.

I didn't ask. Didn't want to know. She stroked her bump.

'Is the baby moving much?'

'Little bugger doesn't stop. Don't know why it's in a hurry to get out. This isn't much of a life, is it!' She threw a look over her shoulder at their hovel.

I opened my cloak. 'I'm pregnant too, Annie.'

'Really?' Her eyes widened.

'Yes. We're in the same boat.'

We hugged.

'I thought you looked fatter.' She giggled and I laughed with her.

'Are you being sick?'

'Not as much as I was. You?'

'No, it's stopped.'

'How about the guard who's sweet on you?'

'Gone, hasn't he!'

We both looked up as a string of geese winged overhead, barking like dogs.

'Big tide later,' I reminded her.

'Yeah, a surge tide. We'll be ready.' We looked up at the stars. I hugged her tightly. 'Keep safe.'

I got up from the step, but she made no move to go back inside. She dragged on the cigarette.

'Yeah, you too,' she called.

The wind hadn't dropped, if anything it was getting stronger. A surge tide would push up the water levels and keep them there for longer than usual. Kit reckoned that the conditions were right for some extreme water levels.

On the bay side things were calmer, as always, but out at sea the tall waves galloped to where the sea met Ede estuary. At Spit Point water churned and exploded as if massive monsters fought beneath the waves. As I walked back along the strand next to the ugly razor-wire barricade, the sea had already crept up and over the groynes and breakwaters, smashing the thorn hedges and some of the dunes, sweeping away the low sand hills and the marram grass that held them together. Suds of sea-foam blew over the bleak landscape and settled like grey fluff, caught on sea holly and samphire. It took all my strength to stay upright as I struggled against the gusts.

Kit wasn't at Shell Shack. The muck from his boots had been swept up, the washing up had been done and the ferret cage was nowhere to be seen.

An hour passed. Darkness was falling. The orange beam of

the searchlight flashed across the window. Surely he must know I didn't really mean him to go back to the yurt to live. Maybe he'd been caught poaching again? He'd be shot this time. No second chances.

I could hardly hear myself call to the chickens above the roar of the sea. I brought the struggling birds into Shell Shack and lifted them up the stepladder to the loft space, where they scratched happily in the straw. They'd be all right roosting on the beams. I wasn't about to lose my brood a second time. I dragged the bags that Grandpa Noah had filled with sand against the door. Just in case. *Kit* should have thought to do that, I grumbled to myself. I climbed in through the window and closed it. I had a few tallow candles, a bucket of firewood and sea-coal stored inside. I closed the shutters against the wind, and hunkered down by the fire, Grandpa's patchwork quilt around my shoulders, wishing I had Manga or even flea-bitten Cat to keep me company. I hadn't seen her since I returned from The Hall. Smoke billowed down the chimney from time to time and made my eyes smart. Through the closed shutters I heard a mournful howl. Wolf? Surely not! We hadn't had wolves on the Spit in my lifetime. Whatever it was, it was close, too close!

Kit where *are* you?

The wind was fearful. I could hear and feel the sea getting closer to my door as the air pressure rose. I wrote in my journal to keep my fears at bay. In the middle of the night, with the stubs of the candles guttering, water started coming in at the door. I had piled stuff on the table in an attempt to salvage household goods – blankets, pillows, pots and pans, and my mother's clothes, but when I could see that it was hopeless, I began to carry things up the ladder to the loft space with the chickens. They were alarmed, as chickens are by anything strange.

I looked around – at the chickens, at my bed, at my life all wrapped up here in Shell Shack. Should I get out, or stay put? I shone my storm lantern to assess the depth of the water and decided it was too late to try and escape. All I could do was to crouch along with the frightened chickens, all of us shivering with cold, hoping that the water would recede. I looked around to see what else had been stowed up here, and in the corner I could see the chest with the Uzi rifles and ammo. Kit must have dug it up this morning and carried it here after I went off. The papers and letters were all there, along with the waterproof DOV overalls. I pulled them on for warmth. There would be no Uzi search tonight. By now, the range fire had drowned, the table was upside down and the linen and china had slipped off into the murky water. Logs or something heavy bumped against the outside walls. With a screech I remembered my mother's portrait and felt around in the dark waters to retrieve it. The digigraph of my parents was safe in a breast pocket, where it always was, along with Barcode's knife and the tin whistle. My journal was in Grandpa Noah's old army rucksack.

By dawn, a barely lightened sky dimly gleamed through the roof window. I knelt to look out, and saw only water. There was no more Spit; the sea had claimed it. How was I to get out now?

CHAPTER THIRTY

MANGA BARKED IN my dream.

'Flora! Flora!' I woke, stiff and cold. I couldn't see Kit but was aware of him calling my name. The roof window had never been opened. I grabbed the journal, covered my arm and hand with the curtain, turned my face away and broke the glass, panicking the chickens.

'Up here.' I cleared the window space of broken glass and climbed out onto the roof. I clung onto the plastic Shell sign. On the other side of the roof a she-wolf cringed, growling, hackles risen, drenched coat in spikes. All around me brown water swirled. Kit stood about a metre or so below in his rowing boat.

'Where have you been?' I yelled.

'Where do you think?' Kit furiously indicated the boat. His hair was plastered to his head and his soaking clothes clung to his thin body. 'Now do what I tell you. Look out for the wolf. Can you climb down?'

'Sure, hang on.' I shrugged the back pack on and scrambled down the side of the house, hanging on to protruding bits of wood and metal. Kit held out a hand and I clutched it thankfully. The wolf sat dejected by the chimney stack, whining like a domestic dog.

My apple tree had disappeared, as had the other trees in the orchard, apart from a few tall branches. The horizon stretched uninterrupted in both directions. No more dunes, no more estuary or spires of Sainsburyness. Eden was all ocean.

'The yurt?' I asked.

Kit shook his head. 'We're lucky to be alive.'

'The chickens! They're all I have left.' I could see that Kit wanted to leave them, but he knew what they meant to me.

'Okay. Got something to put them in?' As he made for the side of the boat it wobbled horribly. I grabbed at the gunwhale.

'Basket in the loft. Mind the glass.' My teeth were chattering.

I took one oar as Kit climbed up with the other, his damaged leg thin and vulnerable. The wolf took one look at Kit's oar, bared its teeth and slid into the waters, swimming away from the boat.

Kit lowered himself through the window and it wasn't long before he reappeared with the basket of chickens, which he slid down the roof towards me. I deposited the unhappy birds in the bilges of the rocking dinghy along with the ferret in its box.

A tree swung by, pulled by the rushing water, a scrap of black fur snagged in the branches. I couldn't tell what it was. Then the bloated corpse of Cat floated past, yellow teeth bared. A grey horse, its hooves sticking up stiff in the air, mane like a pale weed swinging in the stream, rammed the boat with a thwack that nearly capsized us.

'Kit, the guns! We must have them!'

It took time to collect the weapons and stash them in the small boat. Kit looked exhausted as he emerged from the window one final time and shoved the ammo towards me. There wasn't much room with Kit's skim-board shoved under a thwart. Finally, the boat was as packed as it could possibly be. He wriggled down the roof and eased himself onto the stern.

'I'll row,' he said, leaving no room for argument.

As we pulled away from the shack, I watched the water reach the level of the window. There was a sucking noise, as if the place had taken an enormous gulp, and it flowed in, gallons and gallons of it. Then, almost as if it was drawing breath, it retreated, and I watched it pull out the newspapers, my beloved *Pride and Prejudice*, letters and Grandpa Noah's cross-stitch mottoes – all disintegrating amid a swirl of my mother's clothes. Her portrait floated past, out of reach, and disappeared.

'Sorry, Flora. There's nothing we can do.'

'Where can we go now?' I asked.

Kit looked shattered. 'Dunno. Away from here.'

'I suppose the water will go down?'

'Maybe, maybe not. There won't be much of this place left though.'

'Let's head for The Hall. It's the highest point.'

'Yeah, then what? Who knows who else has had that bright idea?'

'What about MacFarm? It's nearly as high up.'

'If we can get there.'

'Be careful, water's coming in,' I warned. Each time Kit pulled on the oars we took in more water over the bows. I baled as fast as I could.

We had thought that the Rice Lords and the Uzi soldiers were our only enemies, when all along we had a much greater opponent. The sea. And it had won. Why did we ever think it wouldn't? I had seen the Spit change shape many times with high tides and hurricanes, but this time it looked like it was gone forever.

'What about the Wangs?'

'They're on a high point.'

Kit was looking on the bright side.

There was a foul smell, cold, foggy, a smell of death. I looked up and below low swollen grey clouds I saw two small white kites, two men stretched out in the harnesses, looking down on us. One waved. I waved back, furiously.

'DOVs. I'm sure they're DOVs. See the tick sign on the sail? Hi! Hi!' I shouted.

'They've seen us. Perhaps they'll send help.'

'You reckon?' Kit didn't sound convinced.

'It's happening!' I exclaimed. 'The revolution! They're taking advantage of the flood. We shall overcome!' I stood gingerly and shouted at the disappearing kites.

Suddenly I felt strong and full of energy.

'Sit down, you'll upset the boat,' yelled Kit, straining at the oars.

Time and again we had to push away logs and dead animals

that threatened to hole the hull of our small craft or capsize us. The bedraggled fowl were silent, soaked in the bilges.

'I'm sure they were DOVs,' I said, forcing myself to sound optimistic. 'They were probably on a reconnaissance flight.'

'If they were they've got more important things to do than look after us. We're okay, anyway.'

'Are we?' I supposed we would find safety soon. When the tide finally ebbed, the hilltops would be uncovered, surely?

I wondered about the rice slaves. Had their cells been flooded? It didn't bear thinking about.

A broken cart swept past, only just missing us. The dinghy was dangerously low in the water. Then we began to see the tops of trees. We had reached the hill.

'What's that?' I yelled above the sound of rain and wind. Someone was stuck in the top of a tree.

'No point,' said Kit. 'No room.'

'It's Mr Wang! We can't leave him there!'

'We'll have to dump the guns then.'

'Okay. If we must, we must.' I began to haul out the weapons.

'It's too late.' Kit had turned to look at the terrified man.

Mr Wang was at the end of his strength. He hung on until we nearly reached him but before I was able to jettison the weapons, his grip loosened and as the tree bent low he slipped into the torrent.

The only other survivors we spotted were four rats clinging to the topmost twigs of a practically submerged shrub. Overhead, pelicans flew around in a state of utter confusion and a flock of parakeets gave shrill vent to their alarm. Almost at the end of our strength, we rowed in over the gate, past the submerged crosses and up to the farmhouse.

CHAPTER THIRTY-ONE

Kit made sure that the Uzis and ammunition were carefully stashed away. The chickens were put in a high barn.

'I knew you'd survive, Flora. You're a strong girl,' Gina said, handing me a large towel.

'Not without Kit, I wouldn't have,' I chittered. 'He saved my life.' I pushed my wet hair out of my eyes. 'We saw Mr Wang in a tree. We couldn't save him.' I began to cry.

The kitchen door flew open and John came in with a dozen half-drowned rice slaves, their eyes full of terror.

Gina bustled from kitchen to bedroom finding blankets and towels, hot drinks and clothes. Trying to pull myself together, I held a little girl for one of the distraught women while she dried herself.

Gina handed out warm clothes, presumably belonging to her own children. The garments drooped pitifully from their thin shoulders and bony frames. They were scared and for the most part, silent.

'How did you escape?' I asked one young man.

'Walls broke. Swept out. Swam for our lives. Don't remember.' He gathered the towel around his shoulders, his teeth rattling.

'We'll hide the women and children in the barns, behind the maize. Come!'

As John led them back out into the pounding rain, some dragged back in terror.

'It's all right, we're friends, we are trying to help you,' I said, but the women couldn't understand and were too scared to go back out into the storm. The young man I had spoken to earlier pointed at my DOV cap and said something in their language. The women spoke together and finally went along, comforting their frightened children.

'There's more of them stranded out there. I've got to go,' I said to Kit. At last I was doing something for the Cause. I was making a difference.

'Not in that matchbox, you won't,' said the farmer when he saw Kit's pram dinghy. He led us out the kitchen door and showed us a large inflatable with an outboard motor at the stern, 'I fished with Noah in this. Knew it would come in useful one day.'

John was also determined to go, but his wife persuaded him to stay, pointing out that he was needed. He showed us how to work the motor.

'Not a lot of fuel in the tank, so go carefully,' he warned, waving us off. 'Good luck!' he shouted and we set off into the downpour.

A while later, above the sound of the wind, we heard gunshots. Hiding the inflatable in the top branches of some drowned trees we crouched down, watching and waiting. There was a large boat in the distance – a land-sea vehicle, Uzi soldiers standing in the bow shooting at anything that moved. There were screams from the boat.

Eden had become a hell.

Had they seen us? It was dark, but they had a flashlight. We huddled together in the bottom of the boat. Kit was trembling. The Uzis seemed to be arguing among themselves. There were more gunshots, more shouting.

'What's happening, I can't bear to look,' I said.

Kit raised his head. 'Dunno, too dark. Something seems to be wrong.'

'Survivors?'

'Can't tell.'

The Uzi boat sped off.

'Let's go see,' said Kit, starting the motor.

We picked up five men and women, all exhausted and terrified. One man told us that the Uzi guns were faulty. They'd blown up in the Uzis faces. Kit pulled the last survivor on board and set off for MacFarm. The fuel lasted until just before we got back. We rowed the final stretch, the men and women who were strong enough paddling desperately with their arms.

By dawn, the waters had retreated a little, leaving hideous scenes of desolation and death. Corpses of drowned slaves, rabbits, cows, pigs and sheep littered the landscape.

Some survivors grieved for lost companions but most were remarkably cheerful, grateful for whatever was given them. People slept on the floor, in chairs, propped in corners, wherever there was room. Gina made sure that our clothes dried over the fire.

Kit and I went outside to see where the waters were.

Down the hill rode Doc, on his horse, black bag on his back. I was astonished to see that he was wearing a DOV uniform. He looked grim.

'How many injured?' he asked.

'None, but check the survivors in the barn. Shock and dehydration mostly.' John Mackenzie shook his head.

'That and near starvation,' said Gina. 'Long before any flood.'

On seeing my baggy DOV uniform, Doc smiled and patted me on the shoulder. 'Well done, child, well done.' He lifted one of Grandpa's medals that I had pinned onto the front. 'Your grandfather would be proud.' He stood to attention, saluted and said 'We will overcome!' It stirred a recent memory. So it was Doc Poliakoff's voice that I'd heard at The Hall.

Tearfully, I told him about Mr Wang. 'You did your best,' he comforted me. He took a gulp of the hot tea that Gina handed him and shook a finger at us. 'And there is good news!' he said. 'The Uzis have no working weapons!'

'What do you mean?'

'Delivery of faulty guns.' He smiled broadly. 'For the past month or so. You'll see.' What did he mean? And then it came to me. The different driver, the man who'd waved, dropped off the carrier pigeon, the bogie driver, with his load of faulty ammo and weapons.

Knowing that there was no risk of being shot, Kit and I rowed back to Shell Shack. Remarkably, it was still standing. We crawled through the upper window, the same one I'd escaped through the previous evening.

Just after we arrived, my boat had practically floated up to the farm door as if I had called it in for the night. It was upside down, but almost undamaged. I took it as an omen. Things were looking up.

To add to our feeling of wellbeing Kit found a skim-board bigger than the one he had – jammed up against an old tractor. He was over the moon. 'Finders keepers,' he chortled.

'I'm worried about the Wangs,' I told Kit.

'Let's go then.'

Gina and John had turned their home into a refugee camp. They'd been preparing for the possibility for years. Kit was full of grim energy. 'We can take both dinghies – there are quite a few children, aren't there? Take one of the guns. I'll take the other. Just in case.'

The fort, barracks and watchtower, where the search light was housed, seemed undamaged, but all were unmanned. It was like an abandoned village. The B&NG flags were shredded and limp. As we rowed by the walls, an Uzi soldier's boot floated in and out, in and out, its laces like thin seaweed. Kit pointed out the razor-wire beneath the waves, stopping nobody.

We tied the boats up by the side of the fort and, clutching the guns, climbed upwards, dodging behind rocks, keeping to the wall. No guards in sight.

Leaving Kit close to the entrance to keep watch I banged on the Wangs' door.

'Annie! Annie!' I called.

I heard a scrabbling and the door was opened by little Ho Wang. He hung onto my legs and pulled me in, gabbling at me in broken Nort, 'Come, come! Help!'

I was not prepared for the scene that awaited us: Annie, lying on a bloody table, her mother slumped over her lifeless body.

Blood everywhere.

Had there been a murder? Then I realised Annie must have died giving birth. And her baby had been stillborn. The little Wangs gathered around me, hysterical. When I coaxed Mrs Wang to come away from Annie, she fell into my arms as frail and light as a bird.

'Kit! Kit!' I cried. I couldn't handle this.

We got the five boys and their tiny mother into the boats. They sat clutching the sides, their eyes staring out of pale faces. When we reached MacFarm, Gina and John lifted them out and carried them in. They asked no questions until the little children were safely inside and warmed up.

Wu, Annie's eldest brother, told us what had happened.

'When rain came and big tide, we batten down hatches. We okay except tha' Pa away. Flood come, Uzis leave in boats. I ask for help but they not take us. Annie start baby. Bad, very bad.'

I couldn't bear it. Doc took the poor boy aside and explained that Kit and I had witnessed his father perishing in the flood. Then he spoke in Mandarin to Mrs Wang. She looked devastated but under the circumstances remained very composed and dignified. Perhaps it was the shock.

Nano and Grandpa Noah, Kit's father, Mr Patel, Mr de Kooning and his wife, their sons Olaf and little Stefan, Mr and Mrs Karim, Sami and Cher. Now, Annie and her father. Thirteen people who had been part of my life and were now gone. Not to forget Annie's baby. Fourteen.

CHAPTER THIRTY-TWO

THE WIND DROPPED. The waters gradually retreated. There were many funeral pyres built. It always took ages to get the wood to catch fire – everything was so sodden. The rice workers wailed and prayed and some tried to throw themselves onto the bodies of their dead.

'It's like the blaring my cows make when we have to take the calves away,' Gina remarked. 'It tears at my nerves.' Her children's memorial markers had floated away, but John and Kit eventually found them wedged into the cleft of a tree and hammered them back into the sticky mud.

Thick black smoke drifted over the land like a malevolent fog. The animal carcasses were piled in heaps and burned. The stench was unbelievable. We went around with rags tied over our mouths and noses.

Constant watch was kept for the B&NG kites. No orange sails appeared. Then one morning, descending slowly through the ghostly fog, came a white kite with the tick mark on its main sail. As it hovered, the Mackenzies, Doc Poliakoff, Kit and I gathered to greet the aeronauts.

Two figures wearing the white DOV uniform disembarked and strode towards us. The bearded man was tall and slim and held himself like a soldier. He wore a black patch over his right eye. The right sleeve of his overalls was sewn back over a missing hand. He had fair hair and a long straight nose. I don't know why – there was no resemblance – but something about him, maybe the way he stood, his head held high, reminded me of Lord Lao. The woman was slightly built, with a newly shaved head. Both were festooned with medals.

Doc and John stepped forward and saluted.

The woman walked swiftly to Gina Mackenzie.

'Gina?'

Gina put her hands to her face. 'Rosa? Rosa! Oh *Rosa*!'

They hugged ecstatically. Then Rosa Dov disengaged herself and came over to me, her eyes resting on Grandpa's medals, which I had pinned on my chest.

'I've met you before. Twice. Once at your mother's funeral, and more recently too, if you remember. I had some hair then. You must be Faith's daughter. You couldn't be anyone else.' A smile lit up her sharp features.

This must be my father's lover, Rosa Dov, Commander in Chief of DOV Freedom Fighters. The woman I had seen with Doc at The Hall. I blushed and accepted her proffered handshake.

'And here's somebody who has wanted to meet you for a long, long time.' She turned to the man by her side. A deep scar ran from his left eye down to his mouth.

'Yes, you do look exactly like your mother,' said Redvers Mandela.

Everyone seemed to want a piece of my father. Except for me. He was a revered hero figure, a living icon of change for them. But I hung back. My own reserve was obdurate, instinctive, but ill-defined. It puzzled me. No one else apart from Kit seemed to notice, they were all so busy.

I was in a strange state generally, still having flashbacks – to Annie and her stillborn child, to the murdered coastguard families, to Mr Wang falling into the torrent, to Barcode and Manga being dragged down by the lurchers. I couldn't shake off these images, they crowded into my mind and infested the few hours of sleep I managed to snatch.

Every so often, Rosa took a break from her military responsibilities and tried to get me to talk, but I couldn't, although I had so many things I wanted to ask her. I kept my distance from my father too. I just wasn't ready for whatever relationship they might offer. Alone, I often took out the digigraph of my parents and looked at it, trying to read their expressions, their body language.

A week passed before I spent any time alone with my father. We sat together on a hilltop, watching workers build a huge barricade at the narrowest part of the Spit out of anything they could find – sheet metal, razor-wire, the collapsed sides of barns.

Red had been organising the fittest survivors all morning. Kit was helping, together with Wu and John Mackenzie. Others were in charge of the children, and there was a team of people forever making large pots of tea and preparing rice for the workers. There was plenty food for the moment – the storeroom at The Hall had been ransacked.

I was having a five-minute break from washing clothes. Keeping clean was difficult and Doc was worried about cholera and other diseases. Some of the rice workers had terrible coughs. They were kept apart from the rest of us, camped down in a barn that had once housed mutan cows. Two of the rice workers turned out to be nurses and they worked side by side with Doc, translating and aiding him with the sick, the injured and the traumatised.

'Why have you asked them to do that?' I asked my father, pointing at the barricade.

'It's your best chance of surviving a renewed invasion by the B&NG troops if they come by land. Next we'll clear the landing strip for our kites.'

Your best chance, not *our* best chance.

'Isn't it over?' I asked, imagining that the occupying forces had turned tail, forced out by the waters.

He shook his head. 'This is only the beginning, Flora. They'll be back. The flood waters will go, they'll need the rice fields. Eden's one of the main paddy fields serving Nortland.'

'So we haven't won, then. This is just a break in hostilities.'

'Spoken like a true DOV,' he replied. 'Fighting an oppressor is hard work. It's only a matter of time, though.' He laughed. 'I did enjoy the operation to get the dud ordnance into the fort.'

'Yes, that was a clever move,' I conceded.

'On one of his communications, our agent described you to me.

That made the pigeon drop possible. With that hair you couldn't be anybody other than Faith's daughter.'

'Your daughter, too.'

'Of course.'

His expression had the same intensity as on the digigraph, the same restlessness.

'You're not aiming on staying?' I tried to sound casual.

'There's significant conflict beyond the Tescopec mountains.' His perspective was that of a fighter, not a father. 'I'm staying on to prepare for our troops when they come.'

No mention of getting to know me.

I changed the subject. 'Where has Rosa gone?' She had kited off earlier that day.

'Back to base. She's our High Commander, in charge of the DOV recovery of Nortland.' He sounded so proud of her.

In charge of an entire army!

'Did you know that my mother had died?'

'Yes, Flora, I knew. I was there. I held you in my arms.'

So he hadn't left before I was born, like Nano said?

'And did you know Rosa Dov before you left the Spit?'

'Yes, of course I knew her. We all grew up together. I took her with me.'

'But, my mother… didn't you love her?'

'Look Flora, by the time Faith got pregnant I'd made the decision to join the resistance movement. She wouldn't consider leaving her parents. I stayed until she had you. Noah and Nano were insistent that I leave you with them. I intended coming back, but then war got in the way. And politics.'

And love, I thought.

'For sixteen years?' Why shouldn't he hear my bitterness?

'Part of my political agenda was to make contact with leaders in other parts of World, and to persuade them to join us in the fight against the fascists. These things take time, Flora.' It was a rebuke.

'Why did you stop printing *The Spit Speaker*?'

'You know about that?'

'I read them all. Nano and Grandpa kept them hidden. I'm afraid they were destroyed in the flood.'

'Independent newspapers were banned. So were radio and digicasts.'

I raised my eyebrows. Could words on paper or in the air really be that much of a threat?

'I made my escape before they could arrest me. I swore to myself that I'd work for the deliverance of Nortland, but in exile.'

'With Rosa Dov!'

'Yes,' he said, unflinching.

'And you love her?'

'Yes, I do. She's an inspiration. When you get to know her, you'll see. She's a brilliant strategist, a courageous soldier, a clever politician.'

It sounded to me more like a speech than a declaration of love.

Before I could formulate my next question, Kit called for Red to come and advise them on the barricade. 'I'd better go,' he said and hurried off.

I walked some distance away so that no one would not see my angry tears. I had not known my mother but he hadn't known her either, I realised. Or loved her. Now I would never really know my father. He'd be off doing his hero thing. My mother must have guessed he was going to leave, that's why she looked sad in the digigraph. Somehow the truth of what had happened, and when, wasn't that important to me any more. I had other things to think about.

Annie's little brothers were being looked after by Gina, who doted on them. She dug out the toys her own children had played with – a football, a garden swing, a see-saw – and put them in one of the barns, out of sight of prying eyes. None of us knew who we could trust and there was always the fear of Uzi kites coming over on reconnaissance flights. Fourteen-year-old Wu was now head of the family, with responsibility for his sick mother and his four small brothers. Most of the time he was at the fringes of things or sat hunched, his eyes heavy and blank.

'It's too much,' I said to Gina. 'He's only a boy.'

'It certainly isn't fair,' she agreed. 'But there's no way of turning back time. I'm sure you wished for that many a time after your grandparents passed away.'

'Yes... but for Wu there's so much more to think about. How will they make a living? There are no crapshacks left to service. Their donkey has perished, the cart's smashed. They have nothing.'

'They have us, Flora.' Gina put her arm round my waist. 'For all that we're living in terrible times, neighbours are neighbours. We'll all need to take care of each other.'

A few days later Kit and I walked hand-in-hand back over the sea-fields – more sea than fields now – in case anything was left that we could salvage of Shell Shack. Our Uzis were slung over our shoulders, an order from my father. Nobody was to leave MacFarm without being armed.

It was a desolate scene. All Kit's work on the fields had gone to waste, the salty water spoiling any hope of a harvest, at least this year. Everything was strange and unfamiliar. No orchard. My mother's apple tree uprooted and swept away. The scent of orange blossom replaced by the stench of shitty mud.

We kicked around in the mud inside and outside what was left of the shack but found nothing, except for one of the suede shoes that lord Lao had given me. Then, just as I was about to suggest that we give up, Kit bent down and uncovered a cola. He rubbed at its coating of filth until a small patch was clear. It was Grandpa Noah's ship in a cola, the only one Nano had kept, all the others having been sold to travs. Kit rubbed some more of the claggy gunk from the glass. There was a painted scene of a village inside and a little red boat with white sails. Grandpa had called it a lost world. Kit rinsed it off in a puddle and put it in his bag.

On the way back we watched swans trying to rebuild a nest on a mound of weed, bending their necks like horses to drink. The sight moved me to tears.

In the distance, something was sticking up out of the rolls of razor-wire on the beach. I was so tired that when Kit suggested going to find out what it was, I refused.

I sat down on a rock while he ran down to the shore and watched as he picked strands of weed and rubbish from the structure. Eventually he released it sufficiently for me to see it was Grandpa's willow dove, amazingly undamaged, stuck on the wire like a sign of peace. It had been released from its barn cage by the flood and now stood for everyone to see for miles around. I clapped my hands with delight as Kit loped back up the slope, grinning from ear to ear.

'The floods haven't been all bad,' Kit said, kissing the side of my head.

When the barricade was finished everybody set to work to clear up the debris left by the receding waters. All kinds of rubbish swept out of houses and barns was dangling from trees and shrubs.

Red organised a schedule to help rid the land of the salt-laden mud. We started with the area around MacFarm, skimming a layer of the viscous topsoil into carts which were then trundled off to be emptied into specially designated Toxic Salt Sites.

'Should you be doing that?' my father asked as he saw me struggling to load up the cart. 'In your condition?'

'Probably not, but I feel perfectly fit.' I was defiant.

'Make yourself useful in other ways,' he more or less ordered. 'There's plenty of planting and hoeing to be done, or you could give them a hand rebuilding sheds, passing tools, holding nails, that kind of thing.'

I needn't have worried that he would embarrass me by giving his daughter special treatment. Red expected as much of me as he did of everybody.

Once the kite landing strip had been made longer and wider, he organised a team to weave huge mats of leaves and thin bamboo branches to camouflage it.

The flood was in the past. Although our lives would never be the same, our hard physical work had lifted us out of our disorientation and grief.

There was still no sign of the B&NG forces returning to retake Eden and although Red constantly reminded us to stay vigilant, it was hard not to believe that they had seen the work of the sea and decided that Eden was no longer a place in which they could make money. Many of the rice fields had been destroyed. There was nothing left for travs to come and gawp at.

The Mackenzies offered to give the survivors a permanent place to live and work – MacFarm was the focus of all our planting, and would be the source of all our veggies and fruit for the foreseeable future. But not all of them wanted to stay. Some were going to chance their luck getting out of Eden, slipping through before the border guard centres were rebuilt; others decided to take over The Hall. There had been well water there, and a sewage system. With some work, they might both be usable and as with so many things, Red seemed to know how to repair them. Because of its position, The Hall had been spared most of the floods, so they could plant and revive some of the rice fields, this time without guards, violence and starvation rations.

Kit and I walked over one day to have a look. I had no desire to return, but Red talked in such glowing terms of the work going on there, and I wanted to see whether my grandfather's sculptures had survived. Most of them must have been taken by the Laos, but his dovecot was still standing, the white doves – only six of them now – displaying themselves prettily on its gilded towers. The liberated slave children ran around the gardens and climbed onto the abandoned checkpoint. Their parents had torn down the razor-wire, removing all trace of the previous regime. The horses, dogs and falcons must have been carried on one of the Laos' freight kites.

I walked silently through The Hall with Kit. I wondered if the telescope was still in the tower? But no, I was told that the Laos had disassembled it and taken it with them. The news saved me having to walk through corridors in which I'd dreamt of escaping my hand-to-mouth existence.

'Shall we go, then?' I was eager to leave.

We walked back towards our temporary home, lost in our own thoughts. I wanted to believe that I had laid the ghosts of my time with the Laos, but I knew there was unfinished business. Yo-yo Lao might not be in Eden, but wherever he was, he was harbouring a vengeful grudge against me. I could never completely relax.

There was no privacy for anyone at the Mackenzies. We were all living too close together for that. Not all the freed slaves had departed to The Hall. Many of them found it a struggle to come to terms with their freedom, preferring to work under guidance, but with masters and mistresses who cared for their welfare and saw that they were healthy and, as far as anybody could be in the circumstances, happy.

The Mackenzies' generosity was boundless and it seemed churlish to complain, but there was something unsettling about living there, not knowing if we could expect this freedom to continue.

John was optimistic that Eden had been abandoned by B&NG. Red was not.

'I think we should give Freeland a try,' said Kit one day. He picked up a skein of soy-flavoured noodles with chopsticks and slid them into his mouth. He was growing a moustache. It was more like a smudge of charcoal, or a wisp of smoke, but he was proud of it.

'Freeland?'

'Red says we'd like it there, Flora. No slavery, no milit dictator, a proper voted-in government, plenty of work.'

Red nodded. 'Democracy,' he said.

Gina ladled more food from a pan into the bowl on the table. She smiled at me, encouragingly. Rosa had returned and was also based at MacFarm, to the delight of her sister. She had warned us all to be vigilant. The B&NG troops would be back. It was only a matter of time.

'Yeah,' Kit enthused, his thoughts obviously still on Freeland. 'You could train to be a kite flyer, Flora, or...' His eyes lit up with ideas.

'You're the one who wants to fly,' I pointed out, 'not me.'

Kit slapped his useless leg. 'Hardly likely, though.'

'That wouldn't be a problem. You *could* train to be a flyer,' Red interrupted. He made no allowances for Kit's mobility problems and Kit loved him for that. 'We need people like you,' Red continued. 'The Cause works in different ways all over World. Choose your destination!'

'Red,' chided Rosa. 'It isn't quite that simple. But yes, Kit, we do need men like you, and women like you, Flora. There is much to do here, too. This is a country that has to be rebuilt, restructured.'

Women like me. Yes, I'm a woman, I realised. No longer a girl.

I thought of the life growing inside me and of the childhood I wanted to offer my child... the sound and sight of seabirds, the windswept dunes, the scent of wild herbs and flowers, bright stars in a clear sky. Without the Rice Lords, surely I could rebuild a life right here, make it good. No need to travel to a new land to start afresh.

That evening as Kit and I got ourselves ready to sleep, I surveyed my worldly belongings. I had an Uzi; the journal I'd been given by Li-li and had somehow managed to hang on to; Grandpa's tin whistle with which Barcode had distracted the guards. I still had the ship in a cola with its dreams of another life; barcode's knife. The digigraph of my parents. A DOV uniform decorated with my grandfather's medals. And of course, I still had my boat. Nothing of Nano, just her voice in my head from time to time.

It was a motley collection, but I wouldn't part with any of it.

'Red says he'll take us with him, when he goes, if you want.' Kit wriggled down under the covers. 'A new life, Flora, think of it!'

'About Red. I don't feel any connection with him, Kit. I don't feel like I'm his daughter. There's no... I don't know... emotional bond.'

'Why should you, Flora? He wasn't around. At least my dad was there, even if he was an old misery. He tried his best, taught me to hunt and shoot, how to work with the ferret. Cooked for me when I was little. All that sort of thing.'

'Grandpa Noah and Nano taught me most of the things I know.'

Kit looked at me.

'You too, of course.'

I thought of how my mother must have felt to be so abandoned by the man she loved. And how betrayed by her best friend.

Annie came into my mind. She hadn't ever been my best friend, but I had been horrible to her when I was at The Hall. I suppose I was a bit of a snob. I'd always thought I was better than her. Poor Annie. What hope had she ever had of bettering herself? I was glad that I had told her about my baby, and that she and I had become friends again at that moment.

The idea of a new life in a new country was exciting, but I also wanted to help make Eden safe. I wanted to be free here, where I had grown up and lived all my life. I wanted to gather cockles and mussels again, I wanted to hear the sea birds crying, to watch the pelicans fishing. I wanted to wake to the sun rising over the dew-drenched sea meadows and watch it set over Eden Bay.

CHAPTER THIRTY-THREE

SIX WEEKS TO the day after my father had come back into my life, gleaming white DOV kites filled the sky above us. The workers rushed to remove the camouflage netting from the airstrip at the Hall. We all went with Red and Rosa to greet the aeronauts.

The DOVs had brought sacks of food and water, and crates with guns and ammunition. Red arranged for us to stand in a row, passing boxes and canisters along to the next person until they reached the large hangars. The system was very efficient.

Rosa requisitioned The Hall as DOV HQ.

'What about the rice workers?' I asked.

'Plenty of room for everyone. They can stay,' said Red.

'Red's amazing,' Kit told me that evening. 'I've never seen somebody like that in action before. He arranged for the rice-worker families to became staff to the DOV milit – which makes sense. Although some of them needed some persuading. The DOVs look just as scary as the Uzis to them, with their heavily armed belts and rucksacks. They all carry BZ63s and they have fearful looking knives and hand grenades.'

I shuddered. 'Will Red need you tomorrow?'

'I've signed up as a volunteer in the Air Corps,' Kit said proudly. 'If it comes to it, I'll be on the front line.' He pulled a gun from a holster hidden beneath his tunic. 'Look,' he said proudly. 'Red gave me this. It's more portable than those Uzis.'

Since when had Kit become interested in guns? 'I want to fight too.' I said, unconvincingly.

'You need to sleep, Flora. You look very tired.'

He was right. My body was languorous, sleepy, slow; my mind full of plans to rebuild Shell Shack. Nest building...

I told Gina. She was pleased that I wanted to stay. The farm was getting back to normal. My chickens were laying along with the Mackenzie's flock. Even Kit's ferret was housed. We were all fed well.

Kit went off to The Hall every morning. He loved it. Red trained him how to handle use our Uzis properly. 'It's just as well that we never actually had to use them,' Kit admitted sheepishly. 'I'll show you the ropes one of these days.'

I would remind him, but for now I was so tired I didn't really care.

One morning, during breakfast, Doc arrived with disturbing news. 'There's fighting in the towns outside, unrest. My sources tell me that scavs and dregs are coming in this direction to get away from the B&NG Justice Trials.'

'We have room...' said Gina but Doc cut her short.

'You don't want to make room for these people, Gina. They are as dangerous in their way as the occupying force we've just lost. Toxics will infiltrate, spread disease.'

So, we had two lots of enemies heading our way – the B&NG Uzi army determined to re-occupy Eden and the diseased and desperate of Nortland. Three – counting the sea, which might close in on us again at any time. After the lull that followed the flood, life was becoming even more complicated and frightening. Once again, Eden was under attack.

Red reassured us when he returned from The Hall with Rosa that evening. 'Nothing Doc told you is surprising in any way,' he said. 'This is what happens. Dispossessed people seek new places to put down roots. If you study World's history you'll find it happens time after time. And those they are disturbing never like it.' He laughed at our concerned faces. 'Now, let's eat!'

He had sent Gina a wild turkey the previous evening and she had worked in the kitchen with a big smile on her face all day. I had helped, sitting to peel potatoes, sieving wild rice, making stuffing from the turkey giblets, bread and herbs. We might be on the verge of war, but tonight we would have a feast.

When everything was ready, we crowded around the table – Kit, Red, Rosa, Gina, John, me and Doc. There was even wine.

John carved the turkey and Kit divided out the vegetables. When everybody was served Rosa stood to make a toast.

'To the success of the DOV Resistance! Deliver Our Victory!'

We all stood and raised our glasses. 'Deliver Our Victory!'

I had thought DOV meant Death or Victory.

'And I would like to say a special thank you to Flora for the maps. Without them we could never have made the progress we have. It was a courageous effort. To Flora Mandela!'

They all drank to me as I sat there, blushing. 'Flora Mandela!' Kit looked so proud he might burst.

Emboldened, I stood and raised my glass. 'To Gina for this wonderful supper!'

'The cook!' they cried.

As Gina and I returned to rejoin the rest of the party after clearing away the dishes, I noticed Rosa bidding farewell to somebody at the back door. She looked pensive as the shadowy figure disappeared into the night.

'Who was that?' I asked, before I could stop myself.

'One of the DOV runners,' she replied curtly. 'One of the bravest girls you'll ever know.' She stood for a moment, as if gathering her thoughts. 'The Laos are back in Nortland.'

I went cold.

I had to hold onto a chair to stop myself from passing out

'We have reliable intelligence that they are leading the fighting in the north of the country, and getting closer. Red sent out some reconnaissance kites and had his suspicions. That girl has confirmed them. Lao and his son are aiming to reclaim the rice fields, basing themselves in The Hall, presumably. He has a considerable army at his disposal. The other Rice Lords have lent their support.'

I sank into the chair next to Kit. There was a murmur around the table. I had my own thoughts. Kit held my hand under the table.

One day it wasn't there, the next it was. Halley's Comet, a bright streak in the night sky. Like a bright star with a fanned tail. I remembered all that Yo-yo had told me about it as if it was yesterday, not months ago. Every seventy-six years it appeared. But I didn't want to share the information with these friends and fellow workers. They had their own interpretation of the comet's appearance. Some of the rice workers said that it was a good omen. Others said it was bad. Maybe they were right because only a few days later, we woke to find the morning sky full of high-flying orange kites. There must have been twenty or thirty of them.

Rosa ordered everyone to take cover, preparing us all for a gunfight. Kit's gun was in his hand, ready. But there were no shots. Instead, a silent fusillade of paper strips spun down like the seeds of an elm tree as the kites disappeared in the direction of Spitsea, the town on the mainland of Eden County.

GIVE UP YOUR ARMS and LIVE.
FIGHT and you will DIE!

'Propaganda,' said Red, screwing up one of the pieces of paper and throwing it over his shoulder. 'A strategy they've borrowed from history, I think. But they won't stop at paper.'

Rosa summoned Red and Kit to The Hall. 'We must go over the plans, we can't leave anything to chance.'

CHAPTER THIRTY-FOUR

'THEY'RE COMING!' THE foot soldier had come across us by the barricade. We'd found a wonderful growth of mushrooms the previous evening and Kit had agreed to help me harvest them before he went to work at The Hall. It had been a few weeks since the B&NG kites had dropped their paper warnings and there had been no sign of them since then. A phoney war. There had been no DOV runners' reports of the Laos either. I'd almost persuaded myself that the intelligence had been wrong. Life had to go on, after all. Doc examined me and said that everything was normal and it wouldn't be long now. I was getting tired, that's all, and needed to rest each afternoon. He gave me vitamin tablets to take.

The soldier's face was clenched and he scuttled through the bushes with his body bent. 'Better take cover, they're on their way!'

I watched him running on ahead of us towards The Hall. Did he mean the B&NG troops or the scavs and dregs?

Kit grabbed my arm. 'No questions,' he hissed. 'Come on…' He dragged his leg as he pulled me towards MacFarm. 'Hurry, Flora…'

I tried to keep up. All of a sudden a stabbing pain shot through my lower back and I stumbled. Kit helped me to my feet and pushed, dragged me to get me going again. We were out of the shelter of the trees, running across open farmland, still waterlogged and muddy and difficult. Kit was hauling me, almost crying with frustration. I was surprised by the panic in his eyes. Surely we'd have had warning of an attack? Surely there was time for us to reach the house before the attack began?

But when I glanced up briefly, I saw that there was no time. Like a flock of giant pelicans, a group of about a dozen orange kites rose into the sky above the horizon but there was already one much closer, heading straight at us.

'Come on!' Kit yelled, pointing his gun up at the kite. Shots rang out.

'I can't, I can't. I've been shot!' I was doubled up with the pain. I couldn't move.

'Flora, come on! You're all right. Come on.'

After a few seconds the pain went as suddenly as it had grabbed.

We stumbled over the last few yards to the farmhouse and threw ourselves in the entrance. Gina slammed the door behind us and ushered us into the room with a view down towards the sea. Adrenalin flooded my veins. This was it! The war had begun!

'I thought I'd been shot.' I laughed hysterically.

'Here come our kites!'

We watched, crouching by the windows with Gina and John as the white DOV kites headed straight at the enemy's. Shots rang out and the sky was full of fire and smoke.

'I should go to The Hall,' Kit said. 'I should be with the DOVs. It's what I trained for.'

Before I could beg him to stay the pain in my back returned, even worse this time. I groaned. During the night I'd had mild waves of back-ache, but they'd been nothing compared to this. I curled myself into a ball when the next wave of agony hit me. There was a strange sensation of pressure inside my abdomen. And then it felt as if I had wet myself.

'Oh!'

I clung to Gina's arm.

'Am I having the baby?' I whispered.

'Yes, it's coming soon, I think. I'll find Doc. Just keep breathing through the contractions.'

Kit grabbed her. 'You can't go out in this,' he yelled. The gunfire was deafening.

'Doc said he'd check on Mrs Wang this morning,' Gina shouted above the noise. 'He might be there now, trapped. It's just across the yard. Look after Flora!' She dashed off towards the back door of the house.

Beads of sweat stood out on Kit's forehead. 'It's not coming now, is it? Doc said another week or so.'

I shook my head. There was nothing I could do now.

The pains were coming every couple of minutes.

'Where's Gina?' Kit was panicking, running from me to the door and back again, like a terrified cat. 'She should never have gone!'

I slipped out of my overalls, grunting and squealing, trying to push the pain out of my body.

Kit crouched by my side and brushed my hair out from my eyes. He was speaking, trying to soothe me, but I couldn't hear him above the noise of battle.

There was a particularly fierce volley of gunfire shots nearby and he left me to go to the window.

'Tell me what's happening.' I demanded through clenched teeth.

He shook his head. The clatter and whine of bullets told me all I needed to know.

Once again, pain grabbed at my back. I was on my knees, pushing down. It felt like the right thing to do.

More shots rang out. Then there was a brief silence.

'I think... looks like we've brought one down,' said Kit. He sounded choked. 'No...'

Flashes of gunfire lit the sky and then stopped. I panted and pushed. This baby wasn't going to wait for the battle to be over. It wanted life, wanted to breathe.

'Kit, Kit!' I screamed through the fog of agony. I could see him standing in the doorway. Was he leaving me? My mind turned somersaults with the pain, and then he was by my side, holding me, his head next to mine.

'He's here, Flora. He's here. I'll protect you.' He sounded scared.

What did he mean? The baby wasn't here yet... 'Where's Doc?' I moaned.

'I found him. Doc's here,' said a familiar voice. 'Yes, help is at hand.' But it wasn't the voice of a friend.

Doc stumbled towards me, as if he'd been pushed. Gina followed in the same manner, sobbing.

I looked up to find Yo-yo Lao standing in the doorway, blood oozing from his thigh.

I closed my eyes, partly to get through the next painful spasm, partly to block out the sight of my dreaded enemy. He was holding a gun in his hand. Kit stepped in front of me, shielding me and a shot rang out. Kit slumped almost on top of me. I tried to take the weapon from Kit's hands but Yo-yo stepped over the body and took it from me as easily as if I was a child. He threw it aside.

'I told you I'd make you suffer, Flora Mandela,' he hissed.

'She's giving birth, can't you see! You animal! The baby…' Doc crawled towards me, but Yo-yo kicked out at him and the old man groaned. Gina crouched in a corner, sobbing.

Yo-yo leaned over me. I saw the livid scar on his ear. I could do nothing except breathe fast, panting through my contraction, forced to inhale the smell of his sweat, his sheer hatred.

Perhaps it was despair that overwhelmed the next thundering contraction, but for a moment my head cleared. In the pocket of my overalls was Barcode's knife. Yo-yo took a moment too long to relish his power over me. I took the knife in both hands and without thinking, plunged it upwards into his chest and twisted it. He reeled back, a look of complete disbelief on his face, gave a tiny, sighing sob, and then slumped onto the floor. I watched him die.

I remember almost nothing after that, except for pain and pushing, the kindness of Gina and the Doc, more pain. And then there was another kind of cry.

Doc put the baby into my arms. 'A healthy boy,' he said, smiling. There was a huge lump on Doc's furrowed temple, his shirt was bloody and his cheeks were colourless. Gina stroked my hair.

'Is it all over?' I implored.

'Shh, shh, rest now,' she whispered and I sank into blessed oblivion.

When I woke, I found that I had been placed in bed, the baby, swaddled in a towel, sleeping next to me.

'Is he all right?'

'He's perfect,' said Gina.

When I woke again, there was only the sound of the baby's breathing, his little grunts and murmurs. He was going to cry. I lifted him to my breast and his lips found my milk. I felt love quicken in my heart. He was so helpless, so small, so perfect.

'You did well, lassie, very well. A fine boy, you have there.' Doc Poliakoff was standing at the foot of the bed.

'Is the fighting over?'

'Bar the shouting,' he said. Doc. 'Yo-yo's was the only kite to land. They've retreated for now. Red suffered a flesh wound, but he'll survive. We've lost some good men...'

The baby cried, quietly at first, then louder and louder. I couldn't comfort him.

'Don't upset yourself, dear. Try and rest, Flora,' Gina stroked my brow, pushing back my damp hair. She took the baby from me, placed him over her shoulder and walked up and down, rocking him and patting him on the back, making soothing noises.

I nodded and closed my eyes.

We've lost some good men. Into what sort of a world had I brought this fatherless baby?

I spent most of the day alone, absorbed by the baby, learning his noises and how to feed him. I felt strangely calm, but always, just out of sight, was a vast black hole of fear and sadness. It was I who had led Yo-yo to this house, with his murdering gun... I used every bit of the little energy I had to force back those thoughts. There was no point now.

I could hear comings and goings, injured men and women brought to the Mackenzies for treatment from Doc, children fed and comforted by Gina. My father, though injured, was up and about, rallying his troops, boosting morale. He had no time to see his grandchild.

I felt utterly separate from it all. I had a baby in my arms, but I was totally alone.

Very occasionally Nano's voice would come into my head, encouraging me, praising me. How she would have loved this child! And then, finally, the voice I believed I'd lost for ever.

'Where's my boy?' Kit's quiet voice.

I closed my eyes and held the baby even closer.

'Can I see him then?' Kit's voice again.

But suddenly his voice wasn't just in my head. It was real. It was Kit!

'I don't want to wake you,' he said, obviously alarmed by my wild eyes. His right arm was in a sling.

'Kit! You're alive!' I screamed his name and clutched at him. The baby flung out his arms in alarm.

Kit recoiled, wincing. 'Steady now,' he said, 'there's a bullet wound healing in there.'

But he was alive.

'I think the other arm's strong enough to hold my son, though.'

Unable to say a word, I passed the baby into the crook of Kit's good arm and we sat, our little family, as he explained that Yo-yo's gun must have been damaged when his kite landed badly, and that its mechanism must have been compromised. 'It fired a bullet all right, but not quite where he expected.'

The wound was in Kit's shoulder, not his heart.

'I thought you were dead,' I sobbed, smiling through my tears.

A few days later, Kit and I stood outside the Mackenzies' house. A string of geese yapped above us. I watched the leader falling back, allowing another goose to take the lead. The sea boomed on what was left of the Spit. The baby lay warm and content in my arms. I stroked his wispy hair and gazed into his almond shaped eyes. Kit counted his perfect toes. The baby shoved his tiny fist into his mouth. I went back inside, gave him my breast and he sucked.

Gina brought me drink of water. 'You must drink lots, for the milk,' she touched the baby's cheek. 'You know, your Grandpa Noah made that nursing chair for me when I had my first child, Rose. She was named after my sister, Rosa.' She sighed and her lips quivered. 'You may have it, Flora.' I smiled at her and touched her hand. What a good friend she had turned out to be.

Rosa and Red joined us. 'How beautiful he is!' Rosa said.

'The first child of the revolution,' Red added.

Since the baby was born I had used every spare moment to

write the story of Eden Spit in my journal. It was his story, after all. I hoped he would read it one day.

'The DOV flag flies over Eden. For now,' Red was saying. 'The maps were vital. We knew where B&NG were coming from. We struck at their air bases and took out their kites.'

'What a victory,' I sighed.

One good thing had come from the Laos' stay. They had left Grandpa Noah's sculptures and most of the books, locked in a vault. The DOV soldiers had broken into it, expecting to find treasure. The bookcases were full again. The Hall library was now a public asset, free to all. It was better than gold.

'You should come to Freeland,' said my father. He was caressing the tiny hands of my baby. 'We have good colleges where you could learn anything you wanted to learn.'

'What about mapping, you seem to have the ability to draw,' Rosa intervened as she sat cuddling my child.

Here was a well-known artist telling me that I could draw! I felt pleased.

'But what about the baby?'

'Take him with you. Plenty of mothers study. There are good crèches.'

It sounded wonderful. I saw myself in a room full of students all passionate about learning.

'Are there books in Freeland?'

Rosa and Red burst out laughing.

'Of course there are, and more being written all the time.'

That decided me. I would go and be educated. And afterwards I would return to my birthplace and really have something to offer.'

'I'll learn about kite-building,' Kit enthused.

Two weeks later, we took off in Red's kite, after a tearful goodbye to the Mackenzies and Doc Poliakoff. Wu, his brothers and Mrs Wang were there too, waving up at us. Wu had been put in charge of the sewage works at The Hall. A regular, secure job. As we rose into the clouds we looked down at the half-drowned narrow spit of land I'd known as home for nearly seventeen years. There was Shell Shack and the pigeon palace, rebuilt on a more secure position, on a hill between bay and sea.

'When we come home, I'll take the boy fishing, teach him how to hunt rabbits. Get him a ferret.'

I threw Kit a look. 'He'll have to keep it in a shed.'

He grinned. His arm was out of the sling, his shoulder wound healing well. He stroked the baby's head.

'I know what we'll call him. Noah,' I said, and the baby gripped my finger, as if in approval. In his other fist he grasped Kit's finger.

'How about Noah Barcode Mandela Patel?' Kit said, smiling at me.

'Look!' I pointed. Below us flapped a dozen pelicans and below them Grandpa Noah's willow dove stood, a survivor in spite of everything – an emblem of hope in the desolate landscape that I loved.

Some other books published by LUATH PRESS

Runners
Ann Kelley
ISBN 978-1908373-62 HBK £9.99

As mankind strives to rebuild society in the wake of climate change, over-population and global food shortages, every day is a struggle for people like Sid and his younger sister Lo. They are 'runners' – people whose very survival the government has outlawed. As they move west, trying to find family or somewhere they can call home, they must work out which of the people they meet on the way can be trusted, and which want to cut their adventure short. Encountering people on both sides of the law, as well as those who seem to exist outside it, Sid and Lo make and lose friends as they fight for their lives and each other.

Tough, tense and moving... Runners *dramatises a society with its back to the wall, which has shucked off any pretence of caring for the weak and vulnerable. It's a disturbing and compulsive read that makes you realise that not so very much needs to change for this to happen here.* HELEN DUNMORE

The Light at St Ives
Ann Kelley
ISBN 978-1906817-6-33 PBK £9.99

France has Montmartre, Prague has Mala Strana and England has St Ives, an enclave where artists can create freely and showcase their works to the world. Costa winner award Ann Kelley has already proved to be an excellent photographer with her previous books *Sea Front: A Cornish Souvenir* and *Paper Whites: Photographs and Poems*. Ann Kelley expresses herself in photographs as if they were words. Her style is simple but special, careful and delicate and her photographs genuinely capture the atmosphere of this beautiful Cornish town.

The Burying Beetle

Ann Kelley

ISBN 978-1-842820-99-5 PBK £9.99
ISBN 978-1-905222-08-7 PBK £6.99

The countryside is so much scarier than the city. It's all life or death here.

Gussie's story of inspiration and hope is both heart-warming and heart-rending. Once you've met her, you'll not forget her. And you'll never take life for granted again.

It is rare to find such tragic circumstances written about without an ounce of self-pity... a circumscribed existence escaping its confines by sheer force of personality, zest for life. MICHAEL BAYLEY

The Bower Bird

Ann Kelley

ISBN 978-1-906307-98-1 PBK £6.99

I now have an amazing scar that cuts me in half almost...

Gussie is twelve years old, loves animals and wants to be a photographer when she grows up. The only problem is that she's unlikely to ever grow up. Gussie needs a heart and lung transplant, but the donor list is as long as her arm...

Winner of the 2007 Costa Children's Book Award.

...lyrical, funny, full of wisdom.
HELEN DUNMORE

Inchworm

Ann Kelley

ISBN 1-906817-12-X PBK £6.99

I ask for a mirror. My chest is covered in a wide tape, so I can't see the clips or incision but I want to see my face, to see if I've changed.

Gussie wants to go to school like every other teenage girl and find out what it's like to kiss a boy. But she's just had a heart and lung transplant and she's staying in London to recover from the operation.

A great book. THE INDEPENDENT

...read it, and it will stay with you forever! TEEN TITLES

A Snail's Broken Shell

Ann Kelley

ISBN 978-1906817-40-4 PBK £8.99

What if I had been born with a normal heart and normal everything else? Would I be the same person or has my heart condition made me who I am?

For the first time in years Gussie can run, climb and jump. Every breath she takes is easier now, and every step more confident, but Gussie can't help wondering about her donor. Was she young? Had she been very sick or was there an accident?

Details of these and other books published by Luath Press can be found at: www.luath.co.uk

Luath Press Limited

committed to publishing well written books worth reading

LUATH PRESS takes its name from Robert Burns, whose little collie
Luath (*Gael.*, swift or nimble) tripped up Jean Armour at a wedding
and gave him the chance to speak to the woman who was to be his wife
and the abiding love of his life. Burns called one of the 'Twa Dogs'
Luath after Cuchullin's hunting dog in Ossian's *Fingal*.
Luath Press was established in 1981 in the heart of
Burns country, and is now based a few steps up
the road from Burns' first lodgings on
Edinburgh's Royal Mile. Luath offers you
distinctive writing with a hint of
unexpected pleasures.
Most bookshops in the UK, the US, Canada,
Australia, New Zealand and parts of Europe,
either carry our books in stock or can order them
for you. To order direct from us, please send a £sterling
cheque, postal order, international money order or your
credit card details (number, address of cardholder and
expiry date) to us at the address below. Please add post
and packing as follows: UK – £1.00 per delivery address;
overseas surface mail – £2.50 per delivery address; overseas airmail –
£3.50 for the first book to each delivery address, plus £1.00 for each
additional book by airmail to the same address. If your order is a gift,
we will happily enclose your card or message at no extra charge.

Luath Press Limited

543/2 Castlehill
The Royal Mile
Edinburgh EH1 2ND
Scotland
Telephone: +44 (0)131 225 4326 (24 hours)
Fax: +44 (0)131 225 4324
email: sales@luath. co.uk
Website: www. luath.co.uk